A VAMPIRE'S SUBMISSION

DEATHLESS NIGHT SERIES #5

L. E. WILSON

EVERBLOOD
PUBLISHING

NOTE FROM THE AUTHOR

This book was previously released as "Blood Submission" with a different cover.

ALSO BY L.E. WILSON

Deathless Night Series (The Vampires)

A Vampire Bewitched

A Vampire's Vengeance

A Vampire Possessed

A Vampire Betrayed

A Vampire's Submission

A Vampire's Choice

Deathless Night-Into the Dark Series (The Vampires)

Night of the Vampire

Secret of the Vampire

Forsworn by the Vampire

The Kincaid Werewolves (The Werewolves)

Lone Wolf's Claim

A Wolf's Honor

The Alpha's Redemption

A Wolf's Promise

A Wolf's Treasure

The Alpha's Surrender

Southern Dragons (Dragon Shifters & Vampires)

Dance for the Dragon

Burn for the Dragon

Snow Ridge Shifters (Novellas)

A Second Chance on Snow Ridge

A Fake Fiancé on Snow Ridge

Copyright © 2017 by Everblood Publishing

All rights reserved. No part of this publication may be reproduced, distributed, or transmitted in any form or by any means, including photocopying, recording, or other electronic or mechanical methods, without the prior written permission of the publisher, except in the case of brief quotations embodied in critical reviews and certain other noncommercial uses permitted by copyright law. For permission requests, email the publisher, addressed "Attention: Permissions Coordinator," at the address below.

All characters and events in this book are fictitious. Any resemblance to actual persons – living or dead – is purely coincidental.

le@lewilsonauthor.com

Print Edition

Publication Date: April 4, 2017

Editing: Jinxie Gervasio @ jinxiesworld.com

Cover Design by Coffee and Characters

ISBN: 978-1-945499-44-9

This one is for you, Tania, my Australian friend.

Thank you for waiting (not) so patiently. It's readers like you that keep me writing and improving. Can't wait to hear what you think!

Much love,

L.E.

1

Dante's hand was on fire. Literally.

Instinctive self-preservation was the only thing that saved it from incinerating in the mid-day sun. As he pulled his hand inch by slow inch down into the grave he'd dug, the desert sand caved in on itself, dousing the flames.

His breaths were soft and shallow, so much so that a human would not have been able to survive the lack of oxygen. He didn't really need to breathe. It was more a habit than anything else, even after hundreds of years. The hot, dry air did little but burn the inside of his lungs, yet he continued the struggle.

He lay absolutely still in his grave. So still, in fact, that he could feel the movement of a creature slithering across the sand above him, tracking it with his heightened senses and by the vibrations in the fine grains. Arresting his breath, lest the serpent sense the predator lying in wait just beneath the desert floor, he forced himself to be patient. If he struck prematurely, before it got close enough to his hand, it would get away. Dante had learned this the hard way.

But this time his skill was dead on. The snake had no time to defend itself or escape before it was pulled down into the grave with him. His fangs—larger than the serpent's own—sliced effortlessly through its protective scales. When he finished draining it of its lifeblood, he pushed the corpse away to join the pile of partially decayed reptiles above and let the burning sand settle over him again.

Dante had no sense of time as he waited to heal. He had no idea how long he'd been there, buried under the hot sand to protect him from the sun by day and insulate him from the freezing cold at night. How long he'd lain in the grave he'd dug for himself with bloodied broken fingers. After he'd jumped from the plane, he'd landed in a heap of shattered bones and lacerated skin, the pain such that he'd never felt before. Not even when he was a young, cocky vampire that had been put in his place more than once.

What he did know was that his bones were nearly healed now, in spite of the meager offerings from the desert. And that he'd been damn lucky the sun had already descended below the horizon, or he would have burned to ash before he'd been able to burrow into the sand.

And he was ravenous for more blood.

Hours, or years, later—he honestly didn't know or care which —he felt the heat of the sun begin to wane. The sand that protected him cooled as quickly as it heated. In the distance, he heard a yip, followed by a howl. Threads of the coyote's voice still hung in the night air when it was joined by others, together forming an eerie, beautiful song.

Dante worked his arm up through the heavy sand, cautiously breaking a few fingers through the surface. He waited a few seconds, and when he felt nothing but a cool breeze caressing his desiccated skin, he pulled his arm back in to his body and clawed at the grains in earnest.

It seemed a losing battle at first, for with every handful of sand he moved, more fell into the pocket of air he'd just created. But over time he made his way to the surface, unearthing himself like something out of a human's nightmare with a little help from the night winds.

The effort exhausted him.

Once free of the heavy weight, he collapsed face first onto the sand and rolled over onto his back. He gathered his energy as he ran his tongue over lips, cracked and dry with thirst. He couldn't even swallow.

Squinting his eyes against the brightness of the moon, he let his head fall to the side. All he saw was sand, sand, and more fucking sand. Turning the other way he saw much of the same. Wait, no. There were a few patches of creosote, and just beyond it some type of round cactus.

Neither of which would ease his particular type of thirst.

Dante studied the bursts of light above him. It had been a long time since he recalled seeing so many stars in one place before. As his eyes followed a particularly fascinating constellation spanning across the never-ending expanse of blackness, they were drawn down to a portion of the night that was brighter, more illuminated than the rest. Only one thing lit up the night sky like that.

A city.

And where there was a city, there were humans. And humans were full of blood. Much more than the scaly creatures he'd been surviving on up until now.

Dante burst to his feet in a flash of movement that belied his exhaustion of just a few moments ago. The thirst burned his insides like the sun burned his skin, and his fangs shot down, readying to feed. Pure vampire instinct took over, and Dante became the predator he had been reborn to be.

2

Laney Moss took her water bottle from the side pocket of her backpack. Unscrewing the cap, she took a long swig of the tepid liquid, wrinkling her nose at the metallic taste. Her white tank top was sticking to the trail of sweat running down the middle of her back, but she could already feel the first drafts of cooler air that would come with nightfall. Eyeing the setting sun, she stuck the bottle back in its designated pocket and set out again.

Maybe not such a great idea to start a hike so late in the day, but nature had called. And after the hectic week she'd had, she'd answered with enthusiasm. So here she was, about thirty minutes south of her apartment in Vegas, hiking through the upper portion of the Mojave Desert.

She saw a distance marker on the trail and squinted at the sinking sun again. If she kept up a good pace, she should be able to reach her car before it completely set. But first, she took just a moment to admire the breathtaking pink and orange hues of dusk streaking the blue sky. Following the reach of the sun with her eyes, she watched as the last lingering rays touched the cactus and other foliage, and tinted the sand with gold, like a painting come to life. Sighing with pleasure at the wonder of Mother Nature, Laney resumed her hike.

She was about a mile from her car when the temperature took a swift dive. The sun had dipped below the horizon, but she could still see well enough. However, she was an experienced hiker, and she knew that when full darkness came, it would be fast and sudden. Which was why she was well supplied with a flashlight, a headlamp, and pepper spray to ward off any nighttime critters that might get too curious.

Stepping off the trail, she took off her pack and set it on an outcropping of red rocks so she could find her gray pullover hoodie. Pulling it out of her pack, she gave it a good shake to make sure nothing had crawled in there during her last break. Sticking one arm into a sleeve, Laney froze, listening.

She thought she'd heard something behind her. Perhaps she'd surprised an animal coming out of its burrow after sleeping the day away. Moving only her eyes, Laney looked from side to side, and then cautiously turned her head to look behind her. She could've sworn...but no, there wasn't anything there. It was probably nothing more than a shifting of the sand, either from the wind or a reptile, but it was enough to set her on high alert.

Still watchful and keeping an eye out for anything that moved, she stuck her other arm through its sleeve and tugged her hoodie down over her tank top. Taking her pepper spray out of the front pocket of her cargo shorts, she slung her pack onto her back and started walking again, holding the small can at the ready. It was probably nothing, but it was always better to be prepared.

She'd been walking about ten minutes when she thought she heard footsteps on the packed mixture of dirt and sand on the trail behind her. Laney glanced back nervously over one shoulder. She didn't see anything, but it was almost full dark now. However, she didn't want to stop to pull out her flashlight. Dammit. Why hadn't she gotten it out when she'd stopped earlier?

Keeping up a brisk pace, she shrugged her pack off her shoulders and started digging around for her flashlight, glancing back every few seconds to make sure she wasn't about to become dinner for one of the coyote that frequented the area. She'd heard them singing to the rising moon just a little while before. It sounded like they were quite a ways away, but she was well aware of how distance could be deceiving in the desert.

Her hand came in contact with the cold steel of her heavy-duty flashlight just as she tripped and stumbled over a displaced rock on the path. With a soft curse, she regained her footing and picked up her flashlight from where she'd dropped it.

A feral growl directly behind her lifted the hair on the back of her neck and froze the blood in her veins a moment before the adrenaline kicked in. Switching on her flashlight, she spun around, swinging the beam from side to side. At the same time, she dropped her pack and lifted her pepper spray in front of her. The light flicked past and then landed on something. Laney blinked hard, her mind unable to comprehend what it was she was looking at.

The thing moved, covering the fifty feet or so between them so fast she had no time to open her mouth to scream. It towered over her in the split second before it attacked, and she caught a flash of crepe-like skin covering a hairless head, long fangs, and red glowing eyes.

The scream tore from her throat as it fell on her. Thin limbs with abnormal strength wrapped around her, cushioning her from the impact as they landed on sand still warm from the sun. With a surge of courage she didn't know she possessed, she swung her heavy flashlight at the back of its head. It landed with a solid thunk, but didn't phase the creature at all. Her eyes widened and she screamed again as it wrapped one hand in her hair, yanked her head to the side, and sank those long fangs into the side of her throat. Pain lanced through her, and she began to fight in earnest. But no matter how hard she struggled, she couldn't get—whatever the hell it was—to release its grip.

And then it began to drink.

Holy shit. This thing wasn't trying to eat her. It was draining her blood. Instantly, she knew what it was: *Vampire*.

Laney knew that vampires weren't just in bad horror flicks. They actually existed. Her father had told her about them before he'd died. She'd even seen one once, years ago, when she was up north on a business trip. A few of her co-workers had invited her out for dinner and drinks after their late meeting, but she'd left the meal earlier than everyone else because she'd wanted to get back to her room and watch a movie while she went through her notes.

Being unfamiliar with the city, she'd taken a wrong turn while walking back to the hotel and she'd stumbled across a scene that was now forever seared in her brain.

A man—a very handsome man—had a woman pressed up against the side of an old bookstore that was already closed for the night. His face was buried in the curve between her head and shoulder, and he was kissing her. One of his legs was wedged between her thighs and the woman was humping it shamelessly while making little sex noises. It had been so erotic: the way he'd held her captive against the wall; the way she'd clutched at his shoulders.

Laney had watched, completely transfixed by the sight of them. In spite of herself, her body had begun to burn and her breathing came in pants. The woman had opened her eyes and looked straight at her, her eyes glazed and her mouth slack with passion. And still Laney watched, desire clenching low in her belly as the woman smiled, closed her eyes again, and orgasmed almost violently in his arms.

As the woman spontaneously combusted, the man lifted his head and leaned his head back, looking up toward the sky. Laney had been shocked to see blood dripping from sharp, pointed teeth. It ran down his chin and landed on the woman's bared breasts.

Laney's desire had gone cold, and she'd gasped out loud before she could stop herself. The man's head had whipped around, following the sound. And when he'd spotted her watching, he'd smiled. Spinning away, Laney had ran back the way she had come, his laughter echoing between the buildings around her.

She'd never told anyone about that night, knowing they'd all think she was nuts or had had too much to drink, or both. And the one person she could've told was gone now.

The thing gave her hair a sharp tug and Laney cried out. She didn't realize she was crying until she felt the tears running down her temples. It groaned with pleasure at the sounds of her distress and sucked harder. She was beginning to feel lightheaded, and knew that if she didn't do something, this thing was going to kill her.

Gathering every ounce of strength she had left, she managed to free her arm from where it was lodged between their bodies. Aiming the pepper spray at its face, she lifted her chin, squeezed her eyes closed, and pressed down on the depressor. For a moment, she was scared shitless that it wasn't going to have any affect on the creature, even though the side of her face and neck was burning like fire. She continued to spray, emptying the entire can into its face and mouth until, finally, it detached from her throat with a roar of rage. Rolling off her, it clawed at its skin as it screamed.

Laney scrambled to her feet. Clutching her pack to her chest, she left the thing writhing on the ground and staggered away. She didn't look back. She didn't want to see it. Tears from the pepper spray blurred her vision, and her hands were shaking so badly that the beam of her flashlight jerked around sporadically on the path. She tripped more than once before she finally reached her car, but each time she staggered back to her feet and kept going. Unzipping her pocket, she dug for her keys, terrified that they had somehow fallen out. But no, they were still there. It took her three tries to hit the button that would unlock her car.

Once inside, she locked all of the doors before starting the engine. Stomping down on the gas, she pealed out onto the road, gravel flying and tires squealing. She didn't think. She didn't try to call anyone. She only concentrated on getting the hell out of there and to the safety of her apartment. If she could just get home, it wouldn't be able to get to her, not without an invitation. And she sure as hell wasn't about to invite it inside of her home.

It occurred to her later that she had run through at least two red lights, but having to pay a couple of tickets was nothing compared to the terror she felt. Surprisingly, she managed to get upstairs and inside without anyone seeing her. Even her pain in the ass roommate was out. When she stumbled into her bathroom and flicked on the light, she realized that was most definitely a good thing.

Dried blood caked her neck, her dark hair, and the front of her hoodie. Tears streaked her dirty face, and her normally olive-toned skin was pale and clammy. Reaching up with shaking hands, she lifted the neckline of her sweatshirt away from her throat, revealing two ragged puncture wounds. Blood still seeped from the holes. She should go to the hospital, but what the hell would she even tell them? It would bring her more attention than she wanted.

Sitting down on the side of the bathtub, she braced one hand on the wall and turned on the water for a shower. As she waited for the hot water to kick in, something brushed against her bare leg. Laney jerked away so hard she almost fell into the tub, her lungs locking up in terror. But it was only Fraidy Cat, her orange tabby rescue cat. He'd gotten his name when he hid under the end table for three days after she'd brought him home. But looking at his brazen attitude these days, you'd never know it. She reached down automatically to pet him, and as she stroked his soft fur and felt the vibration of his purrs, her heart resumed a normal rhythm, and she sucked in a grateful breath of air.

She didn't let herself think about what had happened. Not yet.

Leaving her clothes in a pile on the floor to be tossed out later, she stepped under the hot spray of water. The wound on her neck stung like a bitch, but she clenched her teeth and allowed the water to wash out the dirt and germs. She had to stop a few times because she was so lightheaded she was afraid she was going to pass out, but eventually she managed to get herself scrubbed clean and dressed in her navy "No Wake Zone" nightshirt. Digging the antibiotic ointment out of the first aid drawer, she applied some to a large square of gauze and then taped it over the bite.

Once she looked a little less like an attempted murder victim, she staggered out to the kitchen and opened the fridge to get the orange juice. It took her a couple of tries. The door was amazingly heavy. In retrospect, she probably should have done this first, but she was in shock. Laney recognized the signs, and it explained why the sight of all of that blood had sent her automatically to the shower to get clean.

Fraidy meowed, weaving in and out of her legs as she stood there in front of the open fridge door, wanting his dinner. She looked over at his empty food dish and blinked. The room spun around her.

And everything went black.

3

Dante stood in the center of an empty courtyard. It belonged to a run-down apartment complex that had seen better days before the neighborhood had gone to shit. He stared up at the third floor window. It was the only window that still had a light on at this time of night.

The rest of his meal was in there. He could smell her.

He licked his lips, tasting the remnants of the human female he'd had for breakfast. She'd tasted unlike anything he'd ever had before, and his body had reacted harshly, but not unpleasantly. Or maybe it was just the fact that he was very nearly starved of blood. To the point that his skin felt dry and loose on his bones, and his muscles ached with a weakness he hadn't felt since he was a lowly human. So long ago, he was surprised he even remembered.

He heard a shout to his left. His head snapped around and his gaze narrowed in on a middle-aged human male swinging a bloated trash bag at a loose dog. The dog yelped, skittering away with its belly dragging the ground and its tail between its legs.

Lifting his face to the wind, Dante scented the male. His parched throat immediately began to burn in response. In less than the space of a heartbeat, he crossed the expanse of the courtyard and stood in the human's path. The dog, an ugly little thing with brown and white fur, began to bark crazily at his sudden appearance. Dante smiled in amusement as the ridge of wiry hair on its back rose up into a full mohawk. Ignoring the little beast, he focused on the human that stood wide-eyed and frozen with fright in front of him.

Dante knew it was fright and not just surprise. He could smell the sour stench of fear hanging heavy in the chilly air. The asshole *should* be frightened. Dante had a thing about humans that thought they were better than other creatures.

Without thinking twice about it, he swung out with his right hand and broke the human's neck, then yanked the body toward him and sank his fangs into the warm flesh. He'd have to drink quickly, before the heart stopped beating completely, but that had never been a problem for him.

Dante managed to take only three large swallows before he dropped the corpse at his feet. Leaning over, he gagged, spitting out the blood still in his mouth. The dog, who'd crept closer to sniff his pant leg, jumped back quickly out of the way.

Dante straightened and took some deep breaths, fighting down the nausea. He eyed the dead guy at his feet. Though obviously not an animal lover, he didn't look the type to have a meth cocktail in his veins. But those looks were deceiving, because he'd tasted absolutely vile.

The little dog sat down next to the deceased human. It wasn't nearly such an ass kicker now that it had gotten his scent, or maybe because he'd protected it from the bastard human. Dante ignored the mutt as he tried to clean his mouth of the disgusting blood. But every few seconds, it would raise its soulful brown eyes to his face and whine. It was a pitiful sound coming from such a tough little dude. He stared down at it, and the little beast stared back without blinking. Squatting down, he held out his hand for the dog to sniff, which it did from a cautious distance. After a moment's hesitation, it stood and took a small step toward him.

"Are you gonna gnaw on me if I pet you, little man?" Dante's voice was barely audible, his vocal cords not yet healed. He switched to a different way of communicating.

I won't hurt you.

The dog came another step closer and peered up at him with its sad little face. Carefully, so as not to accidentally harm it, he rubbed its silky ears.

A bizarre feeling crept over him, one he tried hard not to interpret. He knew he must look to be a monster, yet this little guy didn't seem to care in the least. It didn't even care that he'd just killed someone.

Or maybe it did. But dogs, like vampires, tended to be realists. And though it was giving him its finest sad face, it seemed to know that its best bet was to befriend the one that was still alive and could possibly help it find something better to eat than what was in that trash bag.

Dante gave it one last good ear rub, silently wishing it a good hunt. Then he stood and walked away without a backward glance, back to the window he'd been watching. When he got to the same spot he'd been in before, he felt something against his foot and looked down. The little dog had followed and was now sitting beside his boot, staring up at that same window. The barest wisp of a smile crossed Dante's features, then he reached down and picked the little fucker up and tucked it under his arm.

"You're lucky I can climb one-handed." The dog probably weighed in at a good forty pounds, but he barely noticed the extra weight, scaling the side of the building with ease. When he reached the window, he dug the toes of his boots into the worn siding and gripped the sill with the same hand that was holding the dog to hold steady. With the other, he tested the window. It was unlocked. As he slid it open, a fat orange cat waddled out of the kitchen and sat in the middle of the living area to silently watch him with its owlish topaz eyes. A muffled noise came from the kitchen, and the cat flicked its tail.

"My phone. Where the hell is my phone?" A female's shrill voice came from inside the apartment, and a moment later, she rushed into the room, pulling up short at the sight of

Dante hovering outside the window. She had dark hair and skin, and appeared to have just gotten home, as she still had a coat on over her short black dress.

Catching her gaze with his, Dante reached out to her mind. "Invite me in," he commanded.

She dropped the phone in her hand, her eyes as large as the cat's, who sat watching the scene go down with idle curiosity. "Come in," she said in a monotone voice, then stood aside to await his next command.

He lowered the dog in first. Its tail immediately started wagging as it went over to the cat to say hello.

Dante climbed in after him and slid the window shut again. He breathed in deeply, discerning and cataloging the different smells. The scent of the woman he'd tracked there was much stronger now, which meant he'd been correct in guessing that this was where she dwelled.

It was a small apartment. From where he stood just inside the main room, littered with mismatched furniture straight out of a thrift store, he could see the doorway to what appeared to be a small galley kitchen. The entry door to the apartment was directly across from him and a little to his left. To his right were three more doors. One he could see was a bathroom. A pile of clothes lay on the floor. That was where the overriding smell of blood was coming from. His mouth watered and his gums burned as his fangs descended, his stomach clenching with need. Leaving the animals to do their thing, he headed toward one of the other doors, of which he could only assume was a bedroom. He needed more of this human.

As he passed the female that had invited him in, he reached out with one large hand and snapped her neck with a quick twist. He had no interest in feeding from her. She reeked of alcohol and pills.

Walking past the kitchen, something caught his attention out of the corner of his eye—a human limb. A bare, olive-skinned leg, actually. And attached to the leg was the human woman he was looking for. She was passed out cold on the floor in front of the open refrigerator. An unexpected hunger that had nothing to do with feeding assaulted Dante as his eyes traveled from the arch of her petite foot up the curve of her calf to her shapely thigh. It disappeared underneath a sleeping garment that looked to be nothing more than a long T-shirt. Her other leg was bent underneath her and her long dark hair hid her face, damp tendrils of it sticking to her cheek and forehead.

For one frozen second, Dante feared she was already dead. Squatting down on his haunches next to her, he pressed his fingers to the pulse point on her throat, paused his breathing, and listened.

He heard her heart contract and release at the same time he felt a reedy pulse. Removing his hand, he rested his forearms on his thighs as he regarded her prone form. Funny, but now that he'd found her, he was in no rush to finish her off. So it appeared he had a choice to make: he could go ahead and assuage his thirst for this one, and then go hunt for another that tasted as good as she did. Or, he could keep her alive and have the most amazing blood he'd ever tasted ready and available whenever he wanted a sip. At least until he got home. Dante scratched his chin. It wouldn't be hard to bring her with him. Perhaps he'd even keep her for a while.

Decisions, decisions.

Glancing toward the kitchen doorway, he found the animals sitting side by side in silent companionship, waiting for his decision.

"What do you think?" he asked them in his broken voice.

The cat blinked its large eyes at him, not offering an opinion either way. But the dog lifted one front paw and yipped once.

Dante nodded. "Yeah, you're probably right. I should keep her around." *At least until I'm healed enough to take the time to find another as appetizing.* Gathering her up in his arms, he rose and carried her out of the kitchen. The animals followed him.

He stood in the center of the main room, unsure of where to go to wait out the day. Though there was only the one window and it had blinds he could pull down, it was large, and made him feel too exposed. He could cover it with a blanket or something for extra protection, he supposed, but it wasn't enough. Turning on his heel, he opened the door to the first bedroom. It definitely belonged to the female in his arms. Her scent was everywhere. One eyebrow lifted in surprise. Instead of the ruffles and glitter most human females seemed to favor, he found a clean room decorated simply and tastefully in warm blues and browns. Looking down at her, he tried to determine her age. Maybe she had matured past that ridiculous crap. These days, it was much harder to gauge a human's age. In any case, pleasant as it was, there was also another window.

Backing out of the room, careful not to knock her head on the doorframe, he sidestepped over to the bathroom. The room was small but clean. All beige and white, with a deep bathtub, a pedestal sink with a mirror, and just enough floor space for him to sit on the large tiles with his legs stretched out in front of him. And more importantly, not a fucking window to be seen.

It would do.

Lowering his meal into the bathtub, he left her there and went back into the kitchen and found the cat's plastic dishes. He filled one with water and one with some dry cat food that he found in the pantry, and set them both on the floor. That should keep the two of them happy while he got some rest. And cat food had to be a step up from rotting garbage for his new canine friend. Then he retrieved the pillows and the pale blue comforter from the bed and took them into the bathroom with him.

"Behave," he told the two animals. Then he shut the door. The corpse could rot where it was for the day.

Dante arranged the pillows against the wall next to the sink and spread out the comforter. Lifting the woman from the tub, he sat down and settled her across his lap. Her hair fell away from her face as her head fell back over his arm.

Startled by the surge of lust that shot through him, Dante studied her closer. The female was quite beautiful, with the high cheekbones, sculpted full bottom lip, and dark slash of brows common to the women from the old country. Dante frowned, touching her cheek. The skin was cold and clammy to the touch, and had a chalky gray pallor to the natural olive tones. Raising his wrist to his mouth, he bit through the skin until he tasted blood, then laid the open wound over her mouth. He wiggled his arm a little until he got her mouth open and the blood could drip in.

When she didn't respond right away, he scowled, but then she started swallowing instinctively. He re-opened the wound and let her drink a little more, but not more than he could afford to lose. He examined her again. Her color was better, and she seemed to be breathing a bit easier. She would live to feed him again.

Satisfied, he rearranged her on his lap so she was sitting with her back against his chest and her head resting on his shoulder. If she awoke before he did, he would know. He was taking no chances of her getting away.

Dante wrapped his arms around her, slightly amused at how small she was. Her bare feet didn't even reach his ankles. His eyes travelled up her full legs. They reminded him of what he thought of as old Hollywood legs, like the starlets of the nineteen forties and fifties. For as little as she was, she had plenty of curves. He tugged her nightshirt down and pulled one side of the comforter up and over the two of them, then he closed his eyes. It wasn't a bed or even his old mattress back home under the city of Seattle, but it was definitely a step up from being buried alive in sand.

At that thought, Dante opened his eyes again and looked at the tub in front of him. He briefly considered making use of it, but found he couldn't gather the energy. The sun wouldn't be up for an hour or so yet, but he was fatigued from the exertions of the night. He needed to rest.

4

Luukas glanced up from the map on his desk to find four expectant faces watching him closely. There was only one face still missing—Dante's—and he had no fucking idea how to continue the search for the top commander of his Hunters. After he, Nikulas, and Aiden found the abandoned van that had abducted Dante from their apartments, the trail had gone completely cold, even after towing the vehicle back to their garage and going through it with a fine-toothed comb. There wasn't one fucking clue as to where his friend could be at this moment.

But they needed to find him, and quickly, for things were about to become very dicey in their world. And according to Aiden—or rather Waano, the evil entity currently residing inside of Aiden—the demons that Leeha had so foolishly set free from the altar appeared to be waiting for something, and they were becoming restless. What it was, he didn't know.

Nik and Aiden had managed to track down the leader of the group in China by employing some trustworthy vampires over there—the one calling itself "Steven"—and they were keeping close tabs on that group. Though their sporadic movements and killing sprees seemed to have no rhyme or reason as of yet, other than causing mayhem within the city of Dalian and the nearby towns, Aiden was convinced that they were, in fact, looking for something.

In the meantime, the demons that had possessed the vampires still in the area of Leeha's destroyed mountain fortress were laying low. They were unusually inactive compared to their friends across the pond, according to Waano and Luukas's scouts. Which only confirmed his suspicions that they were waiting for something to happen. And Aiden's entity was not forthcoming about any information other than what he'd already told him.

Someone's phone vibrated, and they all turned to look at Shea, cautiously hopeful. The Hunters were all here in this room, who else would be calling her but Dante? And she was his favorite, after all. If he reached out to anyone other than Luukas, it would be her.

Glancing briefly down at her cell, she refused the call. "Wrong number," she told them when she looked up again.

Luukas noticed that she wouldn't quite look at him as she shoved her phone back into the pocket of her jeans. Instead, her green eyes touched on him only briefly and then skittered away. An unusual behavior for his only female Hunter, and one that did not go unnoticed.

Before he could question her, however, Christian broke the silence. "So, what's the next move? Do we concentrate on the search for Dante? Or on trying to figure out what's going on with Leeha's monsters?" As an afterthought he added, "And what about Cedric and his bunch? I bet the wolves would help us. Has anyone asked them?"

"Our werewolf buddies have their own problems to worry about at the moment," Nik said. "So it's just us for this one. As Luukas mentioned when we all came in for this meeting, we already have some of our people in Dalian, ones that knew his vampires before Leeha possessed them," he clarified. "We sent them over right after Aiden and Grace came home. They'll keep us updated on anything they find out."

"Okay," Christian said. "Anyone have any idea what it is they're looking for?"

"I think I might," a female voice said from the doorway.

"*She'ashil.*" Christian jumped up from his chair to greet his mate. Taking Ryan's face in his hands, he kissed her until Nik rolled his eyes, leaned his chair backwards, and smacked him on the ass.

Luukas waited patiently for Christian to release her before he spoke. He understood the need a male had for his mate. "Come in, Ryan. Please sit down." He indicated Christian's vacated chair. With a nervous glance over her shoulder at the empty apartment, she did as he asked, arranging her navy and white tie-dye dress neatly around her legs. Christian took a place standing behind her. He moved her long red hair out of the way and put his hands on her bare shoulders.

Shea made a sound of disgust, but quickly tried to mask it as a cough at a look from Luukas.

"Don't be jealous, love," Aiden teased her.

"I'm not jealous," Shea responded in a sugar-sweet voice. "I just don't like her."

"Enough," Luukas told them sternly. At times, he felt like he was the teacher leading a class full of hormonal teenagers. Turning to Ryan, he asked, "What is it that you think they're looking for?"

She took a shaky breath, her hands twisting nervously in her lap. Christian bent down and whispered something in her ear. Something they all heard, of course, because they were vampires and had excellent hearing.

"*She'ashil*, if you think you know something, you need to tell Luukas."

Ryan nodded. Looking straight at Luukas, she said, "I overheard the other girls say something about a box."

"You interrupted this meeting to tell us about a box?" Shea's snide voice interjected.

"Shea! ENOUGH," Luukas ordered.

"Sorry," she told him. With a sarcastic flip of her hand, she indicated for Ryan to continue.

Ryan narrowed her eyes at the other female, but otherwise continued speaking as if she hadn't been interrupted. "Grace apparently has a box that she brought with her from China, and I heard the other girls arguing over whether or not to tell you about it."

Aiden smacked himself on the forehead. "Bloody hell! I completely forgot about the box!" He looked over at Nik. "Remember, mate? The box I told you about? It has an etching of a dagoba in the bottom of it. Grace took it with the bag that Mojo was in. It's how we met." He grinned broadly.

"What about the etching in the box?" Luukas asked. "What is it there for?" He directed his question at Ryan, as she seemed to be the only one there able to speak sensibly.

"They were saying something about a clue, but they didn't know for what. Just that the demons and the humans were both after it, and that's why they were chasing Grace when she took it." She shrugged.

"So we are now at risk because we are in possession of that item," Luukas mused, mostly to himself.

Ryan shook her head. "No, I don't think so. I think Keira put some kind of protective ward around it."

Nik spun around in his chair to face her. "How is it that you know so much about this, and I don't?"

"Because I'm better at eavesdropping than you are?" she guessed.

"Where are the witches?" Luukas gritted out.

"Emma and Grace are downstairs playing with Mojo. I don't know where Keira is," Ryan told him.

Luukas stood and strode over to the office doorway. Ah yes, his mate was nearby. He could feel her. His teeth ached and he realized he was clenching his jaw, his fangs protruding in his anger. His little witch thought to hide things from him, did she? Did she think him not male enough to handle what was going on? Not sane enough? Or was this just another of her little tricks?

"KEIRA!"

Turning back to his desk, he attempted to silence the doubts running through his mind as he sat down and waited for his mate. His Keira had done nothing but care for him and make him happy since his brother had rescued them both from Leeha's hellish prison. He had no reason to think she meant any malicious intent by not telling him about this piece of information. She was probably just trying to protect him, as usual.

A few seconds later, his raven-haired witch—his angel—came running from the other room. When she saw them all sitting there in the office, obviously waiting for her, she slowed. Her hazel eyes lighted on Ryan and her forehead creased with confusion. "What's wrong?" she asked Luukas. "What's going on?"

Luukas laced his fingers on top of his desk and held her in his steady gaze. "Tell me about the box," he ordered.

Placing her hands on her voluptuous hips, she scowled at Ryan. "You ratted us out?" Then she gazed off to the side, her lovely face scrunched up with confusion. "Wait. How did you even know?"

"I'm sorry," Ryan told her sincerely. "They told me I needed to come here and tell Luukas." She looked seriously upset. Christian leaned over and whispered to her again, and she sniffed and nodded.

"Well, that explains why I didn't know." Nik leaned back in his chair and crossed his arms over his chest with a satisfied smile.

"Ah. The voices," Keira reasoned. "Why didn't you just tell them to shove it?"

"Keira!" The only thing Luukas wanted to hear was what she knew about the box, and where she'd hidden it. "Tell me about the box, witch. Now."

She quirked an eyebrow at his tone, but dropped her arms to her sides and sauntered over to his desk. Coming around to his side, she hopped up right on top of his papers so that her hip touched his arm. She did this on purpose to distract him, knowing how her very nearness affected him.

And he liked it.

Catching his eyes with hers, she said, "I was only trying to protect us. Not hide anything from you. Please don't be angry with me."

Pulling away from her and sitting back in his chair, he repeated, "Tell me about the box."

With a sigh, she conceded, lacing her fingers together in her lap. "Grace just told us about it right before Christian, Ryan, and Shea got home. She'd honestly forgotten about it."

"What. Is. It," he demanded between clenched teeth.

"It looks like an everyday wooden jewelry box with a red felt lining. But if you lift the felt, there's a design carved into the wood—a dagoba, Grace said. Do you know what—"

"I know what a dagoba is," he interrupted. "Go on. What else do you know?"

"When Grace showed us the box, we called Brock. She said he'd freaked out when she'd asked him about it in China, and as soon as he saw it, he knew the demons would be coming for her. The box is the reason he ran with her and Heather, and brought them to Seattle. He said he thinks the etching is a clue."

"A clue to what?"

"He didn't know. Just that when he'd been following the possessed vampires back in China, he had seen them find other boxes like it."

"Is there anything else?"

"No. That's all I know."

"Where is the box now?" Nik asked.

Luukas had nearly forgotten there were others in the room. It was like that when he was anywhere near his witch. She made him forget everything else, even the most horrible memories....

She smiled her sultry smile at him. The vixen knew exactly what she did to him, and she reveled in it. "It's hidden here, in our apartment," she answered Nikulas without taking her eyes from Luukas. "I placed protective wards around it to prevent it from being found."

Aiden stood. "I'll go find Grace and see if we can remember anything else that may have been said when we stole it."

"I'll come with you," Nik told him. Then turned to Luukas. "Are we done here, bro?"

Luukas ran his eyes down the front of his witch, suddenly fascinated with the tiny buttons on her red shirt. A shirt that barely contained her full breasts. "Yes, we're done. Everyone leave, now."

They were still filing out of the apartment when he took the neckline of Keira's shirt and yanked, tearing it down the middle and scattering tiny buttons everywhere.

"I missed you tonight," she told him.

"I missed you, too, witch." Grabbing her by the hips, he pulled her off the desk and onto his lap, groaning when she eagerly settled over his erection.

"You owe me a shirt," she told him with a smile.

Sliding his fingers into the top of her bra, he tore that off her, too.

5

Laney woke to scratching at the door. She tried to open her eyes, but it felt like someone had tied barbells to her eyelashes and applied some Superglue for good measure.

Deciding she was still way too tired to get up and feed Fraidy, she sighed and let herself sink into the firm warmth beneath her. The silly cat would live a few more minutes without his breakfast. He had enough extra body fat to survive the apocalypse.

Her mattress rose and fell beneath her, cuddling her deeper within its folds, the blanket tightening around her middle. Laney froze, suddenly wide-awake and wondering why the hell her bed was hugging her. Maybe she was dreaming. She pried her eyelids open and found herself staring at the tiles above the bathtub.

She was right. It must have been a dream. The events of the previous evening came crashing back into her skull, and a small cry of fright escaped her lips before she could stop it. She tried to slap her hand over her mouth, but she was all twisted up in her comforter.

Heart beating frantically against her ribs, she tried to calm herself.

I'm home. And I'm still here. Still alive. It's okay. That thing can't get me here.

She vaguely remembered leaving the bathroom last night and making her way into the kitchen to get some juice and something to eat. She didn't recall coming back in here, but she must have. Maybe she came in to pee and passed out before she could get to bed.

But then why did I bring my comforter with me?

She must have been cold from the blood loss.

Her bed rose and fell underneath her again, and warm breath stirred her hair. Laney's heart started beating so hard her ears began to ring, blocking out any other sounds. It wasn't any kind of bed that was lying beneath her. It was something alive, and since she didn't have a significant other, and she and her roommate barely spoke, never mind sleep together, the situation she found herself in was raising all kinds of alarms within her.

The vampire from the night before came into her head just as the thing moved beneath her again. A monster stirring from its slumber, perhaps?

With a scream, Laney fought her way from beneath the heavy blanket and kicked it away. Scrambling to her knees, she spun around to find herself face to face with her deepest fear. The monster staring back at her in surprise looked horrifyingly familiar.

It launched itself upright from the mound of pillows and blanket, like a demon rising from the lowest depths of hell, landing on its feet to tower over her. It had to be at least six and a half feet tall. A sound that was somewhere between anger and surprise hissed from its mouth, and it flung its arms out, legs bent in a defensive stance. Its bloodshot eyes shot around the room, searching out the source of danger before landing on her. It glanced around once more and then slowly straightened. Calmer now, it tilted its head to the side and watched her with a guarded expression.

Laney held perfectly still. Her eyes were glued to the thing's face. A face that, although still a bit harsh on the eyes with its blood-reddened eyes and jutting bones, was not as ghastly as she remembered from the night before. When it continued to just watch her without moving, she let her eyes drop, briefly taking in a dusty black T-shirt and black pants that hung from its emaciated frame before she quickly lifted them back up to its bald head. No, not bald, shaved. She could see the hint of dark stubble underneath the layer of grime that covered it.

She was very close to the bathroom door. Her left hand began to inch toward it before she was aware of what she was doing.

When it spoke, its voice was deep and low and sounded like it had swallowed shards of glass. "Do *not* open that door, human."

Her hand froze mere inches from the doorknob, then dropped back down to her lap.

A dog barked from the other room.

Laney didn't have a dog, and for a moment, the noise distracted her. But any random thoughts were chased away by the monster's next words.

"Come. I need to feed." It held out a thin hand to her like it was asking her to dance.

Shaking her head so hard she felt rather like a rag doll, Laney scooted backward on her knees until her toes hit the bathtub. "No," she whispered. Then louder, "No." It wanted to feed on her, like a fucking parasite, and she was supposed to just let it?

I don't fucking think so, asshole.

The bloodsucker, for that's what it was, lifted its upper lip in a snarl to expose fangs as long as her little finger. Opening its mouth wider, it hissed in warning before speaking again. "I said, come." It still held its hand out to her. The gentlemanly gesture oddly out of place with the wordless threats it was making and the predatory gleam in its eyes.

"And I said NO!" Laney told it. Reaching back into the tub, her fingers brushed against the plastic bottle of shampoo. It was full, and rather heavy. Before she could second-guess herself, she grabbed it around the neck and chucked it as hard as she could at the monster's head. It moved to dodge it, momentarily taking its eyes from her, and she reached blindly for the doorknob. Flinging open the door, she was immediately covered in warm sunlight as it flooded in from the large window in the living area. Still on her knees, Laney threw her body forward, out into the light and out of the reach of the vampire. She landed hard on her stomach and froze, unable to make her limbs move so she could scramble completely out of the doorway.

Her roommate, Sasha, lay on the floor in the middle of the living room. Her dark skin strangely ashen, her head bent at an unnatural angle, and her eyes wide and unblinking in death. Fraidy Cat sat near her high-heeled foot washing his tail, unaffected by the corpse next to him.

Laney screamed, then screamed again as a strange dog started barking in her face, its teeth inches from her nose. An iron grip wrapped itself around her ankles. She caught a brief glance of a fuzzy brown face with a long pink tongue hanging out the side of its mouth before she was pulled back into the bathroom. Her nightshirt slid up around her breasts and the cheap carpet burned the front of her thighs and stomach until she reached the cool tiles of the bathroom. The door was slammed in her face and she was suddenly dangling in mid-air for a breath of time before she was again surrounded in steely warmth as the vampire wrapped its strong arms around her from behind.

"Do not do that again," it hissed. And then it sank its fangs deep into the side of her throat.

It had all happened so fast that Laney hung there, limp with shock, for a good thirty seconds. She stared at the bath tiles in front of her without really seeing them as the thing fed on her. The memory of her roommate's face, mouth slack and eyes at half-mast in death, overrode everything else that was happening. So it took a minute for the moaning in her ear and the tugging on her vein to sink in.

When it did, her heart began to thump behind her ribs, quickening her blood, and in response the vampire tightened its arms around her before backing up and sliding down the wall, taking her with it. It stretched out its long legs and settled her back on its lap. The movement jarred her out of her stupor, and Laney began to fight in earnest. Her erratic movements only seemed to excite the creature, however. It moaned with pleasure as it bit down harder, then with a grunt, it captured her arms to her sides to hold her still. Sliding its booted feet in toward her knees, it trapped her legs underneath its heavy thighs so she was well and truly caught.

Laney's eyes burned as salty tears slid down her cheeks and into her mouth. Refusing to give up, she ground her teeth together in anger, and tossed her head back and forth, trying to shake it off her, uncaring that she was probably ripping up her neck in the process. When that didn't work, she tried to reason with the thing. She tried begging it. And finally, she began to struggle in earnest again. It completely ignored all of her efforts. Laney started to feel woozy as she twisted and kicked, her strength quickly waning.

After what seemed an eternity, but in reality was probably just a flicker of time, it disengaged its fangs and lifted its head. Laney fought to stay conscious while it licked her wounds. She had to escape, had to find a way to get away, or she was going to die in her bathroom before the day was over.

The vampire's arm appeared in front of her eyes. She wished it wouldn't hold it there like that, or at the very least would hold it still. It was making her nauseous to watch it. Laney blinked. Its wrist was bleeding.

"Drink," the vampire ordered, then pressed the open wound to her mouth.

Laney tried to turn her head away, but it stopped her by pressing its cheek against the side of her face and tightening its hold around her arms and body.

"Drink," it commanded again, and rubbed its wrist against her lips until it was able to work its way between them.

Laney tasted the copper-laced tang of her own blood from her teeth cutting the inside of her lips as she tried to resist. But then something else mixed with it, something that reminded her of a well-aged, heady wine. Or at least what she imagined one would taste like. Thick and warm, it coated her tongue and dripped down the back of her throat. Without realizing she did so, she moaned aloud at the earthy flavor, swallowing before eagerly sinking her teeth into the wounds and sucking. The creature groaned, rolling its hips into her behind as its blood crept through her body with an erotic heat, slowly making its way down her arms and legs to merge within the very core of her, igniting every sensual nerve ending on its way. Laney moaned and writhed in the vampire's arms, sucking harder, wanting still more.

The vampire growled low in her ear as her behind wriggled deeper into his lap, pressing against the sudden hardness there. With an audible click of its teeth, it pulled its wrist away from her mouth.

"Now sleep, little mouse," it grated out.

Laney felt her eyes slide shut on command, and then there was nothing.

Dante studied the tiny human female in his lap as he breathed through the desire raging through him. He wasn't averse to much, but fucking unconscious women was not his thing. He preferred them to be awake, so he could see the flicker of fear in their eyes.

Even though there were no windows, it wasn't completely dark in the little cave he'd created for them. He could see quite well by the dim light coming from the electric toothbrush that was charging on the sink. The back of her head rested against his chest once again, and her beautiful long hair tickled the inside of his arm. Even without the light, he would recall the vivid color—not an average brown, but with natural strands of red running through it—rich and warm and fragrant. It had tumbled around her shoulders as she'd knelt on the floor, begging for him to bury his hands and face in it.

She was strong, this one. Defiant. He'd been unable to control her until he'd managed to get her to drink from him again. But rather than anger him, the memory of her resistance stirred his blood. Her delicate jaw had been set with a stubborn mien in spite of the paralyzing terror that he'd seen in her tawny brown eyes—expressive, bedroom eyes full of heat and courage. For a few intense seconds, staring into them, he had been completely distracted from feeding. He'd like to see her looking up at him from her knees like that again, but for an entirely different reason.

All in good time.

First, he needed to figure out how the hell he was going to get them out of here. He needed to get the fuck away from this desert and go home. But even without looking in the mirror, Dante was well aware of how he must appear. He estimated it would take a few more days before he would be presentable enough to be seen by humans so he could get on a plane. Even if he covered his head with a hood, anyone that caught so much as a glimpse of his macabre face would run screaming in terror, and rightly so.

Everyone, that is, except the tiny human in his arms that had dared to stand up to him, and even tried to escape. It had been a foolish attempt. The sun wouldn't save her from him. Nothing would save her now that he'd tasted her.

He briefly wondered if the fact that he'd killed her roommate would cause her distress, but then he shrugged it off. She would learn to accept it. Or not. It didn't really matter to him.

The only reason she herself was still alive was for the sole purpose of feeding him. Her blood was potent. He would be healed very soon. His eyes roamed up her gorgeous legs, over her soft belly, and up to the bit of cleavage he could see down the front of her nightshirt. When he healed, he would add fucking him to the list of her reasons to stay alive. Once he'd had his fill of this one, however, he'd snap her neck just like the others. Or maybe not. Maybe he'd kill her slowly, let her screams of terror wash over him like a gentle rain before he silenced them forever.

At the thought of ending her life, Dante's arms tightened around her protectively. The instinct to safeguard her momentarily confused him, but he brushed it off. He was tired, his mind spinning from one thought to the next.

As soon as the sun went down, he would wake the woman he held and find out if she had a car. If so, she could drive them to Seattle. It was the easiest solution. At his age, as long as he was covered from the sun, he would survive the trip. That way, they could leave right away, and he could bring his new canine friend with him.

Maybe he'd even take the cat. The dog seemed fond of it.

With a plan decided upon, Dante closed his eyes and fell into a healing sleep.

6

Laney awoke again, this time to the sound of the shower running. She sat up, pushing her damp hair out of her face and pulling her nightshirt out from where it was stuck under her breasts. She was disoriented at first as she tried to see through the minimal light and the cloud of steam that filled the small room.

The vampire's clothes were lying in a pile on the floor in front of her. She couldn't see him through the curtain, but she could hear him splashing around under the spray. Her eyes immediately went to the closed bathroom door. Hesitating only for a brief second, she got to her feet as quietly as she could and crept over to it. Laney was right next to the shower curtain now, and if she wanted, she could pull it back just enough to peek at the vampire while he bathed himself.

For an insane moment, she was tempted.

Laney frowned at her wayward mind, wondering where the hell *that* thought had come from. Shaking it off, she wrapped her hand around the knob, and very slowly and quietly began to twist it to the right.

"I wouldn't do that, little mouse," came a gravelly voice from behind the curtain.

Throwing caution to the wind, Laney immediately yanked the door open and ran out into the other room, praying it was still daylight. A few steps from the bathroom, she pulled up short, arms pinwheeling like a cartoon character. The sun had set, and the only illumination came from the flickering streetlamp outside. However, it wasn't the lack of sunshine that had interrupted her escape, but rather the chaos that greeted her sudden exit from the bathroom.

The dog from earlier jumped down off the couch where it had been sleeping, leaped over Sasha's body, and charged her. Laney stood absolutely still as the dog barked at her, trying to decide what would be worse: a bite from a dog or a vampire. Fraidy Cat took that opportunity to stroll over to her with his tail straight up in the air and weave in and out of her legs in greeting.

The water shut off behind her, spurring Laney into action. Deciding a dog bite was definitely the lesser of two evils, she scooped up her cat and ran toward the front door, the dog nipping at her heels the entire way. She was still wearing nothing but her nightshirt, but she had no time to grab something to cover herself with. Not if she wanted any chance at all of escaping. She felt surprisingly energetic, considering she'd spent the last twenty-four hours providing meal after meal for the leech in her bathroom and napping on the floor.

Or rather, on the vampire.

As if the mere thought of him had conjured him out of thin air, he suddenly appeared before her, dripping wet and wearing nothing but her lavender towel wrapped around his narrow waist. Laney had no time to stop the forward motion of her body. She slammed right into him, squishing Fraidy Cat, who yowled in protest, between their bodies.

She immediately regained her balance and tried to go around him, hanging on for dear life to the fat cat squirming in her embrace. One muscular arm flashed out and caught her around the front of her shoulders. Wrapping it around her, the vampire spun her around and pulled her back against his body. The water from his chest and stomach quickly soaked through the back of her thin shirt.

"Where are you going?" he asked in her ear.

To her surprise, he didn't sound angry. As a matter of fact, he sounded genuinely curious and rather amused. The dog continued to bark at their feet, but the vampire made a shushing sound, and the mongrel immediately sat down and cocked its head to stare up at him with worshipful brown eyes.

Laney gave up the battle to hang on to Fraidy and opened her arms. He landed on his feet, gave her a glare over his shoulder, and went over to touch noses with the dog before sitting down next to it. His topaz eyes held less worship and more disdain as he looked up at her.

"What the hell is going on here?" she whispered. Laney wasn't sure if she was asking herself or Fraidy.

"They seem to like each other," the vampire whispered loudly in response.

Laney felt her face heat as fear was replaced with anger at the blasé tone in his voice. She felt like she'd been thrown into an episode of The Twilight Zone, made even more terrifying because it was real, and he was...*amused*? The vampire chuckled when she dug her nails into his arm and tugged, trying to get him to loosen his grip on her, but she might as well have been trying to remove the steel safety bar of a roller coaster after it was in motion.

Then the bar suddenly released her, much as she had done to the cat.

For the second—or third—time since she'd met him, Laney landed in a heap on the floor at the feet of the vampire. Jumping up, she spun around to face him, and almost stepped on the cat, eliciting an unhappy hiss from her pet. Fraidy stayed right where he was next to his new friend, however, not deigning to actually move. But he did bat at her leg to let her know he was there.

Laney, on the other hand, felt the need to move far, far away, and put as much distance between herself and the large male in front of her as she could.

For that's what he was. Male. Completely and utterly male.

The monster that had attacked her the night before was nearly gone, and in its place was something that looked like it had just stepped off the cover of Iron Man Magazine—the sadistic, scary vampire issue. The lavender towel that was wrapped tightly around his waist split up one powerful thigh and barely concealed the bulge at the front of his hips. An eight pack of muscle rippled up his abdomen to a wide chest topped with shoulders that looked like they could easily handle the weight of the world and then some. But the thing that drew Laney's eyes the most was the black ink of the tribal tattoos that covered the entire left half of his body, from his temple all the way down to where they disappeared beneath the towel, only to reappear again on his left leg. She hadn't noticed them the night before. Or maybe she had and it just hadn't comprehended. Maybe because he'd been wearing clothes, and she'd been more concerned about the fangs coming at her. They weren't anything like the other tats she'd seen of that sort. These seemed to have a pattern to them, almost like they were symbols from some type of language or something.

"Are you going to run, little mouse? Or are you just going to stand there and squeak at me?"

Laney's attention snapped back up to his face. Eyes like black holes met hers with an unflinching stillness. *No*, she corrected herself. It wasn't the color of them that reminded her of space, it was the utter lack of any type of warmth. There was no soul behind those eyes. And that menacing tattoo twisting up the side of his throat, decorating the edge of his left cheek and temple where it flared out to partially cover his shaved head, only added to his sinister look.

"Are you going to kill me?" Surprisingly, her voice barely shook at all, in spite of the terror running through her veins.

"Yes." There was no hesitation in his voice, not one ounce of remorse on his ruggedly handsome face. "But not today, little mouse." He gave her an ominous smile.

"Why not today?" she asked in a flash of sudden boldness. Or maybe it was stupidity. "Why not just get it over with?" *What are you doing, Laney? Shut up!*

"Because today I need you to drive me home. Do you have a car?"

Okay. Not what she had been expecting him to say. But no way, no how, was she taking this guy anywhere. *Lie, Laney. Lie.* And she tried to. But Laney felt the pull of his control on her mind, trying to force the truth out of her. Gritting her teeth, she fought against it. Her head felt heavy, like it was bolted to her neck, but somehow she managed to shake it back and forth. "No," she told him.

Those black eyes narrowed, and he crossed his arms over his wide chest. She noticed then that he wasn't, in fact, completely healed. His skin still hung a bit loose on his large frame, the color still a bit...off...and that was what gave his face such a rugged look. "You're lying."

"Yes," she answered before she could stop herself, then she clamped her jaw shut before she could admit anything else. Of course he knew she had a car. She'd driven away in it the night before.

He cocked his head to the side and studied her, much as the dog had looked at him earlier, but without the adoration. "Why?"

"Because I don't want to drive you anywhere except back to the gates of hell." This time, she needed no mental prodding from him to tell the truth. And then, as long as she was at it, "And then I want to kick your blood-sucking ass right through them."

Something shimmered in those black eyes for just a fraction of a second, and then it was gone again. Was it anger? Amusement? Laney braced herself for his reaction to her reckless words. But he just headed back to the bedroom, taking her by the hand as he passed, and pulling her along with him. The animals plodded along behind.

Once in her room, he pointed to her bed. "Sit," he commanded.

Laney sat. So did the dog. She scowled down at the ugly thing.

"Don't move," the vampire told her. She re-directed her scowl at him, but he had turned his muscular back on her and was rummaging through her small closet. After perusing her small selection of clothes, he sighed. "There's nothing in here that will fit me."

"No?" she replied sarcastically. "Imagine that. Maybe you should've picked on somebody more your size."

He stiffened, and then his massive shoulders began to shake. Laney was certain that this time the end was nigh. Damn her big mouth. When the vampire turned around, he wasn't laughing, but nor did he look like he was about to add her body to the pile he'd started in the living room.

"You might be right." Planting his hands on his narrow hips, he looked around. "Do you have a washer and dryer?"

Laney shook her head. "There's a laundry mat by the office." She paused. "I don't have any quarters, though." Like that would stop him from hanging around, or convince him to leave her here.

He shrugged. "I guess there's no help for it." Leaving the room, he was back in a few seconds time with his dirty clothes. Shaking the sand out all over her freshly vacuumed rug, he laid them on the blue comforter next to her, then he unfastened the towel from his waist and dropped it to the floor.

She tried not to look, really, she did. But he was *right there*. And her eyes were pulled in that direction by a force so strong it could not have been her own, and maybe it wasn't. Either way, she couldn't honestly say she was sorry.

The vampire's hips were nearly at a level with her face, adjoined by rock hard abs and powerful thighs covered with just a light dusting of dark hair. That strange tattoo, she could now see, continued without a break from head to foot, but it was what was in the center of those hips that drew her attention the most. Even in its semi-hard state, his cock was impressive. Laney swallowed hard as her body reacted to his, a slow burning ache intensifying with each breath deep within her womb. Painfully aware that nothing but a thin nightshirt covered her naked body, she squeezed her thighs together and tore her eyes away to stare at the open bedroom door while he pulled on his pants. Clearing her throat, she managed to mumble, "I'd like to get dressed also." She absolutely refused to say "please."

She felt his eyes on her as he fastened his pants and reached for his shirt. "Go ahead. But be quick. And don't try anything," he added. "It won't end well for you."

Jumping up from the bed and away from his imposing presence, she quickly found a pair of jeans and a green button-down shirt. Grabbing some underthings out of the drawer, she started heading towards the bathroom.

"Where are you going?"

Laney stopped. "I'm going to the other room," she said without looking at him.

"No." His tone was final. "You'll change here."

Laney gritted her teeth. Enough was enough. She spun around to face him. "I have to use the bathroom. There's no window in there, as you well know, so you have nothing to worry about. And that's where I'm going to change." He lifted one dark eyebrow, but said nothing else, so she stomped into the bathroom, and shut and locked the door. Leaning against it, she released a shaky breath, her bravado swiftly leaving her now that she was alone.

"Don't take too long, little mouse, or I'll come in after you," he said from right outside the door.

Jumping away from that coarse voice, Laney switched on the light and checked that she had locked the door. Not, she supposed, that it would keep out a vampire if he really wanted to come in. She wasn't sure just how strong they were, but she had a feeling she didn't want to find out.

Laney took care of her most pressing needs, brushed her hair and teeth, and had her clothes on in record time. Finding a hair band, she pulled the unruly mass back into a low ponytail. Her eyes immediately went to the exposed skin of her neck. He had removed her bandage from the first bite, and there was no evidence that she'd spent the day feeding the creature in the other room, and for that she was grateful. The thought made her rethink the ponytail, but in the end she decided to keep it. It would keep her hair out of her way when she escaped. He wanted her to drive him somewhere? Fine. She'd drive him right into the morning sun, and then she'd stake him for good measure. But in spite of her ballsy state of mind, her stomach clenched and her hands shook. She wiped her clammy palms on her jeans.

"Hickory dickory dock," his singsong voice came through the closed door again. "The clock is ticking, little mouse."

"I'm coming!" Taking a steadying breath, Laney opened the door.

The vampire stood just outside with the dog under one arm and the cat under the other. "Ready?" he asked, as if they were about to leave for a date night. His eyes roved over her from head to toe. When they reached her bare feet, he stated the obvious. "You need shoes. Go get them. And then we're leaving."

Laney's eyes fell to the body of her dead roommate behind him. "What about Sasha?" she whispered.

He didn't bother to look back to see what she was talking about. "Were you attached to the human?"

Laney was a little taken aback by his question. But then she thought about that. Was she attached? Not really. Sasha was a horrible roommate. She ate all of Laney's food, never did her part of the chores, and stole money out of Laney's secret savings jar to blow at the clubs and in the slot machines. No, she wasn't attached. But Sasha was still a human being and deserved better than being left to rot in their apartment. In answer to his question, she only said, "I can't just leave her here. It's not right."

"We don't have time to hide the body, but I can toss it outside if you'd like so it doesn't stink up your apartment."

Laney could do nothing but stare. How could he be so cold? So unfeeling?

She watched as he set the animals down. Picking Sasha up with one hand gripped in the neck of her coat, he dragged her over to the window, opened it wide, and tossed her body down into the courtyard. Laney slapped her hand over her mouth to muffle her cries as he slammed the window shut, locked it, and picked up the animals again.

"Shoes," he said. When she didn't move, he ordered, "Now."

Laney stumbled into her room and dropped to her knees in her closet. Through tear-filled eyes, she searched for her Nikes, finally finding them in the back corner where she'd tossed them. Once she had socks and shoes on, she grabbed her slouchy backpack that substituted for a purse and threw a few extra things in it. Then she went to the nightstand and opened the drawer. She stared at the small book lying there with her heart in her throat, then grabbed it and shoved it into her bag.

The vampire was waiting patiently by the door.

"I need stuff for Fraidy. The cat," she clarified when he gave her a quizzical look. Maybe she could find something to stake him with while she was in the kitchen.

"No need," he said, picking something up off the floor without dropping the animals. When he straightened, he had Fraidy's food bag in one and the litter in the other. "Let's go. I've waited long enough for you."

"You could always leave me here," she tried. "Find someone else to drive you. Lots of people around here have cars."

He gave her that chilling smile. "No chance, little mouse. Now, come."

Laney took one last look around her apartment. Somehow, she had the feeling that this was the last time she would see her home.

7

Dante followed the woman down the stairs and out to her car, still carrying the animals. He had to dodge the drops of saliva that fell from the dog's tongue hanging happily out of the side of its mouth. Its new feline friend drooped over his other arm like a dishrag, purring with contentment to be coming along for the ride.

How had he, the oldest vampire he knew to still survive, come to this?

Dante eyeballed the Dumpster on the right side of the parking lot. He could dump these furballs and be back to his little mouse before she even realized he'd left her. *Little mouse*, he mused. Not really an appropriate name for the human. She was more like a mink, with her agile little body and snapping teeth.

Yet, he couldn't help but admire the way she boldly stood up to him despite the fact that he could smell the stench of her fear. Even when he'd told her, quite honestly, that he planned to kill her, she'd barely flinched. Only her heart had betrayed what she was feeling, skipping a few beats before picking up its cadence again, twice as fast as normal. He could still hear it pounding beneath the fragile protection of her ribcage.

A door lock beeped open as they approached an older black Subaru parked between two newer cars not far from her stairway. It didn't surprise him that she would own something with all-wheel drive, considering where he'd found her. Glancing in the back, he saw a Styrofoam cooler on the floor and an old, faded comforter with obnoxious blue flowers folded up on the seat. The blanket would be sufficient to protect him if an emergency arose and they couldn't stop at a hotel.

Looking back toward the stairway, Dante frowned, thinking about her walking that far from her car to her home, a woman all alone in this neighborhood. Then again, what the fuck did he care? Yet, in spite of his attempt to remain indifferent, it continued to gnaw at him. "You should live in a better neighborhood if you're going to live in an apartment."

She jumped at the sound of his voice directly behind her. Her eyes locked on his, and he recognized the glimmer of guilt. She'd been searching for a way to get away from him.

Run away, little mouse. I fucking dare you.

But rather than the satisfaction he normally felt at striking fear into the hearts of all those he came across, a heavy weight had settled deep within his chest knowing this tiny fighter was that afraid of him. It pressed down on his lungs, and his confusion quickly turned to inexplicable anger. "Open the fucking door." He pointed with his chin at the back driver's side door.

She reached for the door handle and hesitated. He could practically see the wheels spinning in her pretty head. A feral growl rose from his throat, a warning not to fuck with him further that she would do well to heed. Lucky for her, she did. Keeping her eyes averted, she opened the door. Dante deposited the animals on the seat and shut it again. He didn't take his attention off her the entire time. She would soon learn there was very little that escaped his notice.

The female swallowed hard, drawing his notice to the unmarred skin of her throat exposed by the ponytail. Noting the direction of his stare, she raised her hand to hide her fluttering pulse from his gaze.

"You think that will stop me, little mouse?" To prove his point, he lifted her off the ground and spun her around, slamming her back up against the car. His arms had automatically gone around her to take the brunt of the hit, which was a good thing as he may or may not just have left a few dents in her ride. One hand pulled her hips up tight against him while the other tangled in her hair and yanked her head to the side, stretching the smooth skin taught, revealing the blue veins beneath. It had all happened in less than a second's time, and her hands automatically fell to his shoulders and squeezed. She made a small, frightened sound and hung on tight.

As if I would ever drop such a delectable meal as her.

He skimmed one extended fang along that throbbing pulse while inhaling her unusual scent—a mouth-watering scent. "Nothing will stop me if I want you," he rasped in her ear. "It's best you understand that right now." He heard the staccato rhythm of her heartbeat. The sour smell of her fear, though still faint, was now overpowered by the earthy musk of her desire.

Dante growled low in his throat at this unexpected surprise. Her mind may fear him, but her body didn't. Her body liked the way he owned her.

Pressing the sharp tip of one fang through the soft layer of her skin, he drew a single drop of blood. His tongue flicked out to taste it, catching it before it could run down and stain her clothes. She began to tremble in his arms, pushing him away and pulling him closer at the same time. A low groan escaped him as his sex responded to the feel of her. Her fear intrigued him, but not as much as her taste. This human's blood was like none other he'd had before, and Dante had fed from thousands of humans in his lifetime.

Desire rose swiftly within him. Desire to claim her. To tame the wildness within this tiny creature. With a discreet glance around to make sure they hadn't garnered any unwanted attention, he reared his head back and struck hard. The woman cried out, and he covered her mouth to muffle the sound.

With the first pull on her vein, his eyes rolled back in his head. The fantasy of her on her knees before him came out of nowhere to dance behind his closed eyelids. Only this time, her nightshirt was torn open, her breasts exposed to him. And her eyes were not afraid, but filled with the heat of her willing submission. Dante groaned again, and sucked harder, drawing the warm ambrosia into his starving body. It flowed down his throat, hit his stomach, and spread through his body like hell's fire, healing him and slaying him all at the same time. He felt alive, truly alive, for the first time in a long time.

Though it was hard to stop, Dante didn't take much this time. He needed her alert to drive, and he'd only been making a point. After one last sip, he lapped at the wounds. They would heal momentarily. Pressing his lips to her throat, he inhaled deeply; comforted by the thought that he would be able to find her wherever she went by her scent alone, as long as she didn't get too far away. The call of her blood to his would always lead him to her.

Her lithe form felt good against him, and he released her hair but didn't put her down. He didn't stop to examine what he was about to do, or why. He only knew he wanted to taste more of her. His hold on her, though it didn't diminish, changed. One hand slid down from her hips to cup her ass, and the other wrapped around the back of her neck. Dante pressed light kisses to her throat, tasting here and there with a flick of his tongue. Her scent changed even more, becoming something darker, something primitive.

It came to his notice that she didn't appear to be breathing, and he pulled back to look down at her. Wide brown eyes stared back, the pupils so large that they were almost as black as his own.

"What are you doing?" she whispered, drawing his eyes to her lips. For one crazy moment, he was tempted to take her right there on the hood of the car.

With a sigh of regret, Dante loosened his hold and allowed her to slide down his body until her feet were back on the ground. Lust shot through his body everywhere she touched until he had to grit his teeth against acting upon it. Reaching around her, he opened the driver's side door. "Get in."

She stared up at him for a moment, then slid past him without another word and climbed into the car. Dante shut her door, and then got into the back with the animals. The dog wagged his little tail so hard his entire back end nearly slid off the seat. The cat blinked at him from its spot near the opposite door. Leaning forward, Dante reached an arm around her seat from behind and wrapped his hand around her opposite shoulder. The tiny bones felt so delicate in his large palm, like they would shatter with one small squeeze. She stiffened in the embrace, but didn't otherwise protest.

"What's your name, little mouse?"

"Laney," she answered.

"Laney what?"

"Laney Moss."

Why was that name familiar to him? "Start the car, Laney Moss." Her hair smelled like lavender and something he couldn't define off the top of his head. "We're going on a road trip." Leaning closer to her ear, he whispered, "It'll be fun."

Her hands shook, but she managed to get the key into the ignition and start the car. Dante noticed she had just over a half tank of gas. Enough to get them a good distance before they had to stop.

"Why don't you just take the car yourself," she asked as she waited for the engine to warm up. "I'd be more than happy to gift it to you. Or call someone to come and get you. Don't you have a phone?"

Dante didn't answer her right away, though he wasn't sure why. He'd never been ashamed to admit it before. Before the silence became awkward, he said, "I lost my phone." *And never thought to ask to borrow yours.* "And I don't drive. I have others do it for me."

"You don't drive? Or you can't?"

He took offense at her snide tone. "I don't need to," he said with a sneer. "I have minions like you to take me wherever I want to go. And this way I don't have to hunt for snacks. My next meal is right here in front of me whenever I feel the urge to take a drink." He'd said that last part hoping it would shut her up.

Her mouth slammed shut with an audible click.

"Now, be a good little mouse and do as I tell you, and maybe you'll still be alive when we get there."

Laney didn't respond, but he knew he'd gotten to her by the uptick in her rapidly pounding pulse. It sounded loud in his ears.

"Set the GPS for Seattle," Dante ordered.

She did so. And then she took a deep breath and eased out of the parking lot, and out onto the main road.

They drove in silence with only the robotic voice of the navigation system for company until they got onto US-93. Traffic was light this time of night, and they should make good time. He'd have her stop just past Falls City, if necessary. They could get a hotel in one of those little Idaho towns.

To keep himself occupied, Dante stewed on his thoughts. He never lessened his vigil, though. From what he'd seen of this one so far, it wouldn't surprise him if she jumped out of the car while it was fucking moving. And the only one that would get hurt from a stunt like that would be her. Dante had been through things way worse than a measly car crash.

The first years of his vampire life had been…eye opening, to say the least. The vampire that had created him in his image had also been the one to nearly end him when he'd discovered Dante's existence. If it hadn't been for Luukas, he would be nothing but ash in the wind right now. He owed the master vampire everything—his very existence.

Laney's voice brought him back to his current situation. "I need to stop."

"No."

"I need to use the restroom."

"You should have gone before we left the house."

"I did," she gritted out. "I'm stopping."

In spite of her defiant words, she drove past the next exit, waiting for his permission to stop. "Fine. Get off here," he said. Turning on her blinker, she exited the freeway.

Dante could see a rest stop ahead. There was one other car parked in front—a pick-up truck. "Park as far away from that truck as you can."

She pulled up right next to it.

A low growl rumbled in his chest, her flamboyant disobedience lighting him up inside. He needed to do something about this bad habit of hers, now, or he would have to kill her sooner than planned. And that would be a shame. He had plans for this one once he got her home.

Laney turned off the engine and took off her seatbelt. Giving her shoulder a warning squeeze just hard enough to make her wince, Dante removed his arm. As soon as he did so, she bolted.

But he had been expecting it. Dante was out of the car and cutting off her escape before she'd made it all the way out of the car. She'd only fucked herself with her little parking stunt, for now she had nowhere to go, stuck between the cars with her open door behind her and him blocking the only way out. "You weren't going to wait for me?" he asked her sarcastically.

Her eyes shot daggers at him as she closed her door. "I think I can handle this myself."

He told the dog to stay and closed his door as well. "I'm sure. But I'm coming with you anyway." Taking her by the arm, he started walking toward the ladies' room with her shuffling along behind him. "You should know," he said in a casual tone. "By not doing what I told you and parking next to that guy? You just guaranteed his death."

Glancing back over his shoulder at her, he smiled to see that his comment had hit home. She picked up her speed until she was walking next to him. "Please don't hurt them. That person is innocent."

"Too late, little mouse. Besides, I need a drink. And I need you alert to drive."

She ran out in front of him and he drew to a halt, releasing her arm and looking down at her with a challenging lift to his brow. The woman came up to his chest and was half his mass, and she thought she could physically intimidate him? He'd be amused if he weren't so irritated with her...and hungry for something other than her blood.

Placing her small hand on his stomach, she pleaded with her eyes. "Please. I'm asking you not to hurt that person, whoever they are."

Her touch burned through his shirt to the skin beneath. "And I care what you want because...?" He trailed off, cocking his head to the side. He was genuinely curious as to what she would come up with as a reason. And he wasn't disappointed.

"Because you obviously really want me with you for some reason, or you would have killed me the moment you found me. And if you don't spare that person, I won't go with you."

"I don't need your approval to keep you with me. I can make you stay with me."

"Yes, you could. But that's not what you want."

Dante narrowed his eyes at her, surprised to find that she was right. He didn't want to force her to his will. Not with his mind anyway. Or even with physical force. He could think of far more pleasurable ways to bond her to him. A few were popping into his head even now.

Just then, the door behind her opened and a masculine woman wearing men's work clothes came out of the restroom, wiping her hands on her pants. Dante zeroed in on her over the top of Laney's head, his body aching and his throat burning with thirst. He felt Laney's hand pressing into his gut, but didn't take his eyes from his prey. The woman glanced up and opened her overly fleshy mouth as if to say something. But upon seeing his fixation on her, she quickly looked away and hurried past, giving them a wide berth. Indecision wracked him, and the fact that he hesitated based solely upon the pleading look on Laney's face pissed him off.

In the end, he let the woman go.

Grabbing Laney's arm again, he yanked open the door to the ladies' room and shoved her inside. A quick look around told him the only windows were too high for her to reach. "Hurry it the fuck up," he practically spit at her. Then he stepped back to wait just outside the door as the pickup peeled out of the parking lot. He heard Laney go into one of the stalls, and for half a second, he considered chasing down the vehicle. Just to prove her wrong.

But when she came out, he was still standing there staring after the truck. "Thank you."

He didn't deserve her thanks. "All you've managed to do is make it worse for yourself, little mouse."

Dante walked away, not caring anymore if she followed him. He'd never, *ever*, let a human dictate to him what he should or should not do. Quite the opposite, in fact. The extent of his relationships with humans was to happily terrorize them until they broke down and begged for their lives, right before he silenced them forever. Usually in a painful and bloody manner. Humans were only good for two things: easing his thirst and satisfying his carnal lust before he saved them from their own misery. They deserved nothing less after what they'd done to him.

He stopped when he reached the car, out of sorts and unsure of how to proceed. In a few short hours, this tiny female had managed to roust him from the norm of comfort of his dark existence, and he didn't fucking like it. It made him edgy. The dog's brown face appeared in the window, so Dante opened the door and let him out to go shit on the patch of grass between the parking lot and the highway. He looked in at the orange tabby, but the cat didn't appear inclined to give up his spot on the comforter, so Dante crossed his arms and leaned back against the car to wait.

When he looked up, he saw Laney still standing over by the restrooms. She appeared as displaced as he felt as her eyes went from him to the highway to the blackness of the surrounding desert, and then back to him. Dante said nothing. She was a fool if she thought she could get away from him. Apparently, she was intelligent enough to realize it, for her shoulders sagged in defeat, and she got back into the car.

Dante held the door open for the dog and climbed in after him. Resuming the same position as earlier with his arm wrapped around Laney's shoulders, he inhaled her sweet scent. Thirst lanced through him. "We'll stop at the next hotel," he growled in her ear. "I'm thirsty."

He heard her swallow hard, and then she started the car.

Tonight, he was going to trap his little mouse.

8

The demon that now referred to itself as Steven stared at Cheung across the conference table. Refusing to show the thing any chinks in his armor, Cheung stared back with a polite smile. The body the demon possessed was not as formidable in appearance as when he had first done business with it, but Cheung was no fool. He knew that in spite of the deterioration beginning to take place in the physical body, the strength of the demon within was as powerful as ever. As a matter of fact, out of the much larger group he'd started out with, Cheung only had four associates that still had the balls to be anywhere near it or its cohorts. Those four stood in position behind him even now, fully armed and ready to give their lives for the man that fed their families.

"Show me what you have," the demon said to him.

Its voice grated on his ears, and the stench was ungodly, but Cheung just gave it a polite nod. Reaching inside his suit jacket, he pulled out the folded piece of paper where he had written the coordinates. Laying it out flat on the table between them, he smoothed it out and turned it around for the demon to see. "My people tell me that they have set eyes upon that which you are looking for, and can guarantee its existence," he said in Mandarin. He knew the thing would understand him. It spoke and understood all languages.

The demon, Steven, leaned forward in its chair to better see what was written on there. The two on either side of it did the same. Cheung didn't ask where the rest of them were. He was certain he didn't really want to know.

"I know this area. This area is full of human families." Steven looked up at Cheung with watery yellow eyes. "This is in a house?"

"According to my informants, yes."

Steven leaned back in his chair, pulling the paper closer to him as he did so. "And you trust these informants?"

"I do. They know what will happen to them if this information is false." It was one of the reasons why there were now only four others that would come with Cheung to these meetings. They had all seen with their own eyes what the demons were capable of when displeased.

"If it is indeed there, this will be the third clue," Steven said. "Is there any more information on where the fourth clue would be?"

Cheung debated what to say. He didn't want to be misleading. To send these things on a wild goose chase would not bode well for him, or anyone close to him, for that matter. He settled on honesty. He found throughout his dealings with this group that it did no good to lie. "I may have a lead, but I don't want to reveal anything just yet until I am certain that it is not a false one. I would rather wait until I have something concrete to tell you. I should have something for you at our next meeting."

The demon's mind crept into his own, feeling around with slimy fingers, testing the truth of his words. Satisfied that Cheung was being forthright, it pulled out of his thoughts with a sensation of wet string being threaded through a needle. Pushing back its chair, it stood, and the two on either side of it did the same.

"See that you do," it ordered. "As you can see, we are running out of time."

Cheung looked over the emaciated frame of the vampire body it possessed. "You can count on it."

Remaining exactly where he was until it was confirmed that the demons had left the building and were gone, Cheung loosened his tie and allowed himself to take a deep breath. His men sat down around him.

No one spoke. There was no need. Theoretically, they all knew what was going to happen if the demons succeeded in finding what they were looking for. And they all knew what it was they sought through the clues: blood. Specifically, their blood. The blood that had been drained from their bodies when they were forced back into hell hundreds or thousands of years ago. If they found that blood, they would be able to re-animate their original forms that once ruled over earth, and will be able to do so once again.

It would mean the end of the world as they knew it.

But Cheung had seen early on the opportunity that presented itself for him and his people by working with the demons. Although he knew better than to believe the promises it made—for as everyone knows, evil lies more often than not—the chances of him and his people surviving the demon's reign would improve greatly if they were on its good side.

It wasn't a great chance. But he would take what he could get. And maybe, just maybe, if he were very careful, he would survive the mayhem about to come.

9

Under the vampire's order, Laney pulled into the parking lot of a cheap-looking motel. He hadn't taken his arm from around her shoulders since they'd left her apartment, other than those few nerve-wracking minutes when they'd stopped at the rest stop. And that had been hours ago. What did he think she was going to do? Jump out of a moving vehicle?

Wouldn't I? To get away from him?

Sorrow filled her at the thought of leaving Fraidy Cat, her one and only true friend, fickle as he was. But then her thoughts took a different turn. She had to take a chance if it presented itself. Not doing so would just be stupid. He hadn't hurt the animals so far. Actually, he seemed rather fond of them. She had to trust that he wouldn't do so after she was gone. Later, when the sun was up and she had help, she could come back for her pet.

She pulled into a parking space near enough to the entrance to see through the glass doors and into the office, but not too close, and turned off the engine. It was the wee hours of the morning, still full dark, and there were only three other cars parked nearby. And one was probably an employee's. Still, she'd learned her lesson back at the rest stop.

Her mind spun as she tried to think of a reason—any reason—not to spend the day locked up in a hotel room with him. "I don't have enough money to pay for a room," she blurted. Her voice broke, and she cleared her throat and tried again. "I don't have —"

"We don't need money," he growled in her ear. His own voice, though still rough, was getting better. Then again, he hadn't spoken much for hours now. Maybe that was just what he sounded like all the time. "As soon as the other humans leave the lobby," he continued, "we'll go in and I'll get us a room."

On impulse, she asked, "Are you going to kill him? The guy behind the desk?" And then immediately wished she hadn't. But his answer surprised her.

"No. I don't need an army of cops sniffing around while I'm trapped inside."

Laney nodded but didn't say anything else. There was nothing else to say. He was going to secure them a room, probably with that freaky mind control, and then he was going to force her inside of that room and feed from her until she passed out. Or worse. And the thing that really pissed her off was there wasn't a damn thing she could do about it.

"Let's go," he told her.

A chill ran over her skin when the heat of his arm left her shoulders. She took off her seatbelt and grabbed her bag, preparing to make a run for it. But when she reached to open the door, he had beaten her to it. She hadn't even heard him leave the car. It was unnatural, the speed at which he moved.

As if that's the scariest thing about him.

The vampire stood off to the side and held out his hand to assist her out of the car. Laney stared at that large hand. She didn't want to touch him. Touching him was too confusing. It made her feel things that she didn't understand.

Besides, if she was going to die in the very near future, she was going to go down fighting. Ice flashed through her blood at the reality of that thought, instantly cooling the strange attraction she felt.

She was going to die. Soon. Probably within the next few days.

The inevitability of it crashed down on her. Angry at her incompetence to do anything to save herself, and at him for putting her in this position in the first place, she ignored the gentlemanly gesture. Shoving past him, she got out of the car and stepped away from him. Tossing her bag over one shoulder, she waited for him to close the door.

The vampire gave her a look, but didn't say anything. Telling Fraidy and the dog to stay put, he locked the car and closed the door. When he stepped in front of her, Laney tried to look anywhere else but at him. She'd read somewhere that if you didn't look directly at a vampire, they couldn't control your mind. Or maybe it had been on a TV show.

"When we go in there," he said. "You will not scream. You will not run. You will not in any way try to get that male to help you. If you do, I will not hesitate to rip out his jugular and drain him dry. Do you understand, little mouse?"

"Yes."

Gripping her by the chin, he tilted her face up until she had no choice but to look at him. "Do you understand?"

"Yes," Laney told him between gritted teeth, keeping her eyes on his nose.

He searched her face a moment longer, but whatever he saw lying beneath her anger must have satisfied him. "Good. I'd hate to have to hunt down another hotel. I'd be absolutely starving by the time we got there." Still holding her by the chin, he tilted her face away and leaned down to smell her hair. Then he startled her by nipping her jaw and running his nose down the side of her throat. Inhaling much louder than she thought necessary, he moaned aloud. "I'm very hungry, little mouse."

Every nerve ending in Laney's body went on high alert as his voice rumbled over her skin, but not in the way she would've expected. Instead of the impulse to flee, she had the strangest desire to lean into his hard physique until they were connected from head to toe. He wasn't touching her anywhere except where his fingers gripped her jaw, but she could feel him everywhere, as if she had done that very thing. Her head tilted to the side of its own accord, giving him easier access to the vein throbbing in her neck with each eager heartbeat. The warmth of his lips touched her there, soft as a feather, and Laney inhaled on a gasp.

"Little mouse...what are you doing to me?" he whispered.

His words broke through the fog of desire that was spiraling around her. Laney stiffened, snapping back to reality. Her eyes popped open, and she slammed her palms against his chest and pushed him away. He allowed her to move him, taking a step back only to stare down at her with an expression that she could only describe as terrified. But then she blinked, and the emotion was gone so fast that she wondered if she'd really seen it there at all. In its place was his normal cruel facade.

The vampire suddenly grabbed her by the arm, turned, and strode toward the office. Laney had to jog to keep up with him, or risk being dragged along the ground. He didn't say another word about what had just happened.

By the time they walked into the motel a few short seconds later, Laney was convinced that it had been some kind of vampire trick, those things she'd felt when his lips were on her skin. Some kind of thing they did to make their victims complacent. He could control her mind, why not her body? He had forced her to crave his touch. That was the only logical explanation. The only sane explanation.

The vampire walked up to the elderly man behind the desk. As the door swung closed behind them, Laney covered her mouth and nose. The decor looked like something out of a cheap horror film, and to add to the ambiance, it reeked of vomit and piss. She didn't know how anyone could stand working there.

Pulling her up next to him, the vampire tucked her under one heavy arm. "We need a room."

The man's smile was courteous, but his eyes held a hint of suspicion as they went from the vampire's cold stare to her heated face. "Sure, I just need to see some ID and cash or a credit card for the deposit." His eyes kept going back to Laney, and she looked away. She didn't want this man's death on her conscience.

"I don't think you understand," the vampire said, leaning over the desk until he had the clerk's full attention. Locking eyes with the smaller man, his voice had a hypnotic timbre to it that Laney was beginning to recognize. "You're going to give us a room. One that is far away from all of the other guests. And one with a king-sized bed. And then you are going to forget that we were ever here. When you notice the missing key, you will remember that that particular room is under renovations and is not available for guests right now, and that's why the key has been put away."

The clerk smiled. "Yes, of course. One room with a king-sized bed, coming up." He got the key card and laid it on the desk between them. "Paid in full."

The vampire took the card and made to leave, keeping Laney under his arm. As an afterthought, he added, "We will also need food, extra water, and a litter box. And pets are now allowed at this hotel." Then he escorted Laney out of the motel and back to her car.

Laney allowed herself to breathe again once they were outside. Getting back into the car, she drove them around to the back of the motel and parked in front of their room. It was on the bottom floor, and there were no other cars anywhere near it. She turned off the engine and opened the door. She hadn't put on her seatbelt that time, and seeing what was possibly her one and only chance to get away, she took it. She would come back for Fraidy once she had help. Grabbing her bag, she jumped out and started running.

She made it all the way out to the highway before he caught up to her. One moment she was waving her arms and running hell bent toward the headlights of oncoming traffic, and the next she was caught up in tornado force winds. It took her mind only a second to catch up as she was thrown onto a bed. Laney bounced once and landed on her back, then immediately scrambled up onto her hands and knees. Loose tendrils of hair fell into her eyes, and she sat up and pushed them out of her way. Her eyes flew from the dog barking next to the bed, to Fraidy sitting calmly on top of a small table that was supposed to be a desk, to the vampire sliding the chain lock on the door.

He turned around and placed his hands on his narrow hips, dark eyebrows pulled down over obsidian eyes as he scowled at her. He wasn't even out of breath. "Do not do that again," was all he said, and then he came toward her.

Laney crab-walked backward on the bed until her head and shoulders hit cheap metal. The headboard slammed into the wall behind it, the noise startling her. Twisting her body around on the bed until she was sitting, she prepared to jump off the opposite side and run from his wrath. But the vampire just picked up the phone on the nightstand and punched the number nine to get an outside line, then he dialed a number and shushed the dog while he listened to a phone ringing on the other end of the line. Punching another button, he put it on speakerphone and sank down onto the side of bed with his back toward her. His shoulders slumped forward as he rested his forearms on his thighs and waited.

Laney perched on the edge of the bed, completely thrown off balance by his unconcerned demeanor.

A man answered, his voice cautiously hopeful across the distance. "Yes?"

"Luukas," the vampire said. "Just wanted you to know I'm on my way."

"Dante," the man said. The relief in his voice quite obvious this time. "It's good to hear from you, my friend." There was a pause, and then she heard something like, "You don't sound surprised that I'm here."

"I knew Nik would find you. He wouldn't fail," the vampire said. "I'll be there in a day. Two at most." And then he hung up the phone.

Talk about your fuzzy reunions.

There was a knock at the door. Still ignoring her, he got up and went to answer it. He was unusually calm after her latest escape attempt. It made Laney nervous.

When he closed the door again, he had a large, plastic bag in one hand and a cheap plastic litter box in the other. He set the bag on the table, lifting the cat down and placing him gently on the floor when he got too curious about the contents. Laney's stomach growled, and her mouth started to water at the appetizing smells that were quickly overpowering the otherwise stale odor of the room. Taking the plastic box into the bathroom, the vampire filled it with the litter he'd brought from her apartment. Fraidy followed him in and immediately started scratching around. Pulling the bathroom door nearly all the way shut, he left just enough of an opening for the cat to come out again. Then he came out and started pulling takeout containers out of the bag and setting them on the table under the watchful stare of the dog.

Laney watched it all, feeling as if she were in some kind of really messed up dream. Her stomach growled again, letting her know that this was, unfortunately, her new reality, and she barely resisted the urge to run over to the food and start shoveling it into her mouth.

When everything was on the table, he pulled out the chair. "Come here," he ordered. "Eat."

She contemplated telling him that she wasn't hungry, but only for about half a second. Hangry was not a good look on her, and starving herself would accomplish nothing. Sliding off the bed, she made her way cautiously over to the table. She half expected him to grab her and sink his fangs into her throat as soon as she got near him, but he just motioned again for her to sit and even pushed in her chair.

"Eat," he repeated.

Bypassing the burger for now, she grabbed a handful of fries and shoved them into her mouth, washing them down with some bottled water. When the worst of the hunger pangs were gone, she dug into the giant burger. She didn't even care that it had tomatoes on it, which she hated, and took two big bites before pulling them off. The vampire hovered behind her the entire time, putting a damper on the enjoyment she otherwise would have gotten from filling her stomach.

"What is this?" Looking over her shoulder, she saw him holding her bag. In his large hand was the book she'd grabbed out of her nightstand before they'd left her apartment. It was a copy of the child's book *Goodnight Moon*. The rest of the contents were spilled all over the bed.

"That's mine." She tried to sound casual. If he thought it was important to her, he might take it away. "It's just an old keepsake. And I'd appreciate it if you stayed out of my stuff."

One side of his mouth lifted in something resembling a smile. "I only wanted to know what it was that was so fucking important to you that you left me waiting in the other room."

Laney remained silent.

He pointed with his chin to the food in front of her. "Eat." Then he started putting all her stuff back in her bag, including the book.

Turning back around, she did as he told her, grateful that he hadn't pressed the matter. Her nerves were frayed. She didn't think she could handle going there right now if he had demanded an explanation. When she couldn't eat another bite, she wiped her mouth self-consciously.

"Are you finished?"

Laney nodded, and he took the container from in front of her and put it on the floor for the dog to wolf down what was left. When the container was licked clean, he poured cat food into one side and water into the other, leaving it on the floor for the animals. For the first time, Laney realized that while she had been running like the hounds of hell were after her, the vampire had found their room and unloaded the car before bothering to come after her. Including Fraidy and his new friend. And he'd still caught up to her before she'd made it to the highway. Thinking about how he'd accomplished all of that in so short a time left her head spinning. She started to tremble uncontrollably, the fear that had been momentarily sated with food rushing back, for she'd just had a terrifying realization.

Now that her dinner was over, his was sure to begin.

10

Dante was thirsty. So thirsty, in fact, that he knew the female, his main blood source at the moment, would not survive unless he fed her some solid food and let her regain her strength. Even with his blood to revive her, he'd be taking a chance. She was only a human, after all. And the fatigue she'd succumbed to while driving throughout the night had not escaped his notice. Her being too tired to travel any further was one of the reasons he'd opted to stop at this hotel for the day.

But now he wondered if the head drooping and the sleepy eyes had just been a ruse, a way to throw him off track so she could take off on him as soon as she'd seen her chance. A grudging respect was beginning to grow for this human. That little stunt of hers had taken him completely by surprise. Something that rarely happened.

The second reason he'd had her stop was because he didn't trust her to drive through the middle of the day without yanking the blanket off him and letting him fry in the sun. She was frightened of him, but not frightened enough.

Starving her would only impede his own feedings, though. There were other ways to gain control over his little mouse—like that book in her bag. There was definitely more to that than she was telling him. It was important to her, and he would find out why...in time. First, however—

"Stand up," he ordered. His new friend needed to go outside before they settled down for the day, and he didn't trust the woman to stay put if he left her alone in the room. She would run again. He'd never been more certain of anything in his life.

A horrific ache hit him in the direct center of his chest at the thought of her getting away, stealing his breath. Startled by the feeling, and not at all liking what it fucking implied, Dante snuffed the emotion, cloaking it with anger. Tilting his head to the side, his fangs shot down and his upper lip lifted in a sneer as he waited for her to get her ass in gear.

Turns out, she wasn't stupid. She immediately jumped up out of the chair at the sight of his displeasure. Or maybe it was the growl that visibly raised the hair on her arms that spurred her into action. Whatever it was, she obeyed and now stood waiting for more instruction. He took her arm and issued a silent command, telling the dog to follow. The cat meowed at him in question, and he let it know that it could come as well.

When the woman realized they were all heading to the door, she dug in her heels. "Fraidy doesn't go outside."

"He'll be fine."

She glanced back over her shoulder as he opened the door and forced her outside. "But what if he runs out into the road?" A thread of genuine fear was in her voice.

"He won't."

"He will. He does it all the time. Which is why I don't let him out."

Dante stopped and glared down at her, calming his rising temper with effort. "The fucking cat will be fine."

She glanced over at her pet where he was sniffing around the edge of the parking lot with the dog. "But—"

"He won't leave. I told him to stay by us. And unlike his human owner, the cat will actually follow my orders."

Her eyes snapped up to his face. "Unlike his owner, you're not sucking the life from his veins every chance you get, either." A look of horror crossed her features as soon as the words left her mouth, but then she took a deep breath and her jaw set in that stubborn way he was beginning to recognize. Crossing her arms, she refused to back down. Dante narrowed his eyes, but held his tongue. He wasn't about to waste his time arguing with this human, and turned away before he did exactly as she'd accused just for the fuck of it. And if he took her vein out of anger, he'd kill her for sure. Or, at the very least, have to wait days for her to recover, which he couldn't afford to do. With the shape he was in, he'd do best to feed daily. And he needed to get home. Finding a new traveling companion didn't appeal to him, either.

"Why don't you just use your vampire mind control and make me do what you want?" she asked, purposefully provoking him.

He crossed his arms over his chest and smiled down at her. "Because that would take all the fun out of it, little mouse."

The woman paled and looked away. But then she surprised him. Again. "My *name* is Laney."

Yes. *Laney*.

The name meant "torch of light," if he remembered correctly. Unfortunately, there wasn't a light anywhere in the world bright enough to pierce the darkness within him. But he supposed it wouldn't hurt to return the gesture. She wouldn't live to tell anyone about him anyway.

"I am Dante. Dante Gabor." Not wanting to give her any ideas that he was getting soft, however, he added, "Not that you'll ever have the chance to tell anyone about me." He mentally called the animals back to him and ushered them all back into the room before she could say anything else.

Once inside again, the woman—Laney—stood awkwardly to the side as he made sure the heavy curtains were pulled across the blinds that covered the one and only window. The bed was off to the side, and there was little chance the sun would hit him there, but he didn't like to take any chances. Then he locked the door. When he turned around, he found three pairs of eyes looking at him expectantly. He pointed to the corner of the room, and the dog obediently went over and lay down. The cat followed at a more sedate pace, sitting next to it and swatting at the tail that couldn't seem to keep from wagging.

Dante inhaled deeply. *Fear.* He could feel the female's fear. Could smell it from where he stood. It beckoned to the darker side of him, to the ancient predator inside of him that he exulted in letting out. Her fear aroused him. He liked her afraid. He wanted to devour her, literally. And sexually.

And yet, at the same time, the intensity of his cravings for her made him...uncomfortable. He didn't want her to run from him. He wanted her to desire him the way he desired her.

For he did desire her. He wanted her blood, yes, but also her body. Possibly even her soul. The realization was eye opening, and left him staring at the woman trembling in front of him in amazement. Her eyes shifted away when she noticed his unwavering stare, and Dante growled with displeasure that he was no longer the object of her attention.

He approached her as one would approach a cornered animal, admiring the way her spine straightened and how she stood her ground in spite of her diminutive size, and the way her blood pounded through her veins. He could hear it —every beat of her heart. Each step he took made it beat faster until he could visualize the blood rushing through her arteries. By the time he was within touching distance, her breath came in short, erratic pants.

Stopping just inside her personal space, he waited for her to look up. But she refused, keeping her eyes on the center of his chest. "Look at me, little mouse."

Still, she refused. So he took her chin between his fingers and forcibly tilted her face up until she had no choice. He looked into her brown eyes. The rich color tinged with green specks of fear. "I'm not going to hurt you."

Where the fuck had that come from?

But he found that it was true. At least for tonight. Slowly, so as not to make her run, he allowed himself to do what he'd wanted to do since he'd found her collapsed on the kitchen floor. He dropped his hand, palming her breast through the thin material of her shirt. Her nipple puckered into his palm, even through her bra, and he cocked his head and smiled as the blood rushed into her face. He pinched it between his fingers—hard.

Instead of pulling away, her body lurched forward into his touch. She caught herself right away and tried to cover the reaction by stepping back out of his reach, but it was too late. He'd seen her response. He'd felt it. He could smell the scent of her lust rising to mix with the stench of her fear.

Dropping his arm back down to his side, he taunted her. "Are you afraid of me, little mouse?"

She didn't answer him, but her eyes skittered away.

"Good. You should be afraid. I could kill you instantly with little more than a flick of my wrist." Her trembling returned, and a tear leaked from her eye to run down her cheek. Dante tracked it, following its path down over her fragile jawline. It disappeared as it followed the curve of the bone, and then reappeared to make its way down her graceful throat, only to disappear again under the neckline of her shirt. He mourned its loss, jealous of its ability to touch that soft skin so intimately.

Grinding his jaw, he reminded himself that she was not his to care for. This human...this woman...was *more*. She was better than that, deserved more than his depraved existence could give her. Dante recognized her worth, in spite of her being a lowly mortal.

And that made him hate her. Made him want to bring her down to his level. Made him want to prove to her that she was no better than he was. She was human. She was *inferior*. She was nothing.

With one step, he was on her. A quick tug had the hair band out of her hair. The dark strands tumbled around her shoulders, thick and soft, as the fragrance of her shampoo wafted to his nose. Dante cupped the back of her skull, took a handful of that silky hair, and yanked her head back. Laney winced, but didn't cry out. His eyes travelled over her face—eyes tightly shut, but her jaw clenched in defiance—and his admiration for her grew. His eyes dropped to her exposed throat. A groan escaped him as he studied the blue vein pulsing in her neck, clearly visible to him through the near translucent skin. Thirst burned his throat and cramped his still-healing muscles. His hand tightened in her hair, eliciting another wince. He needed to feed. Just enough to ease his suffering.

Drawing his fist in toward him, he brought her closer, and lifted her throat to his waiting fangs. His other arm wrapped around her body to hold her tight against him. She resisted, her hands pushing against his chest even as her feet dangled a foot from the carpet.

"Please," she sobbed. "Please don't kill me."

With an animalistic growl, he struck her throat. The first mouthful of her blood was fucking heaven. The second was even better. He fed from her like a male starving, each swallow hitting his gut and then spreading through his starving body, sending healing power into his emaciated muscles. Nerve endings sparked to life as her blood burned through him in the very best possible way, igniting his senses. His manhood swelled, throbbing within the confines of his pants. Smells became stronger, his sight became clearer, his skin more sensitive until he felt reunited with the elements around him.

Until he nearly felt as one with the woman in his arms. Almost.

MINE. Caught up in the blood lust, the word crashed through him, reverberating like thunder.

"Dante...."

Her plea broke through his sense of euphoria, the sound of his name on her tongue causing him to moan in pleasure.

"Dante, please," she whimpered.

His hand loosened in her hair, just enough so that he wasn't hurting her. He extracted his fangs, licking the wounds to heal them. Before he realized what he was doing, his lips had replaced his teeth, and he was kissing his way down her smooth throat, following the trail the tear had made. He could still taste its salty essence. Laney made a little sound in her throat, part distress and part passion.

Dante tightened his hold on her, carefully, so as not to break her fragile bones, and carried her the short distance to the bed. He didn't stop to think about what he was doing. And even if he had, it wouldn't have stopped him. He just knew that he needed to be closer to this female. Laying her across the bedspread, he released her to pull his shirt up and off. Then his hands went to the waistline of his pants, quickly undoing them to ease the pressure there, but he didn't take them off. Not yet. He wouldn't be able to control himself if he freed his sex pulsing painfully within.

The entire time her eyes travelled over him as if she was just as caught up in the spell weaved around them, her brown eyes wide in her pale face and darkened in passion.

"Take off your clothes," he ordered huskily.

She blinked. Once. Twice. The haze in her eyes cleared. Then she frowned and shook her head. "No. I won't."

Dante's upper lip rose in a sneer, exposing his fangs. "I said, take them OFF."

"No." Pushing herself into a sitting position, she stared him right in the eye.

Dante cocked his head and studied this small female. She had just managed to do something no one else had done for as long as he could remember—knock him for a loop. The color was gone from her skin, and she was so weak that she swayed where she sat, yet she stared up at him with eyes that sparked with glorious defiance.

And Dante found he could do...nothing.

He was caught in a quandary. He wanted her naked. He wanted her naked five fucking minutes ago. But yet, he was hesitant to force her because he knew it would hurt her. Something he'd never had an issue with before.

No, not just hesitant. He really couldn't. He opened his mouth to tell her again to strip, but no words came out. He reached out with his mind, but she had raised her mental shields, and he could find no way around them without the influence of his blood. He couldn't even bring himself to force her to feed from him. For the first time in his long life, he cared about what his victim wanted.

It completely fucking unnerved him.

Turning on his heel, he strode out of the hotel room, slamming the door shut behind him.

11

Laney watched Dante stomp out of the room with his pants still undone, jumping when the door slammed loudly behind him. The dog immediately ran over to it and stood there whining, not happy that he'd been left behind. Fraidy lifted his head, but didn't bother getting up, content to let the dog do all the work.

She started to tremble uncontrollably, her teeth chattering so hard that it hurt her jaw. Scooting over on her butt until she was sitting on the edge of the bed, she attempted to stand on wobbly legs. Laney wasn't quite sure what had just happened, but she wasn't going to just sit there on the bed and wait for him to come back and finish what he'd started.

Bracing herself against the nightstand with one hand, she bent down and picked up her pack with the other and took it into the bathroom with her. She knew she wouldn't get very far if she tried to leave right now. Even if the vampire wasn't nearby, she was in no condition to escape. So she'd settle for the protein bar in her back, some water, and a fast, hot shower. Very fast. The last thing she wanted was for him to return and find her exactly how he'd wanted her.

Right. Shower first. Then food.

Laney knew she probably wasn't in her right frame of mind. But she was so cold. All she could think about was getting warm again, and apparently, running water was soothing to her. So she locked the bathroom door and turned on the water as hot as she could stand it, then stripped off her shoes and jeans. Her hands shook so bad, she quickly gave up on the buttons of her shirt, pulling it up and off, much as the vampire had with his.

She shivered again at the memory of his bare torso, but not from the cold this time. Or even fear. The gruesome monster that had found her in the desert was long gone and had been replaced by a large, virile male. More powerful even than the male that had confronted her in nothing but a purple towel just a few hours before. His shoulders were large and broad, muscle rippled down his flat abs into a "V", and there was not an ounce of extra flesh on him. She could even see the veins on his arms and groin.

Every time he fed, he filled out more. His skin color became richer and darker, his face less rugged and more handsome. No, "handsome" wasn't a word she would use to describe him. Masculine, yes. Charismatic. Powerful. Enigmatic. Terrifying. Even sexy. But not handsome.

Yet, his eyes remained cold and distant.

Because he's not human. He's a monster. No matter what he looks like.

Laney took care of the needs of her bladder, and then stepped underneath the spray of hot water. She managed to wash her hair while on her feet, but ended up sitting in the tub while she washed the rest of her. Then she just sat there for a minute, letting the water rinse away the soap.

Her head fell forward, and her eyes slowly focused on the white, tiger-stripe marks covering her lower stomach. She touched them with her fingertips, tracing the lines as the emptiness threatened to consume her, only to be swiftly replaced by grief. Pushing away the memories, she struggled to her feet and turned off the water. The world shifted around her as she got out and dried herself off, but somehow she managed to keep herself upright and conscious, unlike the night before.

A noise in the other room had her picking up the pace as she dressed with jerky movements in the same clothes she'd had on before and dug around her pack for her brush. Wiping the moisture from the mirror with a shaky hand, she was startled at the reflection she saw there. In her blood-deprived state of mind, she appeared almost otherworldly with her dark hair and eyes, and pale skin. The green of her shirt made the shadows under her eyes more black than blue.

She brushed her teeth, packed up her stuff, and then paused with her hand on the doorknob. Pressing her ear against the door, she listened. If the vampire had returned, she would have no way of knowing until she opened the door. Laney's hand slid from the knob and fell limply to her side. She knew she would have to go out there eventually and face him, but she needed just a few more seconds. Hell, if she was lucky, maybe she *would* pass out here in the bathroom, and then she wouldn't know what was happening when he came back and found her. Fraidy was out there, but she still had no fear that the vampire would hurt him. He'd been kind to the animals, oddly enough. More kind than he was to her. Humans were apparently lower on the food chain than pets, according to vampires.

Unable to take the suspense any longer, she unlocked the door and cautiously pulled it open while her eyes skittered around the small room. The dog's little brown and white body was sprawled across the mattress, Fraidy curled up against its chest. He meowed softly when he saw her standing in the doorway.

Dante was nowhere to be seen.

Laney stumbled across the room to the bed, what little energy she'd had swiftly leaving her. Forgoing the protein bar, and too tired to walk across the room for water, she pulled back the comforter and crawled into the bed next to the animals. She was beyond caring what would happen when the vampire came back. Well, almost.

Her eyes drifted closed.

When she awoke, she found herself tucked up against the vampire, her nose buried in the soft folds of his shirt. It was dark in the room, but she didn't need to see to know that it was him. She knew from his scent. It was impossible to describe, but was as enticing as homemade bread to a starving person. A lure. A way to tempt his victims closer to him, she was sure of it. His heavy arms were around her, trapping her to him, her head resting on one large bicep.

Laney closed her eyes again without moving. She knew he wasn't asleep, and she didn't want him to know that she had woken up. His large hand roved down her back to her ass, then down the back of her thigh and back up to the curve of her hip. He sighed heavily. "You need to drink from me, little mouse," he said. "You're weak."

Guess she needed to work on her sleeping game.

"I'm fine." She tried to pull away from him, her heavy limbs making it difficult, but he only gripped her tighter.

"I shouldn't have fed from you earlier. I took too much, and you can't handle it yet. You need to drink."

Yet?

Brushing her hair tenderly out of her face, he cupped the back of her head and brought her mouth up to his neck. "Drink," he demanded. In the weak light of the alarm clock, she saw something glinting in his other hand as he brought it up to his throat. "Drink," he said again as he moved his hand out of the way and pulled her mouth in closer.

Laney tried to resist, but she was so tired. So she opened her mouth to tell him no, but he took that opportunity to tilt his head away and press her closer. She felt wetness on her lips as they hit the bleeding wound he'd made on his neck, and Laney automatically licked them clean. His vampire blood coated her tongue, and a moan of pleasure escaped her before she could stop it. Her tongue flicked out again, gathering another taste into her mouth. The flavor was indescribable. She'd never tasted anything so wonderful in her life. Laney swallowed, and it flowed down her throat as easy as warm honey, heating her body from the inside out.

A need she couldn't explain consumed her. She wiggled closer and propped herself up on her elbow, her eyes zeroing in on the open wound. She was so thirsty. She had to have more. Taking his broad shoulder in one hand and the top of his head in the other, she pushed them apart, arcing his neck up to give her easier access to the life giving blood. Her mouth clamped down over the wound, and she bit down hard to keep it open.

Dante groaned as his hips thrust forward once, before settling into an erotic rolling motion against her own. He fucked her with their clothes on as she drank from him.

Laney threw one leg over both of his, and he slid a powerful thigh forward until it was pressed against her clit. The seam of her jeans hit the exact right spot, and without even realizing what she was doing, Laney started rocking her hips, riding his leg as she took his lifeblood inside of her. She couldn't stop the little sounds of pleasure from escaping as he squeezed her ass, her breasts, his hands running over her restlessly everywhere he could reach. His scent surrounded her, as did the heat of his body.

"Laney...." Her name was a prayer of wonder on his lips.

The flow of blood was letting up, and Laney bit down again to keep it going. He cried out, his hips jerking forward as he gripped her to him. The sound startled her and she tried to stop, but as soon as he felt her mouth leaving him, he pushed her head back down. With a moan, she latched on again. The pressure built in her womb, waves of pleasure shooting through her as he pushed her down harder against his leg and ground her body against him, squeezing her ass as he encouraged her on.

Laney knew that what she was doing was sick, disgusting, but she couldn't seem to control herself. Her body demanded release, jolts of pleasure surging through her with every drink she took. She rocked her hips back and forth on his thigh, reaching for that elusive peak of pleasure. Faster and faster until she was beyond reason, beyond rational thought. All she knew were the sensations she was feeling, the strength and virility of the male holding her, the connection between them as he shared his essence with her.

The pressure in her womb escalated, climbing higher and higher until, with a muffled cry, she crashed over the edge. Her body convulsed, her head flying back even though she tried to keep her hold on him. Her cries of pleasure mixed with his deep growls as he held her to him and helped her ride out her orgasm.

When she sagged back into the mattress, breathing hard, her muscles still pulsing from the powerful orgasm she'd just had, he pulled his arm out from underneath her and rolled away. The cool air chilled her body where his heat had been just a moment before, causing goose bumps to break out all over. Shame suffused her cheeks and chest as the reality of what had just happened sunk in to her pleasure-soaked brain.

Horrified at what she had done, she jerked upright with a sob. But then he was back, pulling her down with him into the warm bed, and tucking the blankets up around her.

"Sleep, Laney."

She felt his strong arms catch her as blackness descended once more.

When she woke, she again found herself curled up against the front of the vampire. Only this time his breathing was slow and steady. He was sleeping. Laney studied his face. With his eyes shut, the icy remoteness was gone from his features, and in its place was a man like any other man. The small creases around his mouth and eyes made her guess his age to be around thirty or thirty-five years old. Maybe a little older. At least that was about how old he must have been when he'd become a vampire.

That thought led her to wondering how it had happened, and what his life had been like before. Had he been a husband? A father? He must have laughed a lot, before this happened to him, for those lines to be engraved so permanently into his skin.

As if he sensed her rapt attention, his eyes suddenly popped open. Laney was startled to find herself staring into clear brown eyes that were filled with warmth as they gazed upon her, just before they narrowed with suspicion. The light faded as if it had never been there, the color darkened, and they again became cold and bleak. But in that one moment, Laney's breath had caught in her throat.

Untangling himself from her, Dante pushed the blankets back and rolled away. Getting up from the bed, he strode into the bathroom, shutting the door firmly behind him.

While he was in there, Laney freed herself from the blankets and got up to start getting her things together. It took her all of five seconds; everything was already in her pack. So she pulled her hair back again, put her shoes on, and then gathered Fraidy's stuff and piled everything up near the door. She stood there undecided, shifting from foot to foot as she thought about making a break for it, but when she pulled back the curtain to peek outside, she saw that it was already past dusk and well on its way to full darkness. Not enough time for her to get far enough away before he would find her.

Laney had just dropped the curtain back into place and turned away from the window when he opened the door and came out.

She glanced at his neck. The cut was washed clean and nearly healed already. Laney dropped her eyes when he walked past her, not wanting him to catch her staring. But he seemed to be paying her no attention at all as he lifted one side of the curtain just enough to see out, just as she had. She heard a satisfied grunt, and then he dropped it again and turned to give her a once over.

"Take it down," he told her.

"What?" she asked, confused.

He waved a hand in the general direction of her head. "Your hair. Leave it down."

She scowled at him. "No. I like it up."

He growled deep in his throat, a feral sound that made the small hairs all over her body rise up in alarm, but she refused to back down. He might hold her life in his hands, but he wasn't about to start dictating what she did with her hair.

"Are we leaving?" she asked him. "I need to use the bathroom first."

He cocked his head at her, his face emotionless as he studied her exposed throat then her breasts before he spun on his heel and started pacing the length of the room. But he hadn't been quick enough. She had seen the flare of heat in his eyes. "Go on." His voice floated to her as if from everywhere at once.

Laney quickly took care of business, emptying her bladder and brushing her teeth again. When she came out, he was still pacing.

She tried to track him, but the vampire moved so fast that he would only appear for a fraction of a second at each end of the room. He would then turn and disappear, to reappear again twenty feet away less than a second later.

Laney gave up trying to gauge his mood and decided she would do well just to wait, as she was unsure of what else to do. In spite of his earlier eagerness, he seemed to be in no hurry to leave now. But when a few more minutes passed, and he was still wearing out a path in the floor, she spoke up. "Dante?"

The sound of his name snapped him out of whatever deep thoughts he was having and he stopped mid-pace, suddenly appearing directly in front of her.

Laney had to take a step back from his overpowering presence. Clearing her throat to hide her nervousness, she asked again, "Are we leaving?"

His head lifted to look at her, the weight of his stare traveling at a leisurely pace up the length of her body. "Yes," he finally said. Yet he made no move to do so.

Disconcerted, Laney walked over and picked up her bag and Fraidy's food, and then waited for him by the door.

He joined her after a moment, and when Laney looked up, she caught a flash of...something...as the emotion flitted across his features just before they closed off to her again. Laney hesitated, torn as to whether to be eager to leave or not. The sooner she got him where he was going, the sooner she'd be rid of him, one way or the other. He wouldn't want to risk her telling anyone about him. She knew that instinctively. So he would either wash her mind clear of any memory of him, if he could do that, or he would take her out of the equation as he'd threatened. Either way, she would be free.

She reached for the knob, but didn't open the door. "I feel a lot better tonight. I could probably drive right through the day I think, if need be. And I have a blanket in my car. That would protect you from the sun, wouldn't it?" She was babbling. She always talked too much when her nerves were shot to hell.

He narrowed his eyes. "It would. If it stayed over me."

His meaning was clear. He wasn't stupid, and he didn't trust her. But she tried to convince him anyway. "I swear, I wouldn't—"

"So eager to get to our destination? To see the end of your pathetic life, little mouse?" His tone mocked her. "I won't need you anymore once we get to my home."

"At least I'll be rid of you, one way or the other," she said with a show of bravado she didn't feel. "This world is going to shit anyway."

Fraidy chose that moment to jump up onto the bed and meow, demanding attention. Distractedly, the vampire reached over and stroked the orange fur. A flash of irrational jealousy went through her as she watched him being so gentle with her pet. Then she shook her head at herself. It's not like she wished he would touch her like that. Laney would be thrilled if he never touched her again.

You weren't thinking that earlier.

Heat made her cheeks burn, and she turned her thoughts back to her cat. But she had to admit, a part of her was fascinated by the way he could contain his power when he wanted to. She'd felt his strength when he dealt with her, and knew it took a lot of effort on his part to control it. Yet, he did it so effortlessly with the animals. It made her wonder which one was the real Dante. The monster that attacked her? Or the man that so naturally soothed creatures so much smaller and weaker than him?

Maybe they both were.

"Well?" she asked, irritated with herself. "Are we leaving, or are we just going to hang out here all night?" As soon as the words were out of her mouth, she wished she could take them back. She didn't want to give him any ideas. Her traitorous body, however, was in full agreement with those ideas. Ever aware of the male in the room with her, it released a rush of desire that started in her core and crashed through her body, making her breasts swell and her innermost muscles clench. How could she fear a man and desire him all at the same time? What the hell was wrong with her? Then she reminded herself that he wasn't an ordinary man. He was a supernatural creature. A predator of the highest order. She needed to keep her wits about her if she had any hope at all of getting out of this.

He inhaled deeply, and as he did so he seemed to grow larger, his muscles harder, as those cold eyes dropped from her face to her tits to her hips, and back to her lips. The air grew heavy between them, and Laney had to force herself not to fall to her knees and beg for his touch.

But then he sighed, as if the weight of the world were on his shoulders. Striding past her without a word, he brushed her fingers aside and held the door open, indicating with a wave of his hand for her to go out to the car.

Laney hadn't realized until she stepped outside that she had stopped breathing. She gratefully inhaled the cool, fresh air, and headed to the car.

She waited by the driver's side while he gathered up the rest of their stuff, held the door for the dog and Fraidy, and then followed them out, leaving the room key on the table.

12

The drive to Seattle took fucking forever. By the time they arrived, Dante wished he'd taken the chance of being seen at the airport and had had Luukas send a jet for him. Even if a human or two had seen him and freaked out, he could've just wiped their memories. A crowd would be a little harder, but not impossible.

All right, yeah. He was full of shit. It would have been impossible to handle a crowd in the shape he'd been in that first night. But he was healing faster than he thought possible, and it was still easier than being stuck in this box with a constant hard-on and an insatiable blood lust that he couldn't satisfy until she managed to get him home.

They'd had to stop a second night at another out of the way hotel. One look at the double bed—the only size they had—and Dante had locked the woman in the bathroom with a pillow and a blanket. He didn't even bother to feed first. There was no fucking way he could go through another night of denying himself the use of her body. And the line between feeding and fucking was way too blurry for vampires as it was. If she'd been anywhere near him, he wouldn't have been able to control his lust in either situation. He'd learned the night before that though he could drink from her whether she wanted him to or not, forcing himself upon her was just something he could not do. It must be an after-effect of his time in the desert.

But she needed some time to recover if he was going to keep her until they got home. So instead, he'd spent the day staring up at the water-stained ceiling, re-living over and over in his head the way she'd come in his arms with such violent abandon when he'd offered his blood to her. He wanted to make her come like that again. And he would, once he got her back to Seattle and into the underground beneath the city where he dwelled. There, she could scream and beg and try to deny him all she wanted. No one would hear her, and no one would be coming to save her. He could do whatever he wanted with her, make her do whatever he wanted to him, before he bled her dry and tossed her body into the Sound with the rest of the humans that had been unfortunate enough to be invited into his home.

Just imagining her at his mercy in his feeding room made him hard as a rock, but he didn't touch himself. Didn't relieve the sweet agony of his erection. Oh, no. He was saving that for her. She was going to relieve that ache for him.

They entered the city going west on I-90 until they hit I-5, and then he directed Laney north. The tents of the homeless lined the grassy area next to the freeway ramp, the area lit by the distant lights of downtown Seattle. Dante gave his future meals a distracted glance. There was a lot of homeless in this city. It was one of the reasons he was glad Luukas had decided to make it the home of the Vampire Council of the North American territory. There were so many lowlifes wandering around, that when a few disappeared here and there, no one really cared or made much of a fuss about it, if they even noticed at all.

From his place in the back seat, Dante guided Laney through the downtown area to the high-rise apartments that he called home, along with Luukas and the rest of his Hunters. He had her pull into the underground parking garage, the same garage he'd been abducted from weeks before. A group of fucking humans in a black van had squealed to a stop inches from where he'd stood. One had distracted him while another had snuck around and jabbed him in the neck with a needle full of gods-knew-what, effectively knocking him out cold. He'd been out long enough for it to be day when he'd woken up.

His only consolation was that he'd managed to kill one of them and literally scare the piss out of another one before they'd managed to get him into the plane that he'd later jumped out of. Desert sand was not as soft as it looked when you hit it dropping from the sky with no parachute.

"Where should I park?"

Laney's shaky voice pulled him back into the present. "Go down the ramp as far as you can, then just find a spot anywhere," he answered.

She followed his directions, driving past another car that had their reverse lights on without stopping. He saw her glance in that direction, though, desperation clearly evident on her face, and was impressed at how much courage it took for her not to stop and endanger the lives within that vehicle.

The farther down they went, the more her hands shook on the wheel, and the more the stench of her fear filled the car. The dog sat up and whined next to him, clearly smelling it, too. Dante rubbed his head and ears, soothing the canine. When they got to the very last level, he pointed to an empty spot near the back elevator. "There."

Laney pulled the car smoothly into the parking spot and shut off the engine. She didn't move to get out, in spite of the fact that he'd released his hold from her shoulders. Her heart thundered so loud it echoed in the small space. At least, to his ears.

Ordering the animals to stay, he got out of the car and stretched, enjoying the moment. Tormenting humans this way was one of his greatest pleasures. The fear of what was going to happen was often worse than what actually happened. Not in his case, but usually. Where he was involved, the reality of what he did to his victims was way, way worse.

Dante opened the car door. "Get out." He spoke quietly, but firmly, so she would know he wasn't fucking around. The time for games was over. Thirst burned his throat as her scent drifted up to his nose. "*Now*," he added.

The woman struggled to take off her seatbelt, and he let her be, enjoying her terror, though not as much as he thought he should be. She finally managed to release the latch and got out of the car, bringing her backpack with her. Before they left the vehicle, he felt the need to warn her one last time. "If you run, I will catch you, little mouse. If you hide, I will find you. If you happen to see another human and you try to get them to help you, they will die a bloody death right in front of you. And you will join them immediately after."

"And if I do none of those things?" she asked in a whisper.

Dante tracked the tears that were wetting her cheeks, trying to figure out what the fuck that twinge in his chest was. "If you do as I say, and only as I say, I might spare you the pain." Leaning over, he put his mouth right by her ear. "Dying by vampire bite can be a great fucking way to die. I once made a woman come so many times while I drained her that she didn't even realize she was dying."

Her spine stiffened as he straightened again and she looked him right in the eye, in spite of the silent tears running down her cheeks. "Is that supposed to make me feel better about it?" she spit out.

"It's your choice," was all he said before he took her by the arm and started leading her toward the elevator.

"What about Fraidy?" she asked in a small voice. "What's going to happen to him and the dog?"

Reaching the elevator, he pushed the button and glanced around. It was an automatic thing to do, to scan the area for any type of threat that may be nearby. "They'll be well taken care of," he said absently. "I'll keep them upstairs."

She sniffed, and then, "Aren't I going upstairs?"

He smiled down at her, letting his fangs fully show and the blood lust shine from his eyes. "No."

The elevator doors opened, and he pulled her inside. Opening a hidden panel, he punched a button and closed it again. The elevator jerked slightly, and then started descending underneath the city. Dante stood to the left and slightly behind the woman, watching her with a curiosity that he couldn't seem to contain. He found her uniquely fascinating.

She stood tall as they descended to her death, her shallow breaths and silent tears the only signs that gave away what she was feeling. Her unusual mettle made him want to...he didn't know what it made him want to do. A few weeks ago he would've said "destroy it." Slowly. Piece by piece. If she were any other woman, he would want to beat her down until she was nothing but a bloody puddle of babbling fear on the stone floor of his feeding room. But the thought of breaking the spirit in this female left him with nothing but a sour taste in his mouth, and muscles tensed to kick the ass of the bastard who dared to harm her. But there was no one here to confront, except his own self.

The doors opened, and Dante led her out into the Seattle Underground where he made his home. The original city before The Great Seattle Fire destroyed over thirty blocks, it was built primarily of wood and was prone to flooding and sewage backup. So the powers that be had decided to rebuild the city one to two stories higher than the original, leaving a maze of underground alleys and basements to fall into disuse —except by creatures such as he.

Recently, they'd re-opened some of the underground city as a tourist attraction, but Dante turned left, heading deeper into the hidden city where humans were not allowed. This part of the passageway was lit by small squares of opaque purple glass placed in the ceiling at regular intervals, put there by the original builders to allow some natural light. Pedestrians on the sidewalks above walked over the glass, unable to hear or see what was going on directly below them. When he reached the part of the passage that was blocked off from a cave in, he swooped Laney up into his arms without breaking stride and jumped to the top of the pile of bricks and dirt. Balancing her in one arm, he found the hidden latch and released the boards at the top. They swung out on silent hinges, leaving a space just wide enough to crawl through. Pushing the woman through feet first, he dropped her down to the other side and then followed her through the opening.

She stood where he'd set her down, jumping when he landed beside her, his boots making a thud on the old wooden walkway. Her hand reached through the darkness, searching for him, looking for reassurance. Like he was the one that would save her from the monsters hiding in the dark. It made something clench inside of him. He shook it off. She had no right to seek comfort from him. He *was* the monster.

And he couldn't save her from himself.

Ignoring her hand, he took her by the arm again. "Come." Hurrying down the passageway, he kept up a quick pace, dragging her along when she stumbled in the dark. Anger filled him. Anger at himself for being concerned about her and her feelings. Anger at her for touching the last remnants of humanity left inside of him.

She didn't make a sound the entire trip other than her heavy breathing as she tried to keep up with him. When he reached the room he'd made into his own years before, he shoved her up against the wall. "Stay."

She reached for him again when he let go of her, and again he felt that vice tighten in his chest. Kneeling down, he found the matches he kept on a makeshift shelf in the wall where one of the bricks had fallen out. Striking one, he lit the candles around the mattress that he slept on—when he slept at all.

Laney blinked in the sudden flare of light, lifting her hand to shield her eyes. He watched her as she lowered it a few seconds later, taking in her reaction. He shouldn't care what she thought of his home.

Yet, he found that he did.

Her eyes went from the brick walls to the wooden planks of the floor, interspersed with areas that had corroded down to the dirt. Then they found the mattress with the thin blanket on top and rested there a moment. They ended on him, where he still kneeled on one knee on the other side of the small room. She didn't say a word, and he couldn't read her reaction, which bothered him to no end. He wasn't sure what he wanted from her. Disgust? Fear?

Pity?

Enough was enough. Dante stood and went to her, planning to take her down the narrow tunnel behind him that led to his feeding room. He'd dug it out himself. There were devices there that had taken him a lifetime to collect. Devices that allowed him to put his victims through a plethora of fun things before he killed them—from rough sex to something a bit bloodier. Or a lot bloodier.

But when he reached her, he stopped. He imagined her chained and beaten, her smart mouth silenced from the pain. Something he'd been looking forward to this entire trip. Or so he thought. Except now, the image made his stomach lurch.

This...hold...she had on him had to stop. And it had to stop now.

"Laney."

She wouldn't look at him, and he found himself focusing on the top of her head. Her scent rose up around him, the sweet fragrance tinged with the sourness of her fear and the saltiness of her tears. His gums burned as his fangs grew impossibly longer, his hunger for her so intense it was making him lightheaded.

He felt disembodied—watching from a distance as a male that looked like him lifted his hand to her ponytail and freed it from the band. Her long hair fell forward around her shoulders to partially cover her face. Instead of dragging her down to the other room as planned, he picked up a handful of the soft strands and brought it to his nose, breathing in the lavender scent. Lifting his other hand, he buried those fingers in her hair also, sliding them back until he was cupping her head with both hands.

She is only a human. One quick twist, and it would be over. For both of us.

As Dante contemplated that thought, he felt her fingers wrap around his wrists. Her eyes lifted to his—finally!—glassy from her tears, yet the challenge she offered within them was more than clear.

She was daring him to do it.

His hands tightened on her skull until he knew he had to be hurting her, but she didn't make a sound. Just ground her jaw together and continued to goad him on with her silent defiance. Dante's breathing quickened. Such fearlessness in the face of certain death was something he'd rarely seen before. Conflicting emotions ran rampant inside of him. Part of him wanted to break her, and part of him wanted to applaud her.

In the end, he kissed her.

It wasn't a tender kiss. It was too full of thirst, of hunger, of need. Her tongue met his with a tentative touch, and Dante groaned deep in his throat. One hand stayed gripped in her hair while the other fell to her ass and pulled her up and into his aching body. He wanted her to feel what she was doing to him.

She rubbed herself against his erection. It was nearly his undoing.

Enough!

He needed to take control. Breaking off the kiss, Dante put his hands on her shoulders and shoved her to her knees on the floor. Her eyes went immediately to the bulge in his pants, and when they flicked back up to his face they were hungry.

Dante's breath caught in his throat. "Do you want this, little mouse?" He palmed the hard length through his pants, rubbing the heel of his hand over his manhood until the zipper cut into him.

She shook her head. "No." But her eyes were glued to what he was doing. And as he watched, her little pink tongue flicked out to wet her lips.

"You're lying." Releasing her hair, he undid his pants and pulled out his sex. It was thick and long, filling his palm and then some. He guided the head to her sweet mouth. "Take it," he demanded. Her eyes were on his swollen head. Her nostrils flared and her tongue wet her lips. Dante gritted his teeth. He had to calm down. He was too excited, having imagined this very scenario so many times over the last hours, he didn't know if he was going to last long enough to actually feel her lips close around him. When she shook her head again, he cupped the back of her head and forced her to him. "Put your mouth on me, Laney."

He probed her lips with the wide head, and with a moan of defeat, she opened her mouth and took in just the head. Her mouth was hot and wet, and as he pulled out, she ran her tongue around the tip. He pulled her to him again, and this time she opened her mouth wide, sucking hard as he slid inside.

Dante's hips jerked forward as a shout was torn from his throat. Much as he tried to control it, to contain it, the pressure to come continued to build. Exposing his fangs, he hissed in pleasure. Laney's hands went to his hips, and he thought she was going to push him away, but as always, she surprised him. Twisting her fingers into the sagging waistband of his pants, she pulled his hips closer, taking the length of him as far as she could. In and out. Faster and faster. The scent of her desire rose in the air, and he knew that if he touched her now, she'd be wet and ready for him. He was almost tempted, but the pleasure of what she was doing was too good to stop.

Low growls ripped from his chest as he watched his manhood sliding in and out from between her soft lips. The experience wasn't anything like he'd imagined. His plan had been to shame her, to show her how worthless she was, that she was beneath him. A human. There for him to use or abuse as he saw fit. Good for nothing except sex and food.

Instead, she was bringing him to his knees.

Keeping his hold on her head with one hand, he moved the other to his balls and forced her to squeeze. She made sounds of protest in her throat, but he wouldn't let her stop. Pumping in and out of her mouth, he forced her to cause him pain.

His orgasm hit him sudden and hard. Releasing her hair, he jerked out of her mouth and twisted away just in time. Sinking his fangs into his own arm to stifle his shouts of pleasure, he ejaculated all over the wall next to her.

When it was over, he licked at the self-inflicted wound and tried to catch his breath. He could feel the female's eyes on him, but couldn't bring himself to look at her. He was too shaken. Too raw. This place that had been his safe haven for so many years suddenly felt stifling, the walls closing in on him. He had to get the fuck out.

Storming past her, he hit the passageway and ran.

13

Laney stumbled to her feet and looked around without really seeing the barren room that contained nothing but a misshapen mattress, a thick book with a plain black cover, and a few candles. Relief that the vampire had left battled with the raging lust screaming for release that he'd left behind. Laney pressed a hand to her stomach and took deep breaths. She had no idea what had come over her, but she could still taste his sex in her mouth. And she wanted more.

For the hundredth time since she'd been attacked in the desert, she wondered what the hell was wrong with her. There had to be something wrong with her. No normal woman would feel this way. She couldn't seem to decide whether to be terrified or aroused when it came to the monster that had chosen her as his prey.

And he couldn't seem to make up his mind, either. One minute he was threatening her life, and the next he was kissing her like he would never let her go. His emotions, or lack thereof, were giving her whiplash. The outcome remained to be seen, but she wasn't planning to hang around waiting for him to make up his mind. Her very life may depend on it.

Picking up her backpack, a pack of matches, and the tallest candle, Laney cupped her hand around the wick to keep the flame from going out and went back to the passageway the vampire had just tore down in his eagerness to get away from her. Walking as fast as she could without causing the flame to extinguish, she tried not to think about what else might be living down there. Things like bugs. Or worse—rats.

It seemed to take her forever to get to the cave-in. Setting the candle down on the wooden plank way, she eyed up the pile of debris, searching for the best way to get to the top. The right side was the least steep, so she walked over and attempted to get a handhold to start pulling herself up. But every time she grabbed onto something, it would cause a small avalanche of rocks, dirt, and bricks, and she would have to jump back out of the way or risk being buried alive.

After trying every inch she could reach with the same result, Laney had to give up. She now knew why Dante had leapt to the very top, instead of climbing it. But it was at least twelve feet up, if not more. There was no way she could make it up there. She couldn't jump that high, and the walls offered nothing to grip.

Trying not to feel discouraged, Laney picked up the candle and went back the way she had come. She wasn't giving up. There had to be another way out of there.

When she reached the vampire's "room" again, she walked the perimeter, searching for another entrance. The candlelight threw shadows everywhere along the uneven brick walls, but her vigilance paid off. She found a doorway she hadn't noticed at first that revealed a makeshift bathroom of sorts that was really nothing more than an antique commode, and another passageway on the opposite side of the room. No, not a passageway. More like a tunnel. As she walked past the lit candles on the floor, she picked up a second one. Blowing it out, she stuck it in the outside pocket of her backpack. It wouldn't hurt to have a backup.

Laney dropped to her hands and knees, and started crawling down the narrow passage before she had time to talk herself out of it. It was slow going with her holding the lit candle. She had to crawl forward on only one hand, slowly, so it didn't go out. She tried to stay away from the sides, and anything that might be scurrying along outside the ring of candlelight. More than once she thought she heard the scratching of little feet up ahead in the dark, but she gritted her teeth and kept on.

Within a few minutes, a smell that reminded her strongly of copper wafted toward her. Laney wrinkled her nose, but kept going. Shortly thereafter, she came to another room. It felt larger than the one the vampire slept in, the shadows crawling further into the corners. As she crawled the rest of the way out of the tunnel, she lifted the candle and made her way slowly into the interior. Her steps faltered and eventually stopped as she took in the scene around her. Horror froze the blood in her veins.

"Oh my God," she whispered.

Similar to the other room, the walls were made with brick, and the floor and ceiling were wooden planks. To her right were former archways, now closed off with brick. But there were chains anchored into the brick with wrist and ankle shackles on the ends. Laney's eyes travelled the length of the room. Everywhere the candlelight touched, she saw devices made of wood with chains, leather straps, and sometime rope. Some were tables, some were like upright wheels, some were benches. Some she had no idea what they were or what they could possibly be used for. A lone wooden chair with arm and leg straps sat directly in front of her, waiting for its next victim. Its surface had some kind of dark stain splattered all over it. And scattered among the different pieces were hooks on the walls with blades glinting in the flickering candlelight. Knives of every type and length, and other things that she'd never seen before. She could only imagine their purpose.

Moving the candle to the right, she found a flat wooden table covered with things she'd only read about: handcuffs, whips, leather straps with metal spikes sticking out of them.

Laney realized then what the dark stains were. They were bloodstains. A scream began to form in her throat, and she slapped her hand over her mouth to smother it, fighting to get her emotions under control. She needed to get out of there, and she needed to get out of there *now*.

Forcing herself to stay calm and focus on what she was supposed to be doing, Laney walked the circumference of the room with the candle held in front of her, searching for another way in or out. But there was nothing. She even felt along the walls for secret levers or seams not visible to the naked eye. But all she found was old, crumbling brick that nonetheless was completely unmovable. Setting down the candle, she stuck her hands on her hips and looked around for something to use as a ladder that would get her to the top of the cave in. She tugged at the chains, thinking she could throw them to the top and maybe it would catch on something so she could pull herself up. They wouldn't budge. Everything was bolted down or welded together. There was nothing here that would help her.

Grabbing one of the knives down off the wall, she stuck it into her pack, made her way back to the tunnel and got the hell out of that room as fast as she could crawl, for Laney swore she could hear the ghostly wails of the tortured souls that had suffered at the hands of the vampire following her. His words about the woman he'd murdered by orgasm popped into her head. Surely, he hadn't had sex with that woman in that room.

Laney cut off that train of thought as she made her way back to the vampire's room. She searched it again, and repeated her trek up and down the first passageway without any luck. The truth of her situation began to hit her. There was no other way out. She was well and truly trapped.

Physically exhausted and emotionally numb, she went back to the vampire's room. Sinking down onto the mattress, Laney rolled over onto her side and pulled the thin blanket over herself. It didn't do much to keep the dampness out, and she curled herself into a ball. As she lay there trying to get warm, she wondered why Dante hadn't taken her directly to his room of torture. Because her instincts were telling her that this room that she was in was not a place he normally brought "guests." It was a big deal that he left her here. Somehow she knew that. But what she didn't know was if he would change his mind.

She thought about the knife she'd taken out of that room, and it occurred to her that she could take the decision out of his hands. A stillness came over her at the thought of taking her own life, and for a few minutes, she seriously considered it. At least that way she would die on her own terms. But in the end, she couldn't bring herself to act upon it. She was a survivor. She'd survived running from her home with her father. She'd survived his death, and she'd survived even greater loss. And she would fight for her life until she couldn't fight anymore. Because that's what she did.

It was funny, but as Laney lay there in the dark, surrounded by his things, by his loneliness, she felt a sort of kinship with the vampire. He was a killer, yes. But so was she. It was a fault in both of their natures. The only difference being that he did it by choice, and thrived from it. The first life Laney had snuffed out had been necessary. The second had taken her heart and soul with it.

Is this my punishment then?

If it was, it was nothing less than she deserved. She hadn't meant to do it that second time, and as the tears started up again, she wished there was a way to go back before it had happened. So she could hold him once again.

14

Dante burst from the elevator, strode through the lobby, out the main doors, across the sidewalk, and straight out into the street in front of the apartment building. A late night Uber honked its horn as it swerved to miss him, and he slammed his fist into the back end of the car as it passed. Tires squealed as the driver frantically righted the vehicle, then glanced up in the rearview to see what the hell he had hit. Dante bared his fangs at the idiot.

He had to get the fuck out of there. Had to get the fuck away from that woman and the things she made him feel. Taking deep breaths of the cold night air, he backed up a few steps and stood in the middle of the sidewalk, not caring that he made the humans walk around him. There weren't many out this time of night anyway.

He needed to get rid of her. And he needed to do it five fucking minutes ago. So why hadn't he?

"Dante?"

He knew that female voice. A moment later, Shea's concerned green eyes appeared up in his face. "Shea," he greeted her.

"Oh my gods. You're back!" She reached out for him, then thought better of it and dropped her arms back to her sides. He took no offense. Shea was unable to touch a male without paralyzing pain. He knew what her deal was, and he had no desire to cause this particular female any suffering. She was a vampire, like him. And he still needed to change his clothes. A fact that he'd completely spaced on after he'd gotten the woman here. All he'd been able to think of was getting her out of sight before anyone saw her, so he could have her all to himself.

"Are you okay?" Shea interrupted his thoughts. "You look a little…not quite right." She gave him no time to answer. "Where have you been? What the hell happened to you? I came to look for you and Christian, but you were both gone—"

"Where is Christian?" he asked. "Was he taken, too?"

"We all were," she said. "All three of us. But he's back now, too. You're the last one to return. Have you not been upstairs yet?"

He shook his head.

"How long have you been back?" Waving at his clothes, she said, "I would think it was recently, but one can never tell with you." She smiled.

"Just an hour or so ago," he told her distractedly.

Her smile faltered before dying altogether. Shea searched his face for so long that he narrowed his eyes at her. "What."

"Are you all right?" she asked point blank.

He exhaled. "I'm fine. Let's go upstairs."

After another searching look, she nodded. "Everyone will be happy to see you. Luukas told us that you were on your way home." Reaching out to him again, she touched his arm with light fingers for a fraction of a second before yanking her hand away with a hiss. "I'm glad you're home, Dante. And that you're okay. And I'm sorry that I got there too late to help you. I failed you, and for that, I sincerely apologize."

Dante knew the pain that touching him must have cost her, even so briefly. "It's not your fault, Shea. Shit happens." Turning away before she got more emotional on him, he headed back into the apartment building. He didn't wait to see if she would follow, knowing she would. "I have to make a stop in the parking garage first," he said over his shoulder.

Sure enough, he heard her soft footsteps directly behind him as he headed back to the elevator. Punching in the number for the parking level Laney's car was on, he didn't offer up any explanation, just went to get his new friends.

Shea raised an eyebrow when she saw the furry faces in the car window. "So we're an animal rescue now?"

"Something like that." The doors were locked. Smashing his fist through the passenger side window, he unlocked the car and handed her the cat's food and litter while the dog wagged his entire back end with excitement. Dante scooped him up and tucked him under one arm, letting him get in a lick or two before silently telling him to knock it the fuck off. Hanging the cat over the other arm, he kicked the door shut again. Shattered glass fell to the pavement to scatter at his feet.

"Did they come with the car?" Shea asked him. "Where is the driver?" She knew he didn't drive. "I can smell her on you."

Guess that would give it away, too. "Not here. And I found the dog before the car. The cat came with it," he answered.

"The car or the dog?"

"The dog."

"Huh." She shrugged and headed back toward the elevator with her bags.

This time he hit the button for the very top floor—Luukas's penthouse apartment. They didn't speak the entire ride, and that was one of the things that Dante appreciated about this particular Hunter. She knew when to keep her mouth shut. At least with him.

The elevator doors opened and they stepped out in unison. When they reached Luukas's apartment, Dante stopped, threw the cat up onto his shoulder, and knocked twice. Fraidy curled around his neck, purring loudly, and hung over the opposite side to get a lick from the dog. Dante caught Shea's smirk out of the corner of his eye. "What?" he asked.

"Why is it you only knock on Luuk's door? I still need to fix the hinges on mine from the last time you came to visit."

A small smile lifted one side of his mouth. "I only do that for Christian's benefit." He offered no apology. Not that she would've expected one.

"I know," she answered with a roll of her eyes.

The door swung open and Dante found himself face to face with the Master Vampire that he had sworn his allegiance to so many years ago. "Hey, Luukas."

Luukas took in his dusty clothes, the animals he was wearing, Shea behind him holding bags of supplies, and raised one eyebrow. "I hope you weren't planning on leaving those beasts here."

"I was going to put them in my apartment."

"Good." He slapped Dante on the shoulder. "I'm glad you made it back to us," he told him sincerely. Then he stepped back out of the way to let them enter.

Dante strode inside, only to come up short before he'd even made it out of the foyer. His fangs shot down into his mouth as the familiar scent of sweet human blood blasted him in the face, and for a brief second, he thought Laney had somehow made her way up here in the few minutes he'd been gone. He hissed, his eyes shooting left to right as his thirst hit him full force. The thirst he hadn't quenched as he had planned, because he was too twisted up by the other things the female had done to him.

And what he hadn't been able to bring himself to do to her.

Before he realized what he was doing, Dante was standing in the bedroom door. The door that he had just smashed open. A small, dark-haired female was staring at him with wide, hazel eyes. She was wearing nothing but a thin robe that barely concealed her full hips and breasts, her damp raven hair tumbling around her shoulders. At first glance, only her hazel eyes and the pale tint of her skin differentiated her from Laney.

Dante bared his fangs, and she narrowed her eyes in challenge. His thirst raged, the blood lust messing with his head. A growl ripped through the room, and he realized that it had come from him. The female was unmoved. She faced him and smiled.

He took a step toward her, but that was as far as he got before something large and powerful flashed by him, knocking him to the side. Luukas appeared in front of the female, fangs bared and eyes wild. For a moment, Dante was confused, for it seemed that Luukas was threatening *him*. He dropped the dog, forgotten in his arms, and the cat jumped down after him. They were quick to get out of the way. Copying Luukas's stance, Dante prepared to fight for his prey.

"The witch is MINE," Luukas growled in a low voice.

A muscular arm was suddenly around Dante's throat and a quiet voice with a British accent spoke in his ear. "You'll want to back off now, commander."

Dante tried to throw Aiden off, but then Nik's blue eyes cut off his line of vision to the female. Getting right in his face, Nik told him, "Dude. You really don't want to go there."

"Fun as it would be to let Luukas rip your bloody head off, we only just got you back," Aiden chimed in cheerfully. "Let's save it for another day, shall we?"

Dante roared his displeasure at being kept from his meal. She smelled faintly of the female he'd left below ground, and he was suddenly dying of thirst. Hauling back his fist, he punched Nikulas in his pretty jaw and threw his head back in an attempt to shove Aiden's nose up through his skull. Unfortunately, the vampire on his back saw it coming and moved his face out of the way.

"Really, commander? I'm hurt. I really am. I thought I was your favorite."

With Nik out of the way, he had a clear view of the vampire blocking him from his meal. Luukas's eyes glowed with a crazy light as he hissed and snarled from his protective stance in front of the female. She, on the other hand, didn't look the least bit frightened.

"Stop!"

The shout came from his right, and Dante tried to turn his head in that direction, only to find that he couldn't move a single muscle.

"Hallo, poppet," Aiden said as he dropped off Dante's back. "No need to get your knickers in a twist. We had it handled." As he came into Dante's line of vision and picked Nik up off the floor, he saw a tiny, prickly head with a black nose pop up out of the hood of Aiden's ever-present hoodie.

"Is he okay?" the female he couldn't see asked. "Nikulas! Are you okay?"

"I'm fine," he grumbled, wiping the blood from his mouth with his arm. "Dammit, man. Why'd you have to hit me in the face? We never go for the face. It's the rule."

The familiar scent of his female was stronger now, and Dante ground his jaw in frustration from his frozen position.

"Just keep him right there please, Em, until I can calm Luukas down," the dark-haired female said.

"Take your time, sis. I've got this."

Luukas shifted his weight from side to side, ready to pounce at the slightest threat. The dark-haired female moved to stand in front of him. "Calm down, vampire. No one is hurting me."

Luukas's crazy eyes stayed rock steady on Dante's face, fangs bared in warning. But as the female put her hands on him and spoke in soft tones, he eventually stopped snarling, and his eyes lost their glow of crazy, though his fangs stayed distended.

"What the fuck is going on?" Dante gritted out from the haze of his blood lust.

Aiden spoke from where he leaned casually against the wall. "Just that you're threatening to eat the fated mate of our fearless leader."

Fated mate? The words bounced around his head, but he couldn't pin down their meaning. "What?" Fighting to get his own sanity back, he managed to gain enough control over his thirst that the burning in his throat was little more than a strong simmer.

"Keira is Luukas's mate." Nik sounded like he had a mouth full of cotton. "And her stunning sister over here that's keeping you from getting killed is her sister, and my mate, Emma."

"Disgusting, isn't it?" Shea spoke up from behind him. "I was going to let you feed on her."

"Whatever." Keira smiled over her shoulder, but stayed where Luukas could touch her. "You love me."

Shea appeared on Dante's right side to stand next to him, but he noticed she'd walked in a big circle around what he assumed was the girl he couldn't see. Crossing her arms, she shrugged. "You're all right. For a witch."

"Keira, why don't you hang out here with Luukas for a few?" Nik suggested. "We'll take Dante out to feed and bring him back for a proper introduction when he's not being all crazy and shit."

By this time, Luukas had straightened up and had Keira folded in protectively against his chest. His eyes shifted over to his brother. "You don't have to talk about me as if I'm not here. But yes, get him the fuck out of here until he can keep it under control."

"I got this," Aiden said. "Set him loose, poppet," he told Emma. "I think he can control himself now. All right, commander?"

"Don't fucking call me that," Dante ordered.

Aiden smiled. "See? He's fine."

"Nik?" Emma asked.

"Go ahead," he told her, getting into position in front of Dante with his arms outstretched. "On three."

Dante narrowed his eyes at him, wondering what he was about.

Behind Nikulas, he saw Luukas shove the female behind him.

"One, two...now!" Nik shouted.

Dante caught a flash of bright hair and a green shirt out of the corner of his eyes as he was tackled by Nikulas and forcibly taken out of the bedroom. He landed with an *oof* flat on his back with Nik on top of him. Aiden and Shea followed them out, and Aiden pulled the door shut behind them.

"All right, let's go," Nik said.

Three pairs of arms lifted him up and had him out in the hall before he could wiggle himself free between curses. "Put me the fuck down!"

They got him into the stairwell and dropped him. Dante burst back up onto his feet with a snarl, trying to decide which one of them to end first.

"Don't kill them," Shea said. "It really was necessary. You were about to commit suicide in there."

"You ain't kidding," Nik chimed in. "You should know, my brother isn't quite...adjusted yet. When Emma and I found him, he was alive, but his mind was nearly completely fucking gone. Keira is the only thing that keeps him semi-sane, I think. And he's a bit over-protective of her."

"Pfft. Like you don't howl at me every time I say 'hallo' to Emma," Aiden said.

Nikulas turned incredulous eyes his way. "She was *naked* the last time you said 'hallo' to her, and you do it just to fuck with me."

"I needed to speak with you. How was I supposed to know she would be naked?" Aiden asked innocently.

"Seriously?" Nik said, louder now. "We were in the fucking shower!"

Dante listened to their familiar banter, part amused, part wound up, and part pissed off. Without a word, he turned away and stomped down the first flight of stairs.

"Hey, where are you going?" Nikulas asked.

"To feed," he ground out. "I just got home. Tell Luukas I'll be back tomorrow night."

"I'll come with you," Shea offered.

But he spun around and put out his hand. "No." It wasn't like she hadn't seen him in action before. They all had at one time or another, but Dante wasn't going after some random homeless degenerate this time, or some mouthy asshole that deserved everything he did to him.

Well, she did tend to be mouthy. But he still didn't want an audience, for numerous reasons. "I'll be fine," he assured her. "I'll be back tomorrow night."

Kicking it into vamp speed, he descended the rest of the way without giving any of them a chance to say anything else.

15

Laney didn't hear the vampire coming, but she could feel his presence humming through her blood and knew he must be near. This connection to him simultaneously disturbed her and thrilled her. Jacking upright, she scrambled to her hands and knees, backed off his bed and onto her feet, her heart pounding so loud she was sure it was going to bust right through her ribcage. As she waited to see what was in store for her now, flashes of leather adorned with spikes and blades flashed through her mind. She wrapped her arms around herself and clenched her teeth together to keep them from chattering.

He appeared out of thin air. One moment the doorway was empty and the next he was there, filling it with his imposing size. Standing in the shadows, the black ink of the tattoos on his face and neck appeared to writhe seductively in the flickering candlelight. But his eyes held no emotion. No clues to his thoughts. Black depths she couldn't read no matter how hard she tried.

She blinked and he was so close she could touch him, moving so swiftly and silently that she jumped back and nearly screamed when he was suddenly *right there*.

His upper lip lifted into a sneer, exposing his long fangs. "I'm thirsty," he rasped. "I need you, Laney."

The fact that he'd actually called her by name threw her off guard. Though his expression was as closed off as always, his eyes—those black orbs that had appeared so bleak from across the room—were suddenly filled with a hot desperation she hadn't seen since that first night in the desert. Stiffening her spine, she braced for his attack, but it never came.

"Laney—" He paused, waiting.

Was he asking her?

"What do you expect me to say?" she whispered.

"I need to feed," he reiterated. He loomed closer, though she hadn't seen him move at all, growing larger before her eyes. Or maybe it was just a trick of the candlelight.

She backed away another step. "Then go feed on someone else," she spit out. God, she couldn't believe she'd actually just said that. That wasn't what she wanted. She didn't want him to hurt her, but she didn't want him to go after anyone else, either.

But what other choice do I have?

"I don't want someone else," he argued. "I want you."

Tears threatened, and Laney blinked repeatedly, trying to hold them back. It was stupid to cry...again. Tears weren't going to save her. But she couldn't help it. She'd always been a crier. If her emotions spiked in any direction, anywhere other than a happy middle ground, she cried. And right now she was so far off the charts, she didn't know that she'd ever go back to feeling safe again, even if she did survive this somehow. So in spite of her best efforts to not show any weakness, a few leaked out and ran down her cheeks.

Before she could wipe them away, Dante caught one on his finger and brought it to his mouth, tasting the evidence of her fear. But then he did something she did not expect; he cupped her face gently in both hands and wiped away her remaining tears with his thumbs. "Don't do that." His voice was rough, his expression conflicted. He stepped in closer. Tilting her head to the side with a firm grip, he brushed her hair out of the way and exposed her pulsing artery.

Laney squeezed her eyes shut, knowing the end was near. "Just please don't take me into that room," she burst out. "Please."

He stilled for just a second, and then she felt the warmth of his breath on her chilled skin. Bunching the front of his shirt up in her shaking hands, her body swayed toward him of its own accord, craving his touch, at complete odds with the terror rampaging through her mind. She waited for the sharp sting of his fangs to pierce her vein, and had a passing curiosity if he would be kind enough to hold her as he drained the blood from her body until she slipped out of this world and into the icy grip of death.

The pain never came. Instead, something warm and soft touched her jaw. Then her cheek, her mouth—

Laney's eyes fluttered open. It was the vampire, brushing her lips softly with his own. His large body leaning over her and blocking out the light from the candles.

Startled, she pulled away. Releasing his shirt and dropping her arms to her sides, she repeated his order from a few moments ago. "Don't. Don't do that." There was no reason to sugarcoat any of this with kisses. She wished he would just get it over with.

Little mouse.

His nickname for her suddenly made sense. He was the cat, or rather the panther, playing with his prey. But Laney had had enough of his games. Her nerves were stretched taught, and a scream of terror hovered on the tip of her tongue. She couldn't take much more.

"I'm not *playing*," he answered her unspoken thought. "I just —" He snapped his jaw shut, cutting off what he had been about to say. The desperation left his eyes, only to be replaced with the predatory gleam she was more accustomed to. "I just need to feed, little mouse." The corners of his lips turned up in a sinister smile. "Go ahead and scream if you want. No one will hear you."

She caught a flash of fangs as he yanked her hard up against him, right before he sank them into her throat with a deep growl. He wasn't gentle about it, and she cried out in pain as her skin tore with a sharp sting. The vampire latched onto her vein and drank deep.

Laney swayed in his arms, quickly becoming lightheaded. He moaned and sucked harder. She could hear him swallowing, the sounds interspersed with his moans of pleasure. Lifting her up off her feet, he straightened with her held in the vice grip of his arms. Laney gritted her teeth, struggling against him, but she couldn't break his hold no matter how hard she tried.

Dante fell to his knees without releasing his mouth's seal on her throat, taking her with him down to the floor next to the mattress. Her knees went to either side of his hips as he sat her on his lap, and she felt his erection thick and hard between her legs. The pressure on her throat eased off, and he lapped at the wound to close it. His lips pressed against her artery as though in fervent thanks before traveling up over her jaw to her ear.

"What are you *doing* to me?" he groaned. "Laney...." He kissed his way over to her lips, probing for entrance with his tongue.

She wanted to deny him, to beat him with her fists, and scream her rage and terror, whether anyone would hear her or not. But her fear was swiftly turning to desire as her body responded to the change in his demeanor. Her grip on him became as frenzied as his on her. Everything was wrong with this. So very, very wrong. Yet she couldn't find it in her to deny what he was demanding. It was like every feeling and desire that ran through him was her own. His craving was her craving, not only for her blood, but for her body. Like a man starving.

She could *feel* what he was feeling. And he was losing control.

"Let me in, little mouse," he ordered against her mouth.

And she did. She stopped thinking, and let his fire consume her. His kisses were raw, hungry, and she wrapped her arms around his neck and allowed him to overwhelm her. His hips rolled beneath hers, and she felt the heat of his arousal all the way through to her core, even through their clothes.

Dante rose up onto his knees and leaned forward, laying her back on the mattress without breaking the connection between them. Laney opened her legs as he settled his weight between them, even lifting her hips to seek him out, hating having the slightest bit of space between their bodies. His heat seared her everywhere he touched, and she reveled in the feeling of his weight pressing her down into the mattress. He kissed her over and over, demanding her submission, and she gave it to him. Laney arched her body, wanting his hands on her, wanting to feel his skin against hers, moaning in frustration when she didn't get what she wanted.

Breaking off the kiss, he tangled his fingers in the hair on either side of her head. His eyes were feverish as they locked in on hers, his voice hoarse with need, the tattoos running down the side of his face ominous in the candlelight. "Tell me yes," he commanded. "Tell me I can have you."

Laney's attention honed in on his extended fangs. A thrill shot through her as she imagined him biting her again, only this time in the throes of passion. She tried to find a rational thought in her lust-filled brain. One that would tell her that she was insane for even contemplating having sex with him. But she couldn't hear anything past the wild hunger pulsing through her.

"Laney...." Her name tore from his lips. His eyes roved over her face and settled on her mouth, his features tense.

Was she mad? "Yes," she heard herself say.

With a ragged inhale, he stared down at her for a long moment as if he couldn't believe what he'd just heard. But only for a moment. A look of triumph lit his eyes, and he growled low in his throat and took her mouth again, touching her everywhere at once, as if making up for lost time. His hands were rough as they tore at her clothes, stripping them quickly from her body. She had no more time to think about what was happening. His frenzied need hung in the air around them like a living thing as he bared her body to his heated gaze with rapid movements. He made small, satisfied noises at each new reveal, sometimes baring his fangs. But strangely enough, she didn't feel scared. She felt desired, and absolutely alive for the first time in a long time.

The sting of his bite lanced her nipple, and Laney cried out, arching her back in encouragement. She stared down at the top of his shaved head as he began to suckle, part of her in disbelief that this was happening, part of her thinking that he was right—if she was about to die, this was the way to do it.

Removing his fangs, he tugged on her nipple, running his tongue over the wounds, then made his way down her body to pull off her sneakers and unfasten her jeans. Something pricked at Laney's brain, something she should be worried about other than what she was currently doing. But as she lay there with her shirt and bra on the other side of the room alongside his black tee, she couldn't focus on anything except the pulses of desire in her core that desperately needed to be eased.

Her jeans and underwear quickly joined the pile of clothes, yet she didn't feel the least bit self-conscious. Laney rubbed her thighs together, trying to ease the ache between them, her hands fisted in the blanket beneath her. The vampire rose up and sat back on his haunches to admire the sight before him. One hand reached out, and she felt the butterfly touch of his fingers on her belly.

His breath caught in his throat. Black eyes, churning with too many emotions to name, rose to meet hers. "You have a child," he hissed.

She has a child.

Dante traced the pale stripes on her lower belly as long forgotten memories of his human life doused the flames of his desire and stole his breath. The skin had been stretched beyond redemption; hanging loosely between her hipbones where it hadn't quite shrunk back to normal after the birth. It wasn't ugly to him. Quite the opposite. This evidence of motherhood tore at his soul.

It was beautiful. And heartbreaking.

Now he knew why she carried that book with her. It was a children's book. "Where is the child?"

Laney was quiet. Too quiet. Tearing his eyes from the lines on her stomach and the dark, soft curls covering her woman's mound, he searched her expression, but she turned her head away and refused to look at him.

"Where is the child?" he demanded, louder now. He tried to probe her mind, found it impossible. Her shields were up, and she hadn't fed from him since the night before. The thought that he had torn a mother away from her child ripped away at what little was left of his conscience. It disoriented him, making it hard for him to focus.

Laney reached out blindly for the blanket and covered her nudeness as she scrambled out from underneath him. He felt her disappearing even though she was still right in front of him, and he automatically reached out to try to re-establish the connection between them. She shrunk away. "Laney, where is the fucking child?" He shouldn't give two shits about the possible existence of another human. It shouldn't matter. But he had to know. Taking her by the shoulders, he shook her hard enough to set her teeth knocking together. "Answer me!"

"He's dead," she wailed, the words ending on a keening cry. Clutching the blanket to her chest with one hand, she covered her face with the other and began to sob. Heart wrenching sounds that tore at his soul. When she could speak again, her voice was strained and watered down with her tears. "My son is dead." She paused, pressing a hand over her mouth to stifle a sob. "Because I killed him. I killed him because he wouldn't be quiet." Tear-filled eyes half-crazed with grief skittered about in the gloom. "He was just a *baby*." This last was spoken so quietly, he barely heard her. Or maybe it was because of the ringing in his ears.

Dante stared at the female in front of him. Unable to link the self-professed murderer in front of him with the strong, but kind woman he'd observed over the last few days.

He, himself, was a killer, yes. And he took worthless human lives with elation. He could also spot others with a soul just as black as his from a mile away. Laney was not one of those people. She was not like him. She was good. He knew this in the deepest part of his soul. "No." He denied what she had just said, though he sensed she was speaking the truth. "You wouldn't do something like that. You must be mistaken."

She raised swollen, red eyes. They were surprisingly direct as she spoke the next words. "I killed my own child." Her mouth twisted in disgust. "I didn't mean to do it, but I still did it. So the intent or lack thereof doesn't really matter, does it?"

She was looking to him for an answer that he wasn't able to give. "The book belonged to your son."

She didn't answer him. She didn't need to. It wasn't a question.

"What happened?" His curiosity surprised him. He'd never, ever before cared about what was going on in the lives of his current victims, past or present. But he found himself wanting to know everything about this female.

No. Not wanting to know. *Needing* to know.

Her shoulders sagged in defeat, and her expression was so forlorn he wanted to gather her up in his arms again and kiss her until she was able to think of nothing else but him. When she spoke, her voice was robotic. "He was only a few months old, and something was wrong. He wouldn't stop crying." She took a shaky breath. "I hadn't slept for days. I was *so* tired. I just wanted him to be quiet for a few hours so I could sleep." Her voice faded into a ragged whisper.

"What happened, Laney?" he asked again. Reaching across the space between them with his mind, he probed her memories. Intent on her grief, she didn't block him, and he listened to her thoughts even as she spoke them.

"I was rocking him, and he finally stopped crying! He fell asleep." A smile ghosted about her lips. "His little face was buried in my shirt, and I remember thinking that if he would just sleep, just stay quiet for a few hours so I could rest, then it would be okay." There was a dazed look in her eyes as she remembered. "And when I woke up, he was gone."

Dante frowned. "I don't understand. Why do you think that was your fault?"

She started at the sound of his voice, as if she'd forgotten he was there. Her eyes searched him out in the soft light. "Because I sent his soul away to where he'd be happy. He wasn't happy with me. He just cried all the time."

"What do you mean you 'sent his soul away'?" If he hadn't been inside her mind at just that moment, he would have worried about her sanity. But there were no threads of madness, only overwhelming grief.

"I can do that. I'm a monster." That phantom smile was there again. "Just like you."

She was nothing like him. "I don't understand."

"I've done it before, when I was younger. I watched my grandfather's soul leave his body. I forced it out. He hadn't been himself for months. He got mean, and started beating my grandma. I was only eleven, but I knew what was going on. And I loved my grandma. She used to always make me my favorite foods whenever I was at her house, and we'd watch the birds together in her feeders. She knew the names of every single one. So when grandpa went crazy, I protected her." She wiped at her eyes. "I meant to do it that time." This was said with no remorse. "I didn't mean to do it to my son. I was just so tired." She was quiet for a few minutes, then she sniffed and drew herself up. He could see her pulling herself together, and could only imagine how many other times she'd done it, like pulling a protective cape around her pain. "I've never told anyone that it was me. But I guess it doesn't really matter if you know."

He could feel her complete misery, her desperation for him to understand. But he didn't understand. Though he had no doubts that she believed what she was telling him, something wasn't sitting right with her story.

"What did the humans say exactly, about how the baby died?"

She shrugged. "They said it was SIDS." When he looked at her blankly, she added, "Sudden Infant Death Syndrome. Sometimes babies just die in their sleep."

Dante didn't keep up with all of the human illnesses and syndromes; there were just too many these days. Some real, and some created by the pharmaceutical industry to make a quick buck. Plus, he just didn't fucking care. He didn't normally associate with humans, other than to prey on them as they once did him. "And you don't believe them?"

"No," she whispered.

"Why not? There are a lot of human illnesses. It could have been anything."

She shook her head stubbornly. "No. It was me."

Dante didn't know what else to say to her. He wasn't good at this sort of thing. Running his hand over his head and feeling the bristle of new hair, he had the passing thought that he needed to take a blade to it again.

His body's lust was lessened by her grief. Another unusual occurrence. And he could feel her exhaustion, both physically and mentally. "I'm tired," he told her. "And I'm still healing. I need to rest." He paused. "You do, too." Lying down, he pulled her down beside him, arranging the blanket over the both of them. He still had his pants on, but didn't bother to remove them.

She stiffened in his arms. "I want to get dressed."

He almost smiled, glad that the fight hadn't gone out of her entirely. "No. I want to feel you against me." Turmoil continued to rumble around inside of her, but eventually she sighed and relaxed against him. He looked down at her face, noticing for the first time the fine lines on her forehead. "How old are you, little mouse?"

He didn't think she was going to answer him at first, but then she said, "Thirty-eight."

"And when did your child die?"

"Six years ago."

No time at all. "Where is the father?" He tensed, waiting for her answer, and wondered why it mattered to him.

"He's gone," was all she said.

"Tell me again what you think you did."

"Why? It doesn't matter now." Her tone was resigned.

He didn't know why it mattered. All he knew was that he felt this incredible longing to make the sadness go away, and to protect her from anything else that would make her unhappy. Every cell in his body was exceedingly aware of the woman beside him, tuned in to the slightest nuance in her mood. "Just tell me, little mouse. I want to hear the words from you. And don't bother to lie. I will know if you do."

She sighed and tried to pull away, but he wouldn't allow it. Instead, he gathered her in closer to his chest, unconsciously lending her his strength. Giving up, she began to speak, her words muffled against his chest.

"Apparently, I was born with the power. My father told me that my mom was a...she was a witch." She hurried on, as if used to being questioned or ridiculed when she said that. Dante, however, took her at her word. He knew about witches. "I figured it out as a child, and when I confronted him, he didn't deny it. He thought I had gotten lucky, that the magic had skipped a generation. We found out with Grandpa that it hadn't."

"Where was your mother?"

"She was killed when I was a toddler. Some kind of accident. My father moved us to Vegas and raised me by himself. He worked in one of the clubs on the Strip. As did I, up until recently. I was a hostess."

"Is he still alive?"

"No. He came down with pneumonia and died in the hospital last year. It's just me now."

"What did your father say about what happened with your Grandfather?"

"He told me I needed to learn to control my power."

"And did you?"

"I thought so. Until a few years ago."

He played with her hair, running the soft strands through the fingers of one hand while holding her close with the other as he digested all she had just told him. Something about what she'd said happened with her son wasn't jiving for him. As she drifted off to sleep in his arms, he ran over it all again, determined to figure out what it was.

While he mulled over her story, Dante had his own demons banging on the door. But he'd slammed that slab of steel in their faces hundreds of years ago, and he wanted to keep them in there. So he spent the time before sunrise worrying about her. It sufficed well enough to keep his own memories at bay.

16

Dante came immediately awake, but out of habit, he kept his breathing exactly the same and gave no indication that he was aware that something unusual was going on. And a second later, he was glad his natural self-preservation had kicked in when a slight weight carefully straddled his hips and settled over him. Instinctively, he knew it was Laney. He kept up the illusion of sleep, curious as to what she was up to.

A multitude of emotions washed over him from the woman sitting on his stomach. Then suddenly, she shifted her weight in a manner he was all too familiar with. His eyes popped open just in time as he caught a flash of cold steel arcing through the air toward his chest. Moving fast as a striking snake, his hand shot out and wrapped around her small wrist, the bones delicate in his grip. In her hand was a long straight knife she must have found in his feeding room. And the tip of that blade had just nicked the skin of his chest. Right above his heart. He'd stopped it just before she was able to bury it all the way through his ribcage.

With a bellow of rage, he threw the female off him and shot off the bed. A drop of blood trickled down his bare chest, but he ignored it, all of his attention on the woman scrambling to her feet in front of him. She had gotten somewhat dressed before attempting to snuff out his life, and now stood in front of him in her button-down shirt and underwear, the large knife still gripped in her small hand. She was magnificent in her rage. And even in his own anger, Dante found his eyes traveling down her bare limbs to her small toes and all the way back up to her messy, just-fucked hair. His manhood hardened, demanding to give her a reason to look so disheveled. The fact that she still had the knife only excited him more.

So she wanted to kill him, did she? His heart suddenly felt as though she had succeeded in slicing it open.

He stepped off the mattress and stalked over to her. As he advanced, she backed up until she ran into the brick wall behind her. Covering her hand with his, he brought the blade of the knife to his throat, pressing it into his skin until he felt blood welling up and flowing over. She watched it trickle down his skin, her tongue flicking out to wet her lips. "If you want to kill me, little mouse"—he pressed the knife harder into his neck, even as she tried to pull it away—"you'll need to cut off my head." He could feel the blade hitting his windpipe. "Shall I help you?"

She struggled to pull the blade away. "No! Stop! Dante, stop!"

"Why?" he hissed at her. "You obviously want me dead. You just tried to sink this knife into my fucking heart while I was sleeping!"

"I just want to get away from you; I don't want to kill you," she cried.

Dante could feel the truth in her words and her mind, but it was too late for regrets. He laughed without humor. "Little mouse, you can't get away from me. I would find you. It doesn't matter where you run, or where you hide. You are MINE now." Something clicked inside of him as he said those words, but caught up in the emotions of her attempt on his life, he paid it no mind.

He needed to teach a lesson to this one. It was time to take her to the feeding room. Whether or not she ever left it would be up to her.

Pushing the knife away from his throat, he twisted her wrist until she dropped it with a cry of pain. It landed on the dirt floor with a dull thud. He lifted her off her feet with an arm around her waist, holding her on his hip, her arms and legs dangling as she tried to twist out of his grip. Her betrayal seared through him, and the more he thought about it, the angrier he became. But he wasn't sure who he was more angry with: Laney, for trying to stab him, or himself, for allowing her to crack the shield of ice around what little was left of his humanity.

When he got to the tunnel, he put her in, head first. "Go," he ordered. She tried to crawl backwards, to get out, but he was right behind her, blocking her way. "Crawl!" he barked.

She sat up, trying to turn around to face him in the small space. "Dante, please! Please don't make me go in there. I'm sorry!" Realizing his mistake, Dante backed out and she quickly followed him.

He should have gone in first, so he could pull her behind him by the ankles, if need be.

But as soon as she was out of the tunnel, Laney turned and threw herself into his arms. He caught her automatically, landing on his ass and burying his face in her hair. Her entire body was shaking in fear, and he felt another crack in his shield.

"I wasn't trying to kill you," she sobbed. "I wasn't! I just wanted to get away!"

He held her a moment longer, squeezing his eyes shut tight against the way she fit so perfectly in his arms, then firmly removed her from his lap and set her aside. He stared at her for long moments, wondering what the hell was wrong with him.

"I have to go." Rising to his feet he found his shirt and boots and put them on. The tender feelings roiling through him were unfamiliar and unwanted. He'd stop at his apartment upstairs to shower and check on the animals before going to Luukas's. He steadfastly ignored the woman behind him. He had to. Something was wrong with him. Something that had to do with her. He had scared her, and for the first time in a very long time, it wasn't sitting right with him. Without a backward glance, he left, striding down the passageway to the cave-in. She didn't follow or call out after him.

A relentless pain that had nothing to do with the nick on his chest lashed at his insides that she didn't.

Finding himself upstairs in his bathroom with the shower running, Dante didn't even remember how he'd gotten there. He stripped off his clothes and stepped under the scalding spray, wishing it could burn away the fucking memories knocking on the door of the vault inside his head. Memories that he'd managed to shut out for a long, long time.

Papa! Papa! Watch me!

With a growl, Dante shook his head and turned to let the water burn the skin off his back.

Papa, why is Momma not coming back? Where is she?

He turned around again, sticking his face right into the spray.

Papa! Papa, help me! A child's scream of pain and terror tore through his mind.

Rearing back with a roar of pain, he smashed his forehead into the tiles. Blood ran down the wall, turning pink as it mixed with the water at his feet. Blinking it out of his eyes, Dante reached down and picked up the soap. The sting of his injury was a welcome distraction, and with the unrelenting strength of will he was known for, he managed to shove those memories back to the deepest hell of his mind and soul where they belonged. With a breath of relief, he picked up the razor and got rid of the stubble on his head. He had hair, but for some reason, having a huge bald guy with tattoos and fangs coming after them scared the shit out of people more than a guy with hair. Maybe it reminded humans more of the old Dracula movies. In any case, it also gave them one less thing to grab onto as they tried to fight him off.

His new friend whined outside the door, and Dante shut off the water and stepped out of the shower. As he'd expected, Shea must have brought him and the cat over from Luukas's place after he'd left the night before. He should take them outside. Opening the bathroom door, he ruffled the dog's fur and glanced at the clock next to the bed he never slept in, noting he had a good hour before he was expected to show up. He dressed quickly in heavy black cargo pants and a black T-shirt that fit him like a second skin. His combat boots completed the look.

"All right, let's go," he told the animals. The cat meowed in agreement. Tail straight up in the air, he rushed over to the door with the dog on his heels. Dante took them to the elevator and outside. There was a little park with some actual grass not far from his building, and he headed that way.

Forty-five minutes later, he made sure they had all that they needed and headed to Luukas's penthouse apartment, leaving a light lit and the built-in TV on for them. The fresh air had done him good. He had a clear head by the time he walked into Luukas's place.

Immediately, he was assaulted with various scents of human blood, all slightly different and yet very familiar to him. Before he could investigate further, he was met at the end of the foyer by Luukas and the other Hunters.

"Dante," Luukas greeted him. "We were just wondering about you. What happened to your head?"

Dante rubbed the large scab on his forehead. He'd nearly forgotten about it. By the tenderness there, he could tell the wound wasn't quite healed yet. "Nothing. I ran into the door."

One side of Luukas's mouth quirked up in amusement, but he didn't comment further. "We'd like to introduce you to everyone properly."

Dante gave him a nod. "I apologize for last night. I was...thirsty."

"I assume you've taken care of that?"

"Yeah."

Luukas nodded. "Good. Remember, the females that are here are very important to us, and if you think you can control yourself, I'll introduce you and we'll talk about everything that has happened in the short time you've been gone. If you can't control yourself, you will need to find different accommodations immediately."

Dante looked over the group of males. Four pairs of deadly serious eyes stared back at him. They weren't fucking around. "Where is Shea?"

"She'll be along," Christian said. "Told me she needed to do something real quick."

Dante turned his attention to him. There was something different about the male. There was something different about all of them. "Do what?"

Christian shrugged. "I don't know, man."

"Are you ready?" Luukas asked.

Dante gave a nod. Although the humans smelled pretty damn good, enough to tickle his throat, he'd fed from Laney. He no longer had the crazy thirst from earlier.

The group of males turned as one and walked in front of him like a human shield. More than once, he was checked out over a muscular shoulder to make sure he was keeping it under control.

Dante cocked an eyebrow, but said nothing.

"Keira, come here," Luukas said. The wall of brawn split to reveal the dark-haired woman from before. The resemblance to his Laney was still there, but he could see quite a few differences now that he wasn't blinded by blood lust. "This is Keira," Luukas introduced her. "Keira is a Moss witch, as are the rest of the females here. A glitch in a curse that I will explain later."

A Moss witch? No shit? "I apologize for trying to feed from you earlier," Dante told her, dead serious. "I was very thirsty, and you smell very fucking good."

Luukas bared his fangs at him with a hiss of warning. But she put her hand on his arm. "Calm down," she told her mate. "He's messing with you."

Dante gave a little tilt of his head. *Yes and no.*

The female, Keira, smiled at him. "It's good to meet you, Dante. And no apology is necessary. You are what you are. Besides, what Luukas tends to forget is that I'm perfectly capable of protecting myself, especially against powerful vampires. And I can tell that you are very old, and very powerful."

He gave her a small nod of acknowledgement. Inhaling a deep breath, he could scent Luukas's blood in her, and her blood in him, now that he was feeling halfway sane.

The others that were there came forward. He met Emma, Keira's bright-haired sister and Nik's mate, capable of immobilizing a vampire or other creatures where they stood, and the one that had kept him from attacking her sister the night before. Grace, Aiden's mate, had healing powers that may come in handy. Last, he met Ryan, the seductive redheaded female that had finally tamed Christian. When he asked what her magic was, she just smiled. "Keeping everybody in the loop," was her answer. Dante wasn't sure what that meant exactly, but he honestly didn't really care.

"So, where is she?" Aiden asked once the females had gone up to Nik and Aiden's, and the Hunters had gathered behind the glass walls of Luukas's office and found chairs.

Dante cocked an eyebrow. "Who?"

"The female you've mated with."

Dante stared at the male like he'd lost his fucking mind. Which he was pretty sure had happened a long time ago. "Come again?"

"Come on, commander. Don't be obtuse. We can all smell her, no matter how hard you just scrubbed yourself."

Narrowing his eyes, Dante looked at each of them in turn. "What the fuck is he talking about?"

"Aiden." Nik shook his head at his friend with a frown.

But Aiden was not one to take a hint, as Dante well knew. "You show up here in a car that you can't drive. You smell like one particular female who's scent is all over that car. You have her blood inside of you even now, so I know you haven't killed her yet. Shagged her? Probably. Killed her? No. You get your knickers all in a twist the moment you scented Keira last night, who smells amazingly similar to the female you've obviously been getting on with. Almost like she was your"—his eyes widened dramatically—"Mate!"

Denial rose up inside of Dante, fast and furious. "No. That's not how it happened. Or why. I went after Keira"—he glanced at Luukas—"again, no offense,"—then went back to Aiden—"because I was fucking starving."

Aiden sat back in his chair and crossed his arms over his chest. "Bollocks."

"Aiden," Luukas interrupted. "We can discuss this later."

"Actually, Aiden might be right to bring this up now," Christian cut in. "He needs to know. Because if he kills her, he's completely screwed." He turned to Dante with dawning horror. "You haven't killed her yet, have you?"

Dante stood up so fast his chair went flying back into the wall. "What the FUCK are you all talking about." It was a demand. Not a question.

Nikulas stood up and came around to stand eye to eye with him. "All right, look. You've got a female with you that you've been feeding from. Am I right? A human one?"

He narrowed his eyes at the face in front of him that was just entirely too fucking pretty to be on a male. "So what if I do?"

"Have you fed from anyone else since you found her?" Nik asked. "Or tried to? Other than Keira?"

Dante crossed his arms in a defensive pose. The asshole that he'd taken the dog from immediately came to mind. But that had been meth in his veins that made him taste so nasty. Right? "What exactly are you fucking getting at?"

Luukas came around his desk to join his brother. "Have you hurt her?" He didn't seem particularly put out about it if he had, just mildly concerned.

Dante looked between the two of them, and then over to where Aiden and Christian sat leaning forward in their chairs. They all stared at him, waiting for an answer. "No," he finally said. Then he shrugged one shoulder. "Not really."

A collective sigh of relief followed his short answer. Nik nodded. "Good. That's good."

"Where is she?" Luukas asked with a forceful tone.

Oh hell, no. He wasn't answering that one. So they could go down there and take her out? Fuck, no. Laney was no one's concern but his. He stared back at Luukas with a steady gaze and clamped his mouth shut. Luukas had not created him, so he could not make him talk. A problem that arose once in a while. A problem for Luukas, that is. Not for Dante.

Nik gave his brother a look before turning back to Dante. "Look, man. We've all gone through the same thing recently. We can all relate. None of us wanted this—"

"Speak for yourself, Nik," Aiden said. "I knew the moment I saw Grace's derriere sticking out of that doorway that I had to have it all for myself."

"But it's happened," Nik continued, ignoring him. "Luuk still has a problem with being mated to the witch that caused him so much misery."

Confusion crept over Dante. "What?"

Luukas shook his head. "I'll explain that later. Right now, I just want to debrief you and find out what happened."

"And let's not forget about my demon," Aiden said casually. "We need to warn him about Waano."

"Your what?" Dante was beginning to wonder if he was still in the desert. Hallucinating, maybe.

"My demon," Aiden repeated with a cheerful smile. "Waano."

"We'll get to that, too," Luukas said. On his way back to his desk, he paused. "And don't kill the girl. If she *is* yours, you will die without her now."

Dante was familiar with the tales. Once a vampire found his fated mate, and drank from her, he could no longer feed from anyone else. And without her, he would die the true death.

His mate, on the other hand, after drinking his blood in return, would freeze in time and not age until their vampire mate was no longer around to keep them immortal. Then they would begin to age naturally again, though it may be a thousand years from when they were born.

It had always sounded extremely cruel to him. That after losing their mate, the human then had to continue to live without them.

Picking his chair up off the floor and setting it upright again, Dante fell into it.

"Did you happen to catch her name before you dragged her to your cave?" Aiden asked.

"Laney," Dante answered automatically. "Laney Moss."

Christian snorted. "Yeah, man. You're screwed."

"She's a Moss witch," Dante said in that same faraway voice. Laney *Moss*...as in the Moss family of witches. It was all making sense now. That was why he was so attracted to the blood of the women upstairs. They were her family. They shared the same blood. He didn't know how he had missed it before. Of course, at the time he'd asked Laney what her name was, he'd been more worried about his own survival. "Just like your females."

The weight of what he was finally admitting out loud was starting to hit him. He remembered the overpowering feeling of possession he'd experienced earlier when he was with the female. How much he'd wanted to hurt her, to make her beg and bleed, and yet when she'd thrown herself in his arms, he'd felt an overwhelming sense of relief that he wouldn't have to. "Fuck. Me."

Nikulas squatted down on his haunches in front of him. "Yeah. But it's actually kind of cool. Being mated, I mean. The hardest thing about it is worrying about them all the time, and not just because you need their blood to survive. Because you get so damned protective over them."

"Why are they all witches?" he asked Nikulas. "Your mates?" If anyone noticed that he hadn't included himself in the group, they didn't say anything.

"A little caveat that Keira snuck into that curse that Luukas mentioned earlier, although I like to think they would've somehow ended up with us anyway."

"Curse or no curse," Christian said. "I, for one, am completely fucking grateful that Ryan found me. Fucking so many different females every night was seriously getting old."

Luukas cleared his throat. "Can we get on with things now? We need to find out what Dante knows."

"Oh, one more thing. Leeha is dead, by the way," Aiden informed him. "But I have her head if you'd like to pay your respects."

Dante seriously wondered, not for the first time, what the fuck was wrong with the Brit. Of course, some would say the same about him. But at least he had a good reason for being as messed up as he was.

17

Laney sat on the mattress in the candlelight with her knees pulled up to her chest and her arms wrapped around her legs. She stared into the tiny flame in front of her without really seeing it, her shoulders slumped in defeat. She'd gotten dressed as soon as Dante had left, then she'd gone back to the pile of rubble that blocked her way out and dug at it until her nails tore and her fingers bled, not caring anymore if she made it all come toppling down on top of her. It was better than this. Better than the endless waiting.

When that proved to be pointless, she screamed for help under the squares of opaque purple glass. Normal people going about their daily lives walked over that glass. She screamed until her voice went hoarse. Screamed until she sounded like a balloon with a hole in it.

No one stopped in the street above her. No one came running to help her. No one heard her.

Dante had been gone longer this time. She'd slept twice since he'd left, although she wasn't sure for how long each time, or what time of day or night it was. Her stomach growled, more insistent this time. But she had nothing to give it. She'd finished her last protein bar hours ago. If she didn't die by the vampire's hands, she was going to die of thirst and starvation. Either way was fine with her by this point, just as long as it was over with. And there was no more waiting.

Then Laney sighed. That wasn't true. She was lying to herself. She wanted to get out of this rat hole he had her locked up in, yes. But if she were to be perfectly honest, she wasn't so eager to get away from the vampire that was keeping her here anymore. Even when she'd sat with the knife poised above his chest, she'd been fighting an internal battle. Her mind had screamed at her that stabbing him through the heart was the right thing to do and the only way to ensure her own survival, but her soul had cried out in agony even as she'd lifted her arm high above her head and brought the knife plunging down. She'd sobbed with relief when he'd woken up just in time.

He's here.

Warmth filled her from the inside out, every nerve ending in her body jumping to attention. It wasn't unpleasant. More like a feeling of coming home, as strange as that sounded, even to her. Her senses flared to life. The soft glow of the candlelight was suddenly brilliant, the damp mustiness of the underground burned her nose, and ghosts of air touched her exposed skin with sensuous strokes. His footfalls sounded in the passageway as he neared, and she barely caught herself before she moaned aloud in anticipation. Squirming a bit, she tried to ignore the ache flaring between her legs. Laney was fully aroused, and she hadn't even laid eyes on him yet. Her hunger forgotten, she focused on the entryway to the room, waiting for his appearance. And then he was there.

He'd cleaned up and changed, and Laney felt disgusting sitting there in her unwashed clothes with her hair snarled around her face. She could only imagine what she smelled like by now.

The vampire paused in the doorway for a moment, his sharp eyes taking in every nuance of her appearance, from her hair to her sneakers. They narrowed in on the torn skin of her fingers as the muscles jumped from his clenched jaw. She resisted the urge to hide the bloody stumps behind her. Let him be pissed. It was his fault that it had happened. If he would just let her the hell out of here, she wouldn't feel the need to try to dig her way out. As he advanced into the room, her spine straightened even more.

He stopped directly in front of her, and she had to crank her head way back so she could see his face. His expression was unreadable.

"What happened to your fingers, little mouse?"

He sounded different. As if he actually cared. "I tried to dig my way out," she answered honestly. Her voice was still raspy, like she had a cold. "I didn't get very far." She laughed without humor. "As you can see, I'm still here."

He lowered himself down onto the mattress, crossing his legs in front of him and turning to face her. Laney's body angled itself toward his without her consciously thinking about it.

After a minute, he spoke, his voice deep and still a bit grating. "I'm not...overly fond of humans, in spite of the fact that I used to be one. Or maybe because of it."

His words surprised her. "I kind of got that impression." Laney didn't bother to keep the sarcasm out of her tone.

Black eyes flashed with a hint of amusement for a moment before narrowing in on her mangled fingertips again. He took one of her hands gently in his and brought it to his mouth. Laney hissed in pain as he put two fingertips in his mouth and sucked. His eyes closed, but not before she saw the flare of pleasure the moment her blood touched his tongue. Tenderly, he repeated the gesture for all of her fingers, healing her wounds. When he was done, he didn't release her hand, but continued to hold it in his. They both watched as the skin bonded together right before their eyes.

"I'm very old," he continued in a faraway tone. "I don't know if you've figured that out. I was born in Northern India, as one of the Romani people." He glanced up at her with his mouth twisted in a sneer. "You would know us as Gypsies, dirty nomads who survived by stealing and lying." He snorted with disgust. "In reality, we were persecuted for nothing more than being who we were. We were hunted, enslaved, forced to assimilate into a foreign culture." His words faded away, but not his anger. "It only became worse when I was changed into what I am now." His expression glazed over as he stared off into the distance, lost in the past.

"I was hunted. Like an animal. By humans that used to be my family...my friends." His eyes came back to her and he smiled a disparaging smile. "Of course, I gave them good fucking reasons."

"Why are you telling me this?" Laney asked.

He turned his attention back to her. A look of confusion passed over his face as long seconds passed. "I don't know." He shrugged one powerful shoulder. "I want you to know me."

"Why?"

Burning. His eyes were burning as they stared into hers. "Because you are MINE."

Laney was tired, so tired of it all. She pulled her hand from his and threw them both into the air. "What the hell does that even mean?"

He tensed visibly. "It means you can't ever leave me."

She stared at his face, his tattoos menacing in the candlelight. Yet she wasn't afraid. Did this mean he was going to kill her? Or not? "Was that ever an option for me?"

His body seemed to deflate as he relaxed again. "No. It wasn't."

Laney hated to ask, but she needed to know. "Does this mean you're going to let me live?"

Reaching out, his fingers skimmed the top of her breast as he tugged on her hair, running the strands through his fingers.

She felt the heat even through her shirt. "It means I can't kill you now, even if I wanted to."

A surge of hope had her heart doing double-time. She waited for him to say more. He didn't. "You can't?"

He shook his head, the light playing off the tattoos until they appeared to slither and shift on his skin. "No, because you are mine." His tone was matter of fact.

Okay. There was obviously something she was missing here. "I don't understand—"

Tearing his gaze from her hair and breasts, he finally explained. "There are tales, ancient tales, of how vampires find their fated mates. I have never seen it happen in all of my years, and neither had any of the vampires I knew. We all thought they were myths. However, I recently found out that these tales are very much true. A lot has happened while I was gone. To my friends, and to me." He searched her face. "I just didn't realize it until last night."

He wasn't with her last night, but that wasn't the part of his speech that had resonated with her. She was almost afraid to even say the words out loud. "So, you think that I'm your... fated mate?"

"I don't have to think about it. You are." He watched her closely, waiting for her reaction.

"What does that mean? Exactly? And how do you know?" It was important to have all of the facts before freaking the hell out.

Running a hand over his skull, he took a deep breath and exhaled through his nose. "I knew it the moment I drank from you in the desert. Your blood was the best fucking thing I've ever had. I just didn't realize what was going on at the time. I thought you tasted so good because I was in such fucked up shape. I had to have more, and so I tracked you to your home." He paused and frowned. "In retrospect, I should have known when I offed the asshole who was abusing the dog by the Dumpster. After drinking from you, he tasted like shit. I thought it was drugs in his system."

Laney held up a hand to stop him from saying anything else. "You killed one of my neighbors? *And* my roommate?" *God, I'm never going to be able to go back to Vegas.* Then she almost laughed. Two people were dead, and all she was worried about was herself.

His expression was nonplussed. "He was a fucking asshole. The dog was just hungry. He didn't deserve to be hit."

So, he'd killed someone else, but he'd done it to save the dog. She could almost understand that. "And my roommate?"

"I had no use for her after she invited me in." No remorse in his tone for that one.

It was Laney's turn to take a deep breath. She wasn't going to touch that one. "Where is the dog? And Fraidy? Is he okay?"

"They're fine. They're upstairs in my apartment. I just took them outside before I came down here."

A thrill went through her at the mention of an apartment. An apartment meant a real bathroom. With a shower!

He cocked his head to the side. "I'm not taking you up there, little mouse."

She couldn't keep the disappointment from her voice. "Why not? And stop barging into my head uninvited."

Getting to his feet with a growl of displeasure, Dante began to pace the small space. Occasionally, he would run both hands over his skull, but he didn't answer her question.

Laney stood also. "Dante? Why can't I go upstairs?"

"Because you can't leave me," he said without stopping. He was moving so fast the words seemed to come at her from every direction. "If you leave me, I will die."

She wanted to make him stop pacing. "What does that mean? For me?" When he didn't answer, she yelled, "Stop! Stop and answer my goddamn question!"

Surprisingly, he obeyed, coming to an abrupt halt. Scowling down at her, he seemed to come to a decision. "No. I've told you enough. There's nothing else you need to know." Then he smiled, an evil slash of his beautiful lips that she was quickly learning did not bode well for her. "Get used to it down here in your hole, little mouse." Spinning on his heel, he made to leave.

Laney ran behind him. "Wait! Dante! Wait! Please!" She grabbed his arm and hung on. "Please," she begged. "I'm thirsty." His head whipped around, his eyes flaring with heat as they searched for and found hers. "I need water," she clarified. "And food. And a shower. And clean clothes.

And...I want to hold my cat! You can't just leave me down here!"

Those obsidian eyes, cold as the winter sky once more, travelled the length of her. "I'll bring you something to eat when I get back." Pulling his arm from her grasp, he leaned over her. "But get this through your pretty head now, little mouse. I don't care about your comfort. I don't give a shit about what you want. I only need to keep you alive. You mean *nothing* to me."

One second he was there and she was touching him, and the next he was gone as if he'd never been.

Dante left the underground as fast as he could, before he gave in to her and brought her with him.

She's only a human. A means to my survival. Nothing more. He would do well to remember that.

He'd prowled the wet city of Seattle the previous night, not trusting himself to go back to her after he'd left the meeting at Luukas's apartment. Disbelief, distrust, denial, anger—he'd experienced all of these things as he'd headed to his favorite hunting grounds. But after the fifth attempt to feed off a different human, he'd finally accepted the truth. The others were right. Laney, the tiny human woman with the balls of steel, was his fated mate.

It was a good thing he hadn't killed her.

Of course, from what Luukas had told him, it was impossible for him to seriously harm her now. His own vampire instincts wouldn't allow him to harm the only thing keeping him alive. For that's what she was now. Without her blood, he would die, slowly and painfully. Even if he could force himself to drink from another, or from a bag of donated blood, as Nikulas apparently had before he'd finally gone after Emma, it would do nothing but drag out the inevitable. He would still die. It would just take a little longer.

Flinging open the lobby door, he stalked down the street to the nearest store that carried human food. He was thoroughly pissed off, although he couldn't say if it was because he had to go get her food, or because he'd completely forgotten that she needed it. Following the smells, he found a place that was still open and ordered a few sandwiches, remembering to hold the tomatoes. Laney didn't like tomatoes. She'd taken them off her burger that first stop on the road. He grabbed some bottled waters, then almost walked out without wiping the memory of the kid behind the counter.

Shea was approaching the apartments from the opposite direction as he got to the door. It was too late to hide from her; she'd already seen him. Besides, Dante hadn't hidden from anyone or anything since he'd decided to turn the tables on the ones that would hunt him.

Her smile of greeting turned to a look of confusion as she saw the stuff he was carrying. "Don't tell me they have you running for snacks for the witches," she teased.

He snorted with disgust. "No."

Following her inside, he wondered how he was going to lose his favorite Hunter without giving away the location of his little mouse. He'd have to take it up to his place and then take it down to her once he got rid of Shea. "It's for the dog," he told her.

She frowned. "I just got him some dog food last night. And more cat food, too. I left it in your kitchen. Didn't you see it?"

"No," he told her. Truth. "Where have you been?"

"I just went out to feed," she answered.

She was lying, but Dante wasn't going to press the subject. What Shea did was her business; however, his questioning look achieved what he desired.

"I'll see you tomorrow night," she said as she got off on her floor to go back to her place.

"What's tomorrow night?" he asked, sticking his foot in the door so it wouldn't close.

"We're hiding the box, remember?" Shea's forehead scrunched up in concern. "Are you sure you're okay?"

That's right, he remembered now. They were taking the box that Aiden's female had found and putting it somewhere safe, and out of the apartment building. "Right. Tomorrow. I'll see you then." He let the doors close.

After Luukas had debriefed him the night before last, the other Hunters had filled him in on what they'd found out since Luukas's rescue.

Leeha, the bitch that had been made a vampire illegally and banned from their territory, had found a way to capture and hold Luukas in retaliation for his not wanting to make her his queen. She'd done it with a little help from a witch—Luukas's current mate—by threatening to kill her sister, Nik's mate, Emma. And that's where Luukas had been the last seven years, until Nik and Aiden found him and freed him.

While there, Leeha had also been busy attempting to create her own army of demon soldiers. She'd found them chained to an altar buried in the mountains of Western Canada. Not literally, as they were dead, but their spectral bodies. To release them from the altar, she'd had to provide bodies for them to possess. The bodies of vampires created by Luukas, a Master vampire, seemed to work best.

She'd even managed to get one into Aiden, and it was still there, though it tended to stay dormant unless it sensed the other demons and roused. Something was going to need to be done about that.

Any vampires of Leeha's own creation that she'd sacrificed for possession didn't last very long, quickly turning into gray-skinned, rotting creatures that were more demon than vampire. Creatures first seen by Emma and Keira when Leeha had sent her minions to collect the powerful witch. Emma had been left for dead.

These creatures were now all after the box that Grace, Aiden's mate, had brought here with her from China. They thought it held a clue. A clue to what, no one knew. But Luukas wanted it far away from his witch.

There was a lot more to the history of the Moss witches that he had yet to be told, mostly something about how they'd all scattered all over the world when the new High Priest had taken over. Only now, after years of hiding, they were reuniting thanks to a small tweak Keira had put in the curse Leeha had forced her to cast over Luukas and his Hunters. Just a little something extra she had done for shits and giggles.

And Dante had just brought home another of them, out of all the humans he could've found in Vegas.

With Shea gone, he hit the down button in the elevator and took the human her food.

Not just a human. *Laney.*

He would harden himself against his little mouse's wiles to get him to let her out of her hole. If he let her out, she would run away. She would leave him. She would tell others about him. And then his home would no longer be safe. He would be hunted again. They all would. And he couldn't let that happen.

18

Shea knocked on Nik and Aiden's door. Their apartment was on the same floor as hers and Christian's, just on the opposite side of the hall. As soon as the elevator doors had closed, taking Dante with it, she'd done an about face. Watching the numbers above the door, she saw it going down, all the way to Dante's underground hideout.

Leaning back against the wall, she'd debated whether or not to tell anyone. He obviously had a human down there, nothing unusual about that. What *was* unusual was that he was taking the person food. Dante had never gone out of his way to keep someone alive before. Something was up.

Grace answered the door. Her mahogany hair was pulled back in a high ponytail, and her green cat eyes were makeup free. In her hands she held a ball of spines, otherwise known as Mojo, her hedgehog. Or "Prickles," as Aiden called him. "Hey, Shea. What's up?"

Shea smiled. She liked Grace. "I need to talk to Nik and Aiden. Are they here?"

Grace stepped out of the way. "Yeah, of course. Come on in."

The guys were enjoying their downtime by sitting in the living room, watching recordings of MMA fights. Shea plopped down in the plush chair that was near the window. "Guys, I think something is up with Dante."

Aiden held one hand up, palm out in the universal sign for, "You're going to have to wait, something good is about to happen." Sure enough, the guy in red shot out a high kick and hooked his leg back around, effectively catching his opponent in the head with his heel and knocking him to the mat. He didn't get up again.

Jumping up off the couch, Nikulas held out his hand for a high five that never came. "Yes! I told you, man! I told you." Dropping his arm, he settled on clapping his hands together and high-fiving himself.

"Yes, yes, Nikulas. You told me." Aiden rolled his eyes. Obviously, he wasn't as thrilled about the results of the match. "It doesn't mean anything, mate. I'll still kick your arse later, because you aren't able to do that particular kick."

Nik stopped his happy dance and planted his hands on his hips to frown down at his best friend. "What do you mean? I can so do that kick. I just don't when we're sparring because you get all butt hurt if I mess up your pretty face."

Aiden scowled back. "Well, there's no need to be ungentlemanly about it, mate. I thought we'd agreed on that."

Nik sat back down. "We did." Grinning, he looked over at Shea. "What's up, Shea?"

"I think something's up with Dante," she repeated.

"Other than the fact that he returned to us with a mate in tow and now has her locked up somewhere in the bowels of the building and is probably forgetting to feed her?" Aiden asked with an innocent expression.

Shea was confused. "Wait, it's his mate he's got down in his torture room?"

Nik plopped back into the cushions of the couch and glanced over his shoulder to run an appreciative eye over Emma, who'd just come out of their room to join Grace in the kitchen. "Yup. Didn't you smell her on him?"

"Well, yeah, but I thought it was just some random derelict that he'd found and fed from on the way home."

Grace and Emma wandered over, and Aiden held out his hands for Mojo. The hedgehog grunted at him, crawled up his arm, over his shoulder, and curled up in the hood of his hoodie.

"What's going on with Dante?" Emma asked as Nik pulled her onto his lap.

"He found, and is probably currently shagging, another Moss witch," Aiden said. "His mate, it seems, as he hasn't killed her yet."

Grace sat down beside Aiden, a look of concern on her face. "I don't know him, but I've heard plenty. Should we be worried for her?"

Nik shook his head. "No. He won't hurt her."

"Are you sure?" Emma asked him. "He doesn't seem like the type to sit and listen to reason."

"She'll be fine," Nik said. "His instincts won't let him hurt her. Remember how you were all worried about Keira? And see? Luuk never laid a hand on her."

Emma gave him a look.

"What?" he asked innocently. "She's fine."

"Where is she?" Grace asked.

"Probably in his room in the underground," Shea answered. Dante would do what he would do. And no matter what the guys thought, that concerned her.

Grace gave her a confused look. "The underground?"

"It's where the monster dwells," Aiden told her. "The parts where the tourists aren't allowed because it's"—he made quotation marks in the air—"dangerous."

Emma stood up, knocking Nik's hand away from her ass. "And you guys are just going to leave her down there? It's gotta be cold. And wet. She must be miserable."

"He'll bring her up eventually," Nik told her as he tried to pull her down again.

"I don't know about that," Shea said.

Emma and Grace looked at each other, and two sets of Moss jaws set with determination. "We're going to get her," Grace said. "She's family. And even if she wasn't, we couldn't just leave a human being locked away down there. Come on, Em." The two witches got up and started walking toward the front door.

"You two don't even know where you're going," Nik called out.

"We'll find it," Emma answered.

"Don't leave the apartment building," Aiden warned them.

Shea looked at the two guys. They looked back, and Nik shrugged as Aiden turned the fights back on.

"You know there'll be no stopping them now," he said. "Besides, they'll never find it. Might as well finish watching the fight and then we can figure out how we're going to get Dante to allow the female to stay in the protective coven of our witches."

"You two are idiots," she told them, not un-fondly. Getting up, she followed the females. "I'll let myself out."

She caught up to the women pulling on their coats by the elevator. "You two seriously don't want to go down there. Let me talk to Dante. He'll listen to me."

"No, we're going to get her," Emma insisted. "You can make our lives easier and tell us where he's hidden her, though." She smiled sweetly.

Shea couldn't let them go down there. Dante would be furious if they found his home. And he'd kick her ass if she didn't try to stop them. The other Hunters didn't understand why he chose to dwell beneath the city, but Shea did. Sort of. In any case, she respected his wishes to do so. And that he needed his space.

"Please, let me talk to him. I know he seems all hard and tough and unfeeling, but he has his reasons for being the way he is. And he won't take you guys coming down there and removing her lightly. Let me talk to him," she repeated. "And if I can't convince him to take her out of there, I'll even help you get her and keep her safe." She stared at each of them in turn. "But you know, he has to be allowed to feed on her. He'll die if he doesn't. There's nothing we can do about that."

Grace and Emma looked at each other, and Grace gave a small shrug. Emma sighed. "All right. You talk to him, Shea. But if he won't listen to you, then we go after her."

"Agreed," she said. "Give me a night or two. She'll be okay until then."

Emma nodded. "Okay. Two nights. Then I go get Keira and Ryan to join us and we go."

Shea stuck out her hand. "Deal."

"Deal," the witches said in unison as they shook on it.

Now to get Dante to agree.

19

The following dawn, Dante made his way over the pile of rubble that blocked intruders from finding his home. After bringing Laney some food and water during the night, he'd left her alone. His plan had been to check in with the Hunters and then spend the rest of the night lurking in the shadows of the city. He needed something to keep his mind occupied.

Instead, he'd found himself in the passageway on the other side of the cave-in within the hour. He hadn't been able to face her again just yet, though, so he'd taken a seat on the rotting wooden planks that made up the old walkway and kept watch. Nothing would be able to get to her, his hideout was the safest place she could be, but it still soothed him to be near her. He'd stayed there the entire night.

Once, he'd heard her footsteps on the other side of the makeshift wall. She'd called out to him softly. He'd stood up and opened his mouth to respond, but nothing had come out.

A few seconds later, she'd gone back to the room, and he'd sat back down.

To pass the time, Dante worked on hardening his heart toward the female. The heart he hadn't realized he still possessed until she'd thrown herself into his arms of her own free will as he tried to drag her to his feeding room. Or maybe that had been nothing more than a desperate act of self-preservation. He wasn't sure which idea made him feel worse.

Occasionally, as he kept his vigil throughout the night, his mind would drift, and the memory of Laney's nude form—haunting in its perfection—would come to him. He allowed himself a moment or two to enjoy it, however, before firmly shoving the recall away. He couldn't think about her like that right now. Perfect though she might be, the marks on her belly were but a reminder of what he'd once had, and what he'd so violently lost.

Dante tried to remember if he'd ever come across a female with those marks before. Surely, he had. Yet, not one came to mind. Of course, he hadn't paid that much attention to a woman's body in a long time. Even if he fucked them, he barely looked at them. The blood lust would often blind him to their appearance.

When he sensed the rising sun, he stood and stretched. He'd come to a decision during the long night hours. A simple decision, but one he did not make lightly. Scaling the wall, he crawled across the top and dropped down to the other side.

Laney was awake and waiting for him when he reached her. She didn't greet him, just stood waiting expectantly.

He held out a hand to her. "Come."

Surprise shot across her features, but she didn't stop to question him. Hurrying over to her backpack, she picked it up and took his hand, allowing him to lead her out of the room.

Part of him was disgusted at the weakness he was showing, but the other part of him could no longer ignore the fact that he did care somewhat about this particular human's comfort. Therefore, while the others were all sleeping, he was taking her to his apartment to see her pet, and get a shower and some food.

But he was staying with her the entire time, and then he was bringing her back.

Laney was unusually quiet as she hurried to keep up with him. She still didn't ask what was going on or where they were going. But when they got into the elevator and he lit up the button for his floor, her hand tightened on his. He looked down at her. She barely came to his shoulder. Glancing up at him, her expression was cautiously hopeful.

The doors opened and he led her to the apartment Luukas had allotted to him when Dante had agreed to join his Hunters. He'd stayed there for a total of three painstaking days and nights, then he'd burrowed out his own lair below the building. It was too exposed upstairs, too open, too high off the ground. He didn't trust it. It made him twitchy, in spite of Luuk's assurances that it was completely safe for them and the building was secure. The windows even had a special gas between the panes to protect them from its rays, just in case the blackout blinds and curtains weren't enough. In their homes, he'd told Dante, they could enjoy the daylight if they so chose. However, most of them still slept throughout the day, not waking until the sun went down. All except Dante. He rarely slept anymore.

Punching in the code to get into the apartment, he pushed open the door and ushered her in before one of the others on his floor saw them. The animals came running to greet them from where they'd been sunning themselves on the rug in front of the large window, enjoying the warmth.

Laney took one step inside, sucked in a quick breath, and turned and pushed him back out the door. It closed in the dog's face with a soft click. "It's day," she exclaimed. "You can't go in there! The sun—"

"Can't hurt me here," he finished. A peculiar warmth filled him that had nothing to do with the sun flooding the apartment, making his throat swell and cutting off anything more he was about to say. He must be thirsty. Punching in the code again, he re-opened the door and pulled her inside.

She stalled out in the foyer, just outside the ring of sunshine, her hand on his arm. "Dante." The worry in her tone was obvious, in spite of his assurance.

It occurred to him for the first time that she was familiar with vampires. Now that he thought about it, though she was frightened of him at times, she'd never been particularly surprised. He shook off her hand and steeled himself.

Though his limbs suddenly felt like they were weighted down with lead, he forced himself to walk over to the window. The dog followed happily on his heels, tail wagging with excitement. Standing directly in the pool of weak morning sunlight, Dante turned to her and spread out his arms.

See?

She took a panicked step toward him and stopped, watching. Once she had assured herself that he wasn't about to burst into flame, she bent down and picked up the cat that was winding in and out of her legs. Holding him close as he purred with contentment and rubbed his nose on her chin, she came inside.

Dante stepped out of the ring of light, lightheaded with relief. He would never get fucking used to that.

She kept her face carefully blank as she looked around. As he followed her gaze, he could imagine why: the apartment was completely devoid of furniture or decoration. The only room he'd furnished was the bedroom. There was no point in doing the rest of it, as he was rarely there. Not even during those first three days. The place didn't even have barstools.

An unreasonable anger filled him at her continued timidity. "Come," he ordered, and headed to the bedroom. Going into the closet, he found some clean clothes that would fit her—a heavy T-shirt and sweatpants with a string tie. "I don't have any underthings for you," he said over his shoulder when he heard her follow him into the room. "But these are at least clean until we can wash your clothes."

"I have some in my backpack," she said quietly. "Clothes, that is. I just didn't want to change until I could shower."

He put his things back without a word, and tried not to show the disappointment he felt at her refusal of his offer. There was no reason for it. Stepping out of the closet, he pointed to the other door. "The bathroom is there. You should find everything you need."

Laney stared at him in disbelief, but only for a second, and then she set the cat on the bed and went in and closed the door. He heard the lock click, and couldn't help but smile. She knew a lock wouldn't keep him out, but her point had been made. Dante traded looks with the dog, and they headed back out to the other room and gave her some privacy. Careful to avoid the direct light, he hit the button on the wall and kept off to the side as the small motor began to hum, drawing dark curtains across the large wall of windows. It only made him feel mildly more secure.

He pulled out the rest of the sandwiches he'd stashed in the fridge and put them on the counter with a glass of water, then he fed and watered the pets. After that, there was nothing to do but wait. Dante leaned against the kitchen counter and amused himself by watching the cat trying to instigate a wrestling match with his canine friend by batting at the dog's nose.

He remained far away from the windows, even with the curtains closed. His skin was still prickling with unease from the first time. He was too old to ever feel comfortable with the modern conveniences younger vampires enjoyed. Even if the entire apartment was walled in and sun proof, he wouldn't feel safe. It was too far up off the ground. Too dangerous. There was no way out if the elevator stopped and the stairway got blocked somehow. Dante paced the length of the kitchen. He felt trapped.

But he didn't dwell on what he had done by bringing her up to the apartment. What was done was done. She was here. Examining the reasons why would not make him feel any easier about it. And it would not change his mind as to her purpose in his life.

About twenty minutes passed before he heard the water shut off, and it was another seven minutes before Laney came out, not that he was watching the clock. Her hair was damp and she had changed into her own pair of loose, gray, cotton pants and a pullover sweatshirt with a "Save The Earth" logo. The shirt had a "V" neckline and was tight enough to show off her breasts, and the pants did nothing to hide her figure as she walked toward him. Her stride was naturally graceful, and he knew she was completely unaware of how captivating she was to him, no matter what she was wearing. His gums pricked as his fangs extended in response to her scent, even masked as it was with the soap she'd used. He didn't move a muscle, but let his eyes wander up and down her form and back again, glad that he'd changed into more comfortable pants earlier when his manhood responded to the stunning sight in front of him. He didn't even try to hide it.

He pointed with his chin at the sandwiches on the counter. "Eat."

Her eyes dropped down to the growing bulge in his pants, her nostrils flaring as though she found his own scent just as alluring.

"Eat, Laney," he growled.

Keeping the island countertop between them, she picked up a sandwich and unwrapped it. Pausing with it halfway to her mouth, she glanced up at him. "Thank you for the shower." Then she shoved half of it into her mouth, quickly followed by the remainder. Still chewing, she unwrapped another sandwich and stuck it in her mouth.

Dante frowned as he was hit with a sinking feeling. "Am I not feeding you enough?"

Color suffused her face and neck, causing his own blood to heat. The speed of his responses to every little thing she felt made him grind his teeth. She swallowed the mouthful she'd been chewing and her hands, still holding half a sandwich, fell to the counter. "I'm sorry," she told him. "I was just hungry. Not very ladylike, I know."

"I don't give a fuck about you being a lady. Am I not feeding you enough?"

She opened her mouth, but then closed it again without saying anything.

Pushing off the counter, he walked around the island and took her chin in his fingers. "If you are hungry, you need to tell me. I'm not trying to starve you." He was surprised to find that after all of his soul searching the night before, this was now true. "I'm just...I'm just not used to this. To providing for someone other than myself."

Her forehead creased and an expression of uncertainty crossed her features. "You weren't there for me to tell," she whispered. "I thought you were, I called to you, but you weren't there."

A knife, hot and sharp, stabbed him in the chest at her words. His vampire instincts to protect and care for his mate roared to the surface. She had needed him, and he had failed her.

"It won't happen again," he swore with vehemence.

Laney searched his face with wide brown eyes. "Okay."

Feeling slightly off in this newfound role, he nodded, and indicated for her to keep eating. They passed the rest of the time in silence. When she was finished, he said, "Get your stuff."

She stiffened mid-way through crumpling up the third sandwich wrapper. "Where are we going?"

"I'm taking you back underground."

"Why?"

Dante ground his jaw together. He wasn't used to being questioned, especially not by one he considered inferior, mate or no mate. "Because I am." His tone of voice should have warned her that he was not in the mood for a discussion, but true to form, Laney didn't heed the warning.

"I don't want to go back down there. I won't. I want to stay here. I want to have food, and a shower, and a real bed, and my cat."

No. There was no fucking way he was leaving her up here. She wasn't some princess to be kept in an ivory tower. "Do what you need to do and get your bag. We're leaving."

"Dante, please."

"NOW," he roared.

To her credit, she only jumped a little. Without another word she stomped back into the bedroom, coming out a few minutes later with her backpack hanging over one shoulder. Crossing her arms, she stood waiting by the entry. She refused to look at him. Dante could feel the helplessness emanating from her. But overriding it was rage. It appeared a shower and some food had done wonders to revive her sagging spirit.

Thank the gods. Her little submissive act had made his stomach turn. He would be sure to keep her well fed and clean from now on. For he was discovering that he didn't want to subdue his little mouse, after all. Trap her, yes. Break her, no.

Silently telling the pets he'd be back soon, he walked past her and opened the front door. He checked that the hallway was empty before he indicated for her to come with him. With a look that would cower a lesser male, she stalked out into the hall and to the elevator. Luckily, she waited until they were inside before arguing with him more.

"Why do I have to go back down here?"

"Because it's where I live."

"It's not where *I* live."

"It is now, little mouse." With that statement, she deflated in front of his eyes. The elevator dinged, the doors opened, and he stepped out but kept his arm there for her so she could exit. He should've known it wouldn't be that easy.

Staying right where she was, she swallowed hard. With a steady gaze, she stated, "I'd rather you just kill me than keep me here like an animal for the next forty years."

Her words struck him deep. In a gruff voice, he ordered her out of the elevator. "Out. Now."

She backed up until she hit the wall and shook her head. "No."

"Laney," he warned.

"I can't go back in there," she cried in desperation. "I can't!"

"You have to," he insisted.

"Why? Why can't I stay upstairs?"

"Because I want you with me! And it's not safe up there!" Going back in after her, he grabbed her by the arm and pulled her out into the passageway. "No matter what the others think, it's not safe for one like me."

He could feel the weight of her stare as she stumbled along beside him, but he refused to acknowledge it. He didn't want to see the look of pity on her face.

He didn't fully breathe until they were back in his den. Once there, he released her arm and set about re-lighting the candles so she could see.

"Are you?" she asked softly. "Going to stay with me?"

"I don't have much of a choice about it," he replied.

"I mean now. Are you going to stay with me now? I don't like being down here by myself. It scares me."

He stilled as her words broke through the red haze of his anger. "Yes. I will stay with you." Striking another match, he lit the remaining candles.

Dropping her pack on the floor, she sank down onto the mattress.

He ran his eyes over her. "What?"

When she finally lifted her head, her expression was bleak, her eyes filled with tears. "So, this is my life now? Being held prisoner in this cave, with nothing to do except wait for you to feed from me? For you to decide when to give me food or let me shower?"

Dante felt something break inside of him as he stared down at her, so small and helpless...and beautiful. "What do you want from me?" he ground out. "I need you to survive. I can't release you. I can't take any chances that something will happen to you." He threw his arms out to the side, taking in the space around them. "This. This is all I can offer you."

"So this is fate, then."

"What do you mean?"

She was silent then, but not for long. When she did speak, she changed the subject. "Will you tell me more about your life?"

He scowled down at her. "My life?"

"Yes."

Again, he was thrown off balance by this tiny slip of a female. One moment, she was scared to death of him, then railing at him, then wanting him to tell her a bedtime story.

When was the last time anyone had asked him about his long history? The other Hunters knew he was old, and that he'd come from Europe. Luukas had been the only one that had wanted to know anything about him. It had been one of the conditions of his being allowed to join the group.

She scooted back on the bed and patted the mattress in an invitation for him to sit beside her. He gave her a sideways look, but he did so, crossing his legs loosely in front of him. "What would you like to know?"

"I want to know what you were like before you became a vampire."

Memories pounded on the locked door at her innocent words, and he pushed them back. "That was a long time ago, I don't remember much." That was a lie. He remembered everything.

He could tell she didn't believe him, but she thankfully didn't press the issue. "Why do you hate humans so much when you used to be one?"

"Because they're nothing but locusts that consume and destroy everything they touch, and think they're above every other creature on this earth."

"And you don't?"

He turned his head to look at her. "No."

She tilted her head, her tawny eyes inquisitive. "You said something earlier about how your friends treated you when they found out you'd been turned—"

He barked out a laugh. "How they treated me...You want to know how they treated me? Like a stranger. No, worse. Like a wild animal. They laid steel traps in the forest around our home. Traps made to catch a large animal, like a bear. I lost and re-grew two limbs before I figured out to watch for the tiniest glint of metal in the moonlight. If the moon wasn't out, I had to take my chances. They searched for my grave during the day and hunted me with torches and wooden stakes at night. They treated me like I was nothing but a fucking monster."

"And so you became one. You became the hunter rather than the hunted."

She was intelligent, this one. Dante shifted uncomfortably. "Yes."

"Not all vampires are like you, then?" She waved her hand in the air, indicating the apartments they'd just come from and where they were now.

"The others are naïve, living out in the open among your kind. It's going to bite them in the ass someday." He truly believed that. When the humans discovered their kind living among them, they would rise up. They always did. They couldn't stand anything that made them feel inferior. The war would be bloody, and due to their sheer numbers, it wouldn't end until all supernatural creatures were forced into hiding once again if they were to have any hopes of their species surviving.

"How did you become a vampire?"

He didn't respond at first, those memories banging—pounding now—on the door.

"Dante?"

Without meaning to, he began to speak, his voice monotone. "I was turned by a stranger that came to our camp just after dark one night. He claimed to be a necromancer, and he wanted some of us to join him, to fight whatever battle he was fighting. We refused his offer, but welcomed him into the fold to rest and eat because that was how my people were. I woke during the night and went out to piss. The stranger was still awake, roaming our camp, and I found him walking away from my wagon. I called out, and asked him what he was doing. When he saw me there, he came toward me, moving so fast I couldn't follow. He just appeared next to me, like magic. He was angry that we had refused him. The tips of his fangs were showing, and he looked different. Larger. I asked him again what he was doing roaming around our camp while we slept. Was he stealing from us after we offered him food and shelter? He told me he was hungry, and then he jumped on me. I tried to fight him off, but he was too strong. The commotion woke some of the others...."

Papa? Papa!

Stay inside! No! Leave my son alone! Leave him alone!

Dante stared into the flame of the candle in front of him, lost in the horrors of his past. "He threw me to the side and got a hold of a child," he rasped. "My son."

"What happened to him?" she whispered.

His voice dropped to match hers. "He tore him apart right in front of me, as I crawled through the wet grass, trying to get to them. To save him. But I was too late. Then he came to finish me off, only I had the misfortune of surviving."

"And his mother?"

Blinking hard as he came back to the present, Dante couldn't speak for a moment. He cleared his throat. "She was already gone. She died the winter before from an illness."

"How old was your son?"

"Nine."

Laney was silent then, and Dante was glad. Still locked in the past, he rose to leave.

She jumped to her feet as well. "Where are you going?"

"I need to go."

"Please don't," she said. "Don't leave me here alone."

There was something different in her expression as she looked up at him, something that pulled at his insides.

MINE. The word pounded around his skull, chasing away the sadness of his past. "No more questions."

"No more questions," she agreed.

He waited for her to say something stupid, something like, "I'm so sorry for your loss," as humans were inclined to do. But she didn't. She just gave him a small, tired smile and went back over to lie down. A few seconds later, he followed her and blew out all but one candle before joining her on the bed.

"Are you not going to feed yourself?" she asked quietly once he was on his back beside her.

A sharp, instant burn hit his throat as his fangs punched down in his mouth. It was intense, as if he hadn't fed in months.

"You can, if you need to," she said, and held out her wrist. "You're looking a little peaked."

Dante turned his head to stare at the female beside him calmly offering him her wrist. He wasn't sure what to make of her offer, or how to accept it. This had never happened to him before. He'd always had to hunt for his food and take what he needed, and he rarely left his victims alive. Unless they were especially deserving of it and he wanted them to be plagued by nightmares for the rest of their short years. They weren't apt to offer to feed him again, however.

"Go ahead," she urged. "Drink."

"Why are you doing this?" He smelled no fear, only her natural mouth-watering scent.

She gave a little shrug. "I just figure that if we're stuck together now, that we might as well get to know each other and try to make the best of it."

"You want to be friends with a monster?" Though the words were lightly spoken, he found he was nervous as he waited for her reply.

"I don't think you are a monster. I think you did what you felt you had to do to survive, and now you don't know anything else. And maybe...." She bit the inside of her lip and lowered her eyes.

"What?"

She caught her gaze with his. In it, he saw no pity, just understanding. A linking of similar souls. "Maybe we can offer each other comfort. We both carry the burden of not protecting our children as we should have. And we have to live with that until we can see them again." A tear slid down her temple as she offered her wrist again.

Dante's heart pounded, and he grew lightheaded from the blood rushing through his head. He'd never once in all of his years thought he would be so lucky as to find someone to share this long, lonely life with.

"Take it, Dante." Laney snapped him out of his thoughts as she waved her wrist in front of him.

He inhaled the sweet smell of her blood. "Thank you," he whispered in awe. The words sounded foreign on his tongue. Taking the delicate bones between his fingers, he brought her offering to his mouth, and with a hiss of anticipation, he sank his aching fangs into her flesh. Immediately, her honeyed blood filled his mouth. He savored the taste for a few seconds before swallowing. It burned through him, lighting him up inside like a slow-burning fire. Opening his eyes, he saw her small hand clench into a fist, saw particles backlit by the candlelight floating in the air around them like a snow globe. The burning hit his sex, and the semi-hard length instantly became a massive hard-on. He drew up one leg to ease the pain of his erection, the soft rasp of his clothing on his sensitive skin only making it worse.

But overriding it all was the scent of his female. His nostrils flared to take in more. Her sex was aroused, the musky smell consuming her normal fragrance until he was aware of nothing else. He eased his fangs out, only to bite her again, harder this time. Laney gasped, but didn't cry out. Her free hand gripped the side of his shirt and hung on.

Taking one last drink, he sealed the wounds. Laney moaned as he licked the delicate skin of her inner wrist. Turning his head, his eyes clashed with hers. They were filled with a hunger that matched his own. With a low growl, he reached for her and pulled her on top of him. Her slight weight was barely noticeable. He felt raw inside, vulnerable, the past and the present banging around inside of him with her words.

She tried to rear up, to slide off him again, but he wrapped his arms around her and held her to him. "No, Laney." He lifted his head off the bed and captured her mouth with his, kissing her until she became pliant. "Take what you want from me," he told her against her mouth.

"I can't," she whispered.

"Why not?"

"Because I...." The words drifted off as she tried to think of a good argument.

"You are MINE, Laney." He paused. "And I am yours. Take it." And then he kissed her again. One hand slid inside the back of her shirt, the bare skin of her back soft beneath his rough palm. Her breath caught as he slid that hand down to cup her ass. He squeezed, and she rolled her hips up, pushing her curves up into his palm. He moved his hand lower, sliding his fingers between her legs from behind and pressing, manipulating her through her pants. The cotton material was no hindrance at all. He could feel every fold of her pussy right through it. Her body responded to him instantly, and she bit his lip even as she wiggled against his fingers. He raised his hips so she could feel the hardness of his sex, could feel what she was doing to him. He rolled his hips against her over and over while his fingers continued to move in circles on her clit. Not too hard, but just hard enough.

He broke off the kiss, nipping at her jaw. "Laney...." Her name hung in the air between them. He slid one powerful thigh between hers, opening her to him. "Say yes, Laney," Dante demanded. "Tell me yes."

Laney was panting on top of him, her face pressed into his neck.

His large body curved beneath her so he could feel as much of her as possible. "Say it." Her hips kept rocking against him, helping his fingers along. He knew she was almost there. He suddenly removed his fingers and Laney cried out in protest, her head lifting and her eyes popping open only to be caught and held by his. "Tell me I can have you," he demanded through gritted teeth. "Tell me you want me."

When she didn't answer him, he went for her mouth again, kissing and nipping in between words. "*Tell me*, Laney."

"Yes," she finally said. "Yes."

Triumph flared within him. He smiled, purring with anticipation. Her eyes widened and her heart pounded as she stared down at him and realized what she'd just agreed to.

It's too late now, little mouse. You won't be getting away from me this time.

Gripping the bottom of her shirt, he yanked it up and off, and her bra soon followed. But it wasn't enough. He needed to feel her skin on his.

He rolled to the side, taking her with him and laying her on the bed before rising up to his knees. His eyes roved over the smooth skin of her breasts—quivering with her panting breaths—the curve of her shoulder, the graceful arc of her collarbone, her slender arms. Not wanting to disrupt the sight in front of him for even just the short time it would take him to get his shirt off, he gripped the neckline and tore it from his body.

Throwing it to the side like so much trash, he bent down and took one hard dusky nipple between his teeth. Laney arched into his mouth, her hands flying to his arms and her nails digging into his biceps. Dante bit down, releasing the sweet nectar from the blue veins just beneath her skin, then sucked and teased the hard bud until she was squirming and lifting her hips to his. Working his way down her stomach, he paused when he reached the drawstring of her pants, the memory of the marks on her belly threatening to remind him of things he didn't want to think of right now. Or ever.

With a growl of denial, he untied them and yanked them off, along with her shoes and socks, until she was gloriously nude beneath him. Skipping over the disturbing stretch marks, he looked his fill of the rest of her, something he hadn't done last time because he'd been too distracted by the horror of thinking he'd taken her from her child.

And if you had, would you have released her to mother that child?

No. He would have gone for the child and brought him back, also. For he would've been his now, just like his mother.

To have a child again. The words filled him with joy, and sadness because he knew it would never happen.

Pushing the thought aside, Dante spread her legs wide, revealing the damp folds of her womanhood nestled beneath soft dark curls. She tried to bring them back together, to cover herself and hide from him, but he wouldn't allow it. His mouth watered just looking at her, and unable to resist, he leaned over and ran his tongue from back to front, enjoying the way her hips jumped when he hit her sensitive spot. The skin within the folds was as soft as satin, and tasted nearly as good as her blood. Her hands landed on his skull, and she couldn't seem to decide whether to push him away or pull him closer.

He gave the hard bud one last flick, and then unbuttoned his pants and shoved them down off his hips. Sitting down, he yanked off his boots and pulled his pants off. This was done so fast, Laney had no time to sit up or move before he laid back down beside her and pulled her up against him. His fingers tangled in her long, dark hair as his other hand gripped her lush ass and pulled her tight into his hips. He took her mouth in a hungry kiss, groaning with need when his fangs nicked her lips and her blood trickled into his mouth.

His skin felt too tight, and not just on his swollen sex, but everywhere. He tried to pull her in closer still, and was about to roll her onto her back when she threw one shapely leg over his hips and pushed hard against his shoulder. He broke off the kiss and rolled onto his back, instantly missing the feel of her flesh on his. But he didn't have long to wait. His little mouse climbed over him, straddling his hips as she had when she'd attempted to stab him. The wet heat between her legs coated his manhood. She moaned as she rocked her hips.

Placing her palms on his chest, she sat up, a Madonna with her long hair partially hiding her breasts and the curve of her hips flaring out from her waistline. Laney let her eyes roam over him much as he had her. With shy fingers, she traced his tattoos, following the pattern from his shoulder down to his hip until she ran into her own thigh and could go no further. He lifted his head to watch as she trailed her fingertips over his hipbone to lightly touch the swollen head jutting from between her legs.

Dante gritted his teeth and dug his fingers into her legs. He went to sit up, but she pushed him back down and shook her head.

"No," she commanded.

He fell back onto the mattress, helpless to disobey her. Playing the submissive had never been a turn on for him, not even in his human life, but giving up his power to Laney excited him to no end. Dante didn't understand it, but she didn't give him any time to stress about it.

Going back to what she was doing, she gripped the head of his sex, her small hand unable to wrap completely around it. "You're so big," she said with awe.

He almost came in her hand. "Ah! Laney…take me." He was begging her now. His instincts were screaming at him to throw her down and make her his completely, but he was afraid that he would hurt her. And he found he was unable to take the chance of doing so. He was in her small hands to do with what she would. "Take me," he growled. His upper lip lifted off his fangs, showing her how much he wanted her.

Slowly, she leaned down over him, but instead of kissing him like he thought, she brought one dangling breast to his mouth. He rose to meet the full globe, sucking her nipple into his mouth and holding her where he wanted her with his hands around her ribcage. Her hips lifted up and off him, and he moaned with disappointment even as he opened his mouth wide and sank his fangs into the soft flesh. Laney cried out and pressed her breast closer. Dante drank greedily, and then she gave him the other side to do the same.

He kissed the wounds clean. "I want to taste all of you, little mouse." Urging her to move up over him, she quickly caught on, crawling up his body until her pussy was poised over his mouth. Dante breathed in the earthy scent and dove in with a rumble of pleasure. She was wet and warm and tasted better than any woman he'd ever had before. He pressed his tongue into her opening, fucking her with it before licking his way up to the tight bundle of nerves. It was swollen, begging for his touch. Dante flicked it once, twice, and again. She cried out and tried to press closer, but his hands on her hips held her still above his mouth.

"Dante." His name was both a plea and a command.

Unable to deny his female, he gave her what she wanted, swirling his tongue around the hard nub faster until her body tensed above him. When she started to tremble with the strain, he bared his fangs and bit her clit. Blood mixed with her come as she orgasmed, jerking above him, her breathless cries making him so hard he thought he was going to pop from his skin.

Dante could wait no longer. Lifting her hips from his mouth, he moved her back down his body where his sex was rock hard and ready. He took himself in his hand and found her entrance as soon as she settled back over him. With a thrust of his hips, he plunged deep inside of her with a shout. She was tight, but wet, and he had no worry that he was hurting her. Especially when she immediately took over.

Taking his hands in hers, she removed them from her hips and pressed them down on either side of his head. She held him there as she rocked above him, her breasts swaying above his face, urging him toward his own orgasm. He rose to meet her with each thrust, his heart pounding, his breath coming in pants.

"Oh, God," she groaned. Releasing his hands, she rose up above him and took her breasts in her palms. He watched as she pinched the nipples into hard peaks, her hips rocking faster now, her dark hair falling down her back to tickle his thighs as she threw her head back. Her eyes closed, and he was glad, for he felt sure that if she were to look at him now, she would see all the way down to his black soul, raw and exposed and hungering for her.

Gripping her hips again, he held her still as he pounded into her, deep growls tearing from his throat.

"Dante...oh, God...I'm coming!"

Her cries echoed around him as he felt his balls tighten and his own orgasm traveled up his length to explode inside of her with a hoarse cry of his own. He came so hard his head smashed back onto the mattress, and his hips bucked beneath her uncontrollably.

After the longest orgasm of his life, Dante caught his breath as Laney collapsed on top of him.

He held her close as she cried.

20

The demon known as Steven pulled the hood of his black jacket farther down over his face, as did the other demons following him. Still, humans gave them strange looks as they entered the airport in Dalian, China.

Was it the way they looked, or the way they smelled, he wondered.

The vampire bodies they possessed were deteriorating rapidly now. It could mean only one thing: the female vampire who created them, Leeha, was dead. He couldn't say that he would miss her. She was nothing but a means to an end, and he'd never had any plans of keeping the promises he'd made her. No. She would've been one of the first ones he eradicated once he had no more use for her and their reformation was complete.

Steven hefted the duffle bag he carried onto the counter.

"Be right with you," the human male said in a too-cheerful voice. Placing the last traveller's suitcase on the conveyor belt behind him, he turned around with a wide smile. "Good evenin—" He inhaled sharply, his mouth hanging open, shock and horror filling his features.

Steven caught his gaze and burrowed into his mind. "We need tickets to the next available flight to Washington in the United States. If it's full, you will make room for us." It had taken them all a while to learn the new geography of the earth, so named by the humans. It was ridiculous, of course, they owned nothing and had no right to fly their flags or stake out parts of the earth for their particular group. African, American, Russian…it didn't matter. They were nothing but gnats, soon to be removed from this planet.

The human put a hand to his head, squinting like he had a headache, but he smiled and said, "Of course. There's a flight leaving in thirty minutes. How many would you like?"

"Five. In the front of the plane."

"First class, then?" the human asked, typing away on his computer.

"Yeah, whatever. Just make sure they're at the very front of the plane."

"I'll just have to bump these guests…okay. We're all set." He handed Steven the tickets he'd just printed. "May I check your bag?"

"No," Steven answered. "The bag stays with me."

"Of course," he said again. "Can I do anything else for you today?"

"Yes." Reaching in with mental razor blades, he removed the memory of this conversation from the human's mind. "You never saw us." As the human searched for something to catch the blood running out of his nose, Steven turned on his heel and left the counter, waving at the others to follow.

Bypassing the security lines with a wave of his hand and a mental suggestion that the skinny young nerd punch the woman behind him until he pulverized the bones in her face, they headed for the gate.

Fellow travelers gave them a wide berth, which was lucky for them. When they reached the gate, they were the last ones on the plane.

"Why don't we just take over the entire aircraft?" one of the others asked him.

Steven gave him a look. "It's not time to draw that much attention to ourselves. Yet," he added with an ominous smile, made more so by the cracked, discolored skin around his mouth. "We need to try not to draw an overdue amount of attention until we have the final clue and find what we need."

"Are you sure it will lead us to our blood?"

Steven clicked his seatbelt. "It better, or we'll be stuck in these rotting corpses we currently inhabit."

"And if it no longer exists? What if the ones that drained us and chained our souls to that fucking altar got rid of our blood somehow?"

"It exists," Steven told him. "And we will find it." The flight attendant did a double take as she walked by doing a final seat check. "Take care of her," Steven said. Then he leaned back in his seat and settled in for the long flight.

When the plane landed at the Seattle/Tacoma airport, the captain taxied in to the gate and took off his seatbelt. Laughing with the co-pilot, he unlocked the cabin door. His wife was waiting for him, but he liked to watch the passengers disembark before he left the plane.

Opening the door, the smile froze on his face. A moment later, his hand clutched at his chest over his heart as he stumbled back away from the bloody carnage that filled his plane.

21

Grace rolled over in the bed she shared with Aiden. Stretching out an arm, she patted around on the mattress next to her. It was empty.

Rubbing her eyes, she sat up and looked around the bedroom. Though it was just past dawn, the room was dark thanks to the blackout shades. "Aiden?" she called softly. She heard movement on the other side of the bed and reached over to turn on her lamp. Her hedgehog poked his nose out of his house next to the nightstand and grumbled about being woken up. "Sorry, little dude." Rolling back over, she found Aiden standing next to the bed in his red boxer briefs. He had his back to her.

The tiny hairs rose on the back of her neck as she watched him. "Aiden?"

When he turned around, she realized she wasn't talking to Aiden at all. Shadows darkened his grey eyes until they appeared more like a storm cloud than a morning mist. "Waano." She spit out the detested name. Sitting up, she was glad she'd kept her PJ's on last night. Normally, her vampire mate liked to feel her skin against his, even if they didn't have sex, but she'd fallen asleep reading a medical textbook this morning. She'd decided to go back to school the previous week.

Anger overcame her in a rush. "Why are you here?" she demanded. "What do you want?" She hadn't seen this particular side of her mate since it had tried to force Aiden to commit suicide by crazy obsessed vampire bitch in a desperate bid to gain its freedom. It didn't want to possess Aiden any more than he wanted to be possessed. But they seemed to be stuck with each other until they could figure out how to get it out of him.

Waano cocked Aiden's head at a strange angle as he studied her, causing chills to skate over her skin. "What do you want?"

"They're here." Aiden's British accent was gone. "We have to warn him."

"Who's here?"

"The others. They came for the box. For the clue." Aiden's body walked toward the bedroom door.

"Wait!" she cried after it. "Where are you going with him?"

"I must tell her to warn him," it said, and left the bedroom.

Grace scrambled out of bed, pushing her long, red hair out of her face. She followed Aiden, or rather Aiden's body, out of the apartment and to the stairs. "Nikulas!" she screamed from the hallway. "Emma!"

Nik's blonde head popped out of the apartment and Grace looked back at him with frantic eyes. When he saw her following Aiden into the stairwell, he shoved Emma back into the apartment. "Stay here!" he ordered. "I mean it, Em!" Then he closed the door in her face and followed Grace.

She held the heavy door open for him and kept her eyes on Aiden. He was heading up the stairs. "I think he's going to Luukas's."

"Yeah, that's not going to end well," Nik answered. "Especially not with those obnoxious undies he's wearing. It's going to be like flashing a red cape in front of an enraged bull. Only worse."

"How do we stop him?" she asked as she began climbing the stairs. The concrete was cold on her bare feet.

"I don't think we can," he said. "But we can stop Luukas from killing him." Adding under his breath, "I hope."

But Grace heard him. "You should've let Emma come. She could help —"

He cut her off with a slash of his hand and a quick shake of his head. "No fucking way."

"Nik, her powers are growing. She stopped Dante. You need to let her help us."

"Not today," he sang.

"Nik."

"NO."

Grace sighed, but didn't argue with him further. They were approaching Luukas's door.

Waano didn't knock. One well-placed front kick broke the lock, tore the door from its hinges, and sent it flying into the apartment. Aiden/Waano calmly walked in after it, with Grace and Nikulas on its heels.

"Dammit, Nikulas! We just fixed that door!" Keira's voice came from the glass-walled office just as over six feet of pissed off Master Vampire filled the doorway at the opposite end of the foyer. He wore nothing but a pair of black lounge pants, the muscles jumping in his chest and arms as his upper lip pulled back to reveal long fangs ready to take a bite out of whoever it was that had just busted into his home.

One look at Aiden and Luukas hissed in fury, fisting his hands at his sides and dropping into a fighting stance.

Nik got between him and Aiden just as he was about to attack. "Luuk! Wait! He says he needs to tell you something. He hasn't threatened anyone."

"Her," Waano clarified. "I need to tell her, the witch."

Keira appeared behind Luukas. "What is it you need to tell me?" Laying a hand on Luuk's arm, she tried to get him to let her pass, but he wouldn't budge. With a sigh, she stood behind him and peeked out from over his shoulder as he rocked on the balls of his feet, ready to pounce at the slightest indication.

In that moment, Grace was very grateful that Waano had come so close to succeeding in killing Aiden, for it was Luukas's blood that had saved him. And that re-established blood bond was the only thing saving him now.

"Not her," Waano said. He pointed past them into the office Keira had just left. "*Her.*"

Grace looked to where he pointed, as did everyone else. Ryan, Christian's female, stood in the doorway, her face pale and her eyes wide with fright.

"They're coming," Waano told her. The same thing he had told Grace.

"Who's coming?" Keira asked.

He directed his words at Ryan. "The demons. They're here, and they're coming for the box. You must not let them find it. Your older brother. Tell Shea she must contact him. They must not find the last clue."

Keira frowned. "Who must Shea contact?"

Waano smiled, an evil grimace that was nothing but a morbid replica of Aiden's normal cheeky grin. "She will know of whom I speak."

"But who is 'he'?" Keira asked.

Waano's head whipped around toward her. "I'm not speaking to you, witch!" Grace rushed forward, as did Nik. But before they could reach him, Luukas shoved Keira back and rose to his full height. Throwing out his hands, he roared with rage and knocked the demon back a few steps without ever touching him. The fact that he was only able to throw him a few steps spoke of the demon's power.

The demon narrowed his eyes, but stayed where he was. Looking around the angry vampire, he repeated to Ryan, "Tell her. She will know." Then he smiled at Luukas again. "Until next time, *Master* Vampire."

Grace held her breath as Aiden's eyes rolled back in his head. His body sagged as the thing that was animating it slithered back to wherever it normally hid. His knees buckled and he collapsed to the floor just as she and Nik rushed forward to grab him.

Aiden gagged as he pulled his knees into chest. "Bloody hell," he moaned. "I think I'm going to retch."

Tears filled Grace's eyes as she pulled his head and shoulders into her arms. He could 'retch' on her all he wanted, as long as she had him back. Out of the corner of her eye, she saw Luukas walk to the window and knew Keira would be watching him with a worried expression. Though his state of mind had gotten much better since they'd come home, it was never a good sign when he stared out the window.

Ryan came out of the office, looking as confused as Grace felt.

"Who is your brother?"

Ryan shook her head slowly, her brow furrowed in confusion. "I don't have an older brother. Only a younger one. I don't know where he is."

"I need a shower, love," Aiden groaned. "Get me home, please. I need a shower."

"Okay." She kissed his forehead. "Nik, would you help me, please?"

"I'm on it." Bending down, he pulled his best friend from her arms and threw him over his muscular shoulders in a fireman's hold. He pointed with his chin at his brother. "You got him?" he asked Keira.

She nodded. "He'll be fine." To Ryan, she said, "We need to figure out what the hell Aiden's alter-ego was trying to tell us, who it is he wants you to warn."

"I guess we need to ask Shea," Ryan said. "He said she could get a hold of 'him', whoever that is."

"Let's go," Nik told Grace, and she fell into step behind him.

As they waited for the elevator, Grace looked up at Nik. He smiled down at her, but she could tell he was distracted. "I wonder why he didn't just go straight to Shea?"

Graced shrugged. "Do you think he meant what I think he meant?"

"That the demon-possessed vampires Leeha created have figured out we have the last clue they're looking for, and that they're here in Seattle to get it, leaving a path of rotting bodies behind them? Yeah, I think that's exactly what he meant."

The elevator opened and they got inside, Grace making sure Aiden's head didn't slam into anything. "What are we going to do?"

"We planned on taking the box out of here tonight. We'll still do that." He frowned. "We'll have to bring all of you with us now. There's no fucking way I'm leaving Emma here by herself with the threat of those things finding their way in."

"Keira has wards in place. I don't think they could get in."

"I'm not taking the chance."

Aiden groaned from his prone position.

"Aid isn't either," Nik translated. "We'll all go, and we're bringing you females with us."

That was just fine with Grace. She never liked being left behind. When the doors opened, she rushed ahead of Nik and ran to open the front door for him, but when she got there, Emma had beaten her to it.

"Is he okay?"

"Hallo, poppet," Aiden managed with a wink, then started to dry heave as Nik carried him past her.

Emma smiled with relief. "Oh, good."

"He'll be fine," Nik confirmed. "Just needs to wash the demon out of him."

"Can I do anything?" Emma asked Grace.

She smiled at her new friend. "Some tea would be great." Emma had a big heart, and she didn't like feeling helpless, Grace knew.

"Whiskey," Aiden said, and started gagging again.

"On it," Emma told them with a smile, and headed into the kitchen.

Grace followed Nik into the room she shared with Aiden. Laying his friend on the bed, he straightened and gazed down at him with a worried expression while she went in to start the shower. When she came out, he was still standing there while Aiden fussed at him.

"Stop it, Nik."

"What?" Nik asked. "I'm just waiting for Grace to get the shower on so I can drag your happy ass in there for her."

"You're hovering," Aiden argued. "Again." He struggled to push himself up into a sitting position, and Nik quickly reached out and helped him, maybe a little over exuberantly. "Not so fast, you bloody Estonian. I'm not kidding about the retching."

"Sorry," Nik told him with no remorse whatsoever. "Shower ready?"

"Yup, bring him in. And I think I can handle it from there."

Emma came in with a cup of tea in one hand and a bottle of whiskey in the other. "Here you go." She set the drinks on the nightstand, and bent down to let Mojo investigate her fingers before carefully rubbing his head.

Grace got on one side of Aiden as Nik hauled him to his feet. He didn't need her help, she knew, but she needed the reassurance of being able to touch her mate.

They got him into the bathroom and Nik propped him up against the wall. "You're looking a little green, Aid. You sure you don't want to wait and do this later?"

"Absolutely not," Aiden rasped. "I feel like I've just swallowed the rotten insides of a fish. Or a bucket full of them." Then he fell to his knees over the toilet and heaved up his insides.

"He's all yours," Nik told Grace. Giving her a light pat on the back, he left, closing the door behind him. It opened again almost immediately. Nik placed the bottle of whiskey on the sink and shut the door again.

Grace got a washcloth out of a drawer and wet it with cold water, then waited for Aiden to be done. Still hovering over the toilet, he stuck out an arm and she handed it to him. He waved his hand back and forth, the universal sign for "Not that, the other thing," and she took the cloth back and handed him the whiskey.

Aiden hit the button on the back of the tank to flush, then fell back onto his ass and opened the bottle. Taking a large swig, he wiped his mouth with his forearm. "I'll take that shower now, love." His eyes roamed over her T-shirt and boxer shorts, damp from the steam and sticking to her body. A light of interest sparkled within the gray orbs. "I think it would be best if you got in with me. I still feel a bit wonky. I might fall over and bash my pretty head."

The last of her nervousness settled, and she grinned at him and shook her head. "You're going to be the death of me."

"I think you have that backwards, love. I do believe I am the life of you. The immortal life, that is. Now, start stripping before we lose the hot water." His boyish grin appeared.

Laughing, she helped him to his feet and out of his boxer briefs, noticing that at least one part of him was feeling just fine. As he got under the spray of hot water, whiskey in hand, she took off her pajamas and pulled her long, mahogany hair up into a high bun. When she pulled the curtain back, she found her strong vampire propped up in the corner, shaking. "Aiden?" She took his face between her palms and made him look at her. "Aiden? Are you okay?"

Haunted eyes, though thankfully free of dark shadows, rose to meet hers. "I hate this, Grace. I don't know what I was thinking, asking you to be with me when I have this thing inside of me. Putting you in danger. What if, tonight, he had —" He clenched his jaw, unable to continue that thought. "If I wasn't such a bloody coward, I would remove myself and my bloody demon from your life."

Tears welled and she blinked them away. Forcing a smile, she tried to reassure him. "Just try it, dude. You won't get very far."

He sniffed, then narrowed his eyes at her. "What do I tell you about calling me 'dude'?"

"Well, stop talking shit and I won't have a reason to." As he took a swig of the whiskey, she reached behind her and got the soap and her scrubbie. "Besides, Mojo would never forgive you if you left him." Without another word, she helped him scrub himself clean. "Better?"

"Much," he said. "Thank you, love."

"To bed?"

His eyes fell to her breasts and she smiled. He was completely obsessed with her chest, but that was all right with her. "I think bed sounds like a fine idea," he told her.

Shaking her head, she helped him out and got him dried off, then herself. As he stumbled out to the bedroom, she grabbed her robe off the back of the door and followed him, grateful to find the tea Emma had left her. She took a few sips, hoping it would help her get back to sleep, then took off her robe and climbed into bed beside her vampire. But when she reached to turn out the light again, his voice stopped her.

"Leave it on. I want to see you, Grace."

He curled up behind her. Pulling the band from her hair, he ran his fingers through the damp mass, fanning the strands over the pillow. "I love your hair. Almost as much as I love your breasts...and the soft reddish curls between your legs... and the taste of you...." His large palm ran up her leg and over the curve of her hip. "But it was this brilliant derriere that won me over the moment I first saw you." She felt his lips, warmed from the whiskey, kiss her shoulder. "I'm thirsty, love."

Rolling over onto her back, Grace opened her arms and welcomed her vampire to her throat. A soft hiss rent the air just before he struck, his razor sharp fangs slicing through the skin easily and with only a quick prick of pain. Then it was all pleasure as he began to drink, every pull on her vein sending sparks of lust straight to her groin until her moans of desire blended with his.

22

Laney watched Dante as he slept. He'd drifted off once she'd finished sobbing like an idiot after the best sex of her life. But it wasn't just the sex that had made her emotional. It was that he'd actually opened up to her and exposed a softer side of himself. His story still ricocheted around in her head, each new discovery fighting for dominance over the other. But one thing stood out above all of the rest: he'd had a child, too. A son. Now she understood why he'd acted the way he had. Why he'd freaked out when he'd seen her stretch marks. She even kind of got why he did the awful things he did. Sort of.

But it was more than that. For the first time, she'd acknowledged the connection between them was more than just their unusually high sexual attraction. There was a bond here, an attachment to him she'd been fighting. And it wasn't the usual case of Stockholm syndrome, though she had wondered about that more than once since she'd woken up in his arms the first time. It was something much, much more. She knew that now. Her soul soared every time he was near her. It overrode the fear, the frustration, the anger.

She now knew that in spite of what had happened here in the past, he wasn't keeping her in this damp underground to be cruel. He kept her here because he thought it was safe. It was where *he* felt safe. He was trying to care for her the only way he knew how, and he'd never really hurt her. Honestly, she had to admit that she didn't think he ever would.

His horror at forgetting to feed her flashed through her mind. Well, she might have to make sure he didn't accidentally starve her, but still, he was trying. She ran her fingers down his bare chest, and he sighed, tuned into her even in sleep. She was coming to realize that he had just given her a gift of the highest proportions. He'd given her complete control over him while he was vulnerable with lust. He'd given her his trust.

That said more to her than anything else. He claimed that she was his? Well, whatever the supernatural phenomenon that had brought them together, he also said he was hers, too. So she just had to figure out how to get him to let her out of this damn cave.

That may be easier said than done. She'd noticed the difference in him earlier almost immediately. The entire time they were upstairs, his eyes had constantly shifted around the room, even when he spoke to her. And a nervous tension had radiated from him. Nervousness that she once would have mistook for menace. It made her jumpy. Except for when he'd shown her that the sun wouldn't hurt him, he'd stayed far away from the windows. He felt exposed up there, and it obviously didn't sit well with him. Of course, now she knew why.

So, it appeared she had a decision to make. She could stay with him, and hope that maybe someday he would think twice before he ran around snapping people's necks. She could accept him for who and what he was, or she could leave—one way or the other.

That last idea didn't hold the appeal it had just a few hours before.

A phone began to ring and Dante's black eyes popped open. His upper lip lifted in a snarl, exposing his fangs, before he sat up and searched her out. Upon finding her next to him, he did a quick scan of her face and what he could see of her body above the thin blanket. Seeing her looking back at him with a smile, he scowled, then rose to walk completely nude over to where his pants lay. Pulling a cell phone out of his pocket, he answered it. "Dante."

Once Laney could tear her eyes from his powerful legs and backside and think coherently, the smile fell from her face. He'd had a cell this entire time? But the thought fled as he turned to face her with the phone still to his ear, something akin to fear on his face before he quickly turned away again. Pulling the blanket around her, Laney got up and started pulling on her clothes without having to be told. Something major was going down. He watched her from the corner of his eye, but didn't stop her as he spoke to the person on the other end.

"I'll be right up." Hanging up, he ran a hand over his skull.

"What is it?"

Grabbing his pants, he pulled them on.

"Dante?"

When he continued to ignore her, she put a hand on his arm. His eyes closed at her touch, his shirt hanging forgotten from his hands. He inhaled deeply, and opened them again. But he wasn't angry. His eyes roved over her face. "I'm trying to decide what to do," he finally said.

"About what?"

"You."

"What about me?"

"Don't worry about it."

Laney put her hands on her hips and glared up at him. "Don't worry about it?" she repeated. "If something is going on that involves *me*, I think I have the right to know."

He went to put on his shirt, then tossed it aside when he saw it was torn in half. Powerful muscles rippled in the dim light of the candles. "I'm not used to this, little mouse."

She raised her eyebrows in an unspoken question.

"This," he said, moving his hand back and forth between them. "I've been alone for a long time. I'm not used to this. Especially not with a human."

He *had* been alone. She could see that. But it was his own doing. In spite of all of the others around him, he had placed himself in a type of self-exile. So she chose to ignore the "human" remark, for now. "Okay. I get that. But you need to talk to me, Dante. I have a right to know what's going on."

Both hands rubbed his skull this time.

"Dante."

"All right," he ground out between gritted teeth. Then he took a breath. "All right. But we don't have time to get into a long fucking discussion right now."

"So just give me the main points."

He searched her face again. For what, she didn't know. But he seemed to find what he was looking for. "I told you about the whole fated mate shit, and that you're mine."

"Yes." Crossing her arms over her chest, she tried to be patient. Instinctively, she knew to give him his space if she wanted him to open up to her, strange as that sounded.

"There's more to it than what I told you earlier."

She waited for him to elaborate. He didn't. "Like what?" she prompted.

He stared down at her, and then paced away. Keeping his back to her, he stared out the doorway and down the dark passage. Whatever it was, he didn't want to tell her.

After a few seconds, he turned around, but still kept his distance. "I told you that I knew the moment I tasted your blood, you were meant for me."

"Yes."

"I told you I needed you to live."

"Yes, you need to drink blood to live. I get that. I'm familiar with vampires, although you're the first one I've actually met."

"No, little mouse. I need *your* blood to live. I can no longer drink from another and survive. Once mated, a vampire can only feed from his mate." He glanced up toward the ceiling. "Well, let me re-phrase that, I could choke down their blood if I was desperate enough, but I would still die. It would just take a little bit longer."

"So, if something happened to me, it would mean the end of you."

"Yes." As Laney absorbed the fact that his life was now, literally, tied to hers, he added, "There's more."

She couldn't imagine what more there could be, but she asked anyway. "What?"

"As my mate, you are now as immortal as I am."

Her arms fell to her sides. "Would you repeat that, please?"

"You're immortal now, little mouse. You will stop aging. You won't get sick. You won't die of natural causes."

"How does that happen?" she asked. "Just from you drinking from me?"

"No. From you drinking from me."

Oh. "So, if I don't drink from you—"

"Your body will pick up where it left off and you will start to age naturally again. You will also become susceptible to illness once more. But as you can see, it would behoove me to keep you alive. The longer you live, the longer I can survive."

"So in a way, my life is as dependent on you as yours is on me."

"No, for you would continue your natural existence if and when I die. I would not, if anything were to happen to you."

A sharp pain shot through her at his words. "Don't talk like that, Dante."

His black eyes narrowed on her. "Why not? If I die, you will be free of me. Isn't that what you want?"

He was right. The thought should make her happy. Yet, it didn't. Not at all. It did nothing but cause her pain.

"Little mouse," he whispered, his expression reflecting the anguish she was feeling. Between one heartbeat and the next he was across the room and right in front of her again. "What are you saying?" His voice was raw to her ears. One hand reached out to touch her, but dropped it before it made contact.

She stepped away and refused to look at him. Not ready to reveal the chaos of her feelings just yet. Besides, it appeared she didn't really need to. He invaded her feelings just like he invaded everything else. "I don't think I said anything."

"Laney—" His cell phone rang again. With a growl of displeasure, he answered it. "I'm coming. No." His jaw set in a stubborn gesture. "I said no," he growled. "I need a minute." Hanging up, he shoved the device back into his pocket. "I have to go upstairs, there's some shit going on."

He sounded worried. The nuance in his voice was slight, but she caught it. "What's happening?"

"I don't know yet, but they wanted me to bring you upstairs."

"And you're not going to." She didn't bother trying to keep the disappointment out of her voice.

"No. It's safer for you here." He went over to get his boots.

"But what if it's not?"

He stopped, looked back over his shoulder, and then he was suddenly in front of her. The heat of his chest made her breasts tingle, even through their clothes, the warm masculine scent of him heady in the small space. Vampires were not cold at all. Tilting her face up, he leaned down until his lips were but an inch from hers. "We will talk more. Later. For now, I need you to trust me, and do as I say." His eyes bore into hers with a possession that was frightening in its intensity.

"Okay," she breathed.

"But be ready. Just in case." He kissed her gently, his lips soft and warm on hers, then he released her and finished putting his boots on.

Beginning to feel really scared now, Laney also put on her shoes. After what he'd recently admitted to her, she knew he wouldn't be taking her out of here unless there was a very good reason. One that threatened one or both of their lives.

"Do you have a jacket in there?" he asked, indicating her backpack on the floor.

She shook her head. "No."

"I'll get you something upstairs if I need to come get you."

"Okay," she said again.

He stared at her as if he wanted to say more, but was uncertain as to whether he should. Laney didn't press him, knowing by the look on his face that he would either tell her or he wouldn't. He made to leave, stopped, and turned back again.

"The room that you found, the one where you got the knife." He paused.

Laney didn't want to ask, she really didn't, but she needed to know. Shoving her hands in her front pockets, she shifted her weight nervously. "What happens in that room, Dante?"

His expression hardened. "What do you think happens in that room, little mouse?"

"I'd prefer to hear it from you." Laney waited. Waited for him to tell her that all of that stuff was here when he'd moved in. Waited for him to tell her that he didn't use the diabolical equipment in there. Waited for him to tell her that people weren't tortured and killed by his hands. That he was a collector. That he had a good reason for that room.

He gave her none of those things. Offered no excuses. Displayed no regret.

"The bench, the one with the leather straps in the back corner. There's a hidden latch under the front end. If you release it, you can lift the seat to reveal a tunnel that I dug out. There's a ladder, but be careful. It will take you all the way out to the Puget Sound, if you find the need to run...for any reason."

He was giving her a way out. A way to escape. "What is it exactly that I should be afraid of?"

He was in front of her again, running the tips of his fingers down her cheek. But all he said was, "No one will hurt you, little mouse."

"Including you?"

"I am what I am, Laney. And I'll make no apologies for it."

A vampire. A beautiful, seductive killer.

As she watched him leave, she took a shaky breath and tried to calm her racing pulse. He looked back over his shoulder once, running his eyes up and down her form, and then he was gone.

Laney's accusing eyes haunted Dante as he walked down the hall to Luukas's, pulling a clean shirt over his head. He halted in front of the door, one eyebrow lifting in surprise that it wasn't attached to its hinges, but rather propped haphazard in the doorframe. Moving it out of the way, he let himself into Luukas's apartment. They were all gathered there waiting for him, lounging silently on the overstuffed furniture. Except for Christian, who was sitting on the fireplace near Ryan's chair.

"Where is Laney?" Emma asked him from the couch she shared with Nikulas.

It appeared they'd been talking without him. "She's none of your concern," he told her.

The look of surprise that flashed across her features was quickly replaced by a stubborn skew to her jaw that he was becoming well acquainted with from these witches. "She is so my concern, you big oaf. She's family."

Big oaf? Dante cocked a half-amused eyebrow at the female.

"Em." Nik put his hand on her knee. "I guarantee that she's fine." He looked up at Dante, daring him to say differently. "Isn't that right?"

"Is there a point to this little get together?" Dante gritted out. He didn't know why he was letting their lack of faith in him get under his skin so much. As they were all aware of his past run-ins with humans, and how they normally ended—with him well-fed and what was left of the human feeding the fish in the Sound—he couldn't really blame them for their concern. Yet, it still irked him. Laney was not like the other humans. She belonged to him, and his very survival depended on her staying young and healthy. He would protect her with his life.

Aiden sat near Grace with his back to Dante. He cranked his head around. "Why don't you come inside, commander, before I get a crick in my neck?"

Luukas nodded at him from his place by the windows, so Dante came inside, but only to the edge of the area rug. Stopping near Shea's chair, he was careful not to touch her. She gave him a smile.

"Alrighty," Aiden threw his arm around Grace's shoulders and leaned back. "So you missed all the fun, commander. My demon made an appearance this morning," he told Dante. "Overcome with brilliant intentions, he busted in here to give Ryan a warning and/or possibly a piece of advice."

"Explains the door," Dante commented.

"Ryan," Luukas said, indicating for her to take the floor. "Please fill in those that weren't here."

She stood up and went to stand next to Christian. Wiping her palms on her jeans, her turquoise eyes glanced around nervously.

"Go on, *she'ashil*," Christian encouraged.

She cleared her throat. "For those of you that don't know," she said, glancing at Shea and Dante. "Early this morning, I was up here with Keira working in the office. We're trying to piece together our families' histories since our coven split apart."

"Since the new High Priest took over and the families that escaped in time scattered," Keira clarified.

"Right," Ryan agreed. "Anyway, Aiden came crashing through the door—"

"Not me," Aiden said. "My demon."

"We know that, Aid," Nik told him, rolling his eyes.

"Just want to make sure we're all on the same page," Aiden said.

"Aiden's *demon* came crashing in," Ryan corrected. "He said he wanted to warn me that 'they' were here, and they're coming after the box that Grace brought with her from China. He also told me to tell my brother what he said, except I honestly have no idea who that is. Just like I didn't know about all of you. If I have a brother, I never knew about him. But he said that you, Shea, would know how to get a hold of him."

All eyes turned to Shea. Uncrossing and re-crossing her legs, she showed no outward reaction to Ryan's words. "I have no idea who you're talking about." She looked to Luukas. "Honest. I really don't."

He watched her with sharp eyes, but gave no indication as to whether or not he believed her.

Nik spoke up. "Originally, I was going to send a few of you to a safe place to put the box. We've just been trying to decide where. But with this new threat, I think we should all go, including the witches. It's not safe to leave anyone here."

"I don't think that's necessary. Those that didn't go would protect the others," Dante said. He didn't want to go anywhere at the moment if he didn't have to. He had his own shit to work out here.

"We're not taking the chance," Luukas said. "*Everyone* is going." He said this while looking straight at Dante.

Nik nodded. "I don't think the demons would be able to overcome our security system, which includes the wards put up by Keira, but I'm not taking the chance of leaving my Emma here. I'll feel better with her along. And I know you all would feel the same."

There was a rumble of agreement from the other males. All except for Dante. "Why don't we just burn the fucking thing? Then there's nothing for them to find."

"I want to know what it is first, and why they want it so badly," Luukas answered. He paced away from the window. "Then we can use it to get them where we want them."

All eyes turned to him.

"Things are moving at a faster pace than I had hoped. We're not ready to face this threat yet, but we might have to. This group appears to be the leaders, as they are the ones taking the initiative to gather the boxes of clues, or whatever the hell they are, while the rest of them are biding their time. We've sent out patrols to track the ones in this area, and to try to keep their killings to a minimum. Mostly they've just stayed hidden. But if you haven't noticed, none of them are straying very far from Leeha's mountain, from the chains of the altar they were only just released from. Does that not seem strange to you all?"

Aiden rubbed his chest. "They've had it planned all along. To meet back there."

"Exactly," Luukas said. "We need to arrange it so we're there to greet them."

"But we don't even know why they're after the box," Christian said. "How are we supposed to stop them if we don't know what they're after? Even if we destroy the bodies they're in, they'll just find new ones to possess, and we'll have no idea who they are."

Luukas looked at Aiden. "Can your demon recognize his kind in whatever body they're in?"

Aiden nodded. "When he deigns to let me know, yes."

Holding his hand out to Keira, Luukas waited for her to join him. His eyes roamed over her features, the look in his gray eyes so warm and intimate that Dante felt like he was intruding. Yet he couldn't look away. He could practically see the connection between them.

"Are you ready for this, witch?" Luukas asked Keira. "I hate having you anywhere near those things again, but I see no other choice."

She just smiled. "We discussed this already, Luukas. You worry too much. My girls and I will be fine." Rising up on her toes, she kissed him. "Besides, we have our big strong vampires to keep us safe."

"Keira, if anything happened to you—"

"It won't," she assured him.

Luukas swallowed hard, and with one last kiss on his mate's nose, he released her and straightened. The tenderness was gone from his expression as quickly as it had appeared. "We need to leave as soon as possible."

"I'm coming alone," Dante informed him in no uncertain terms, and Shea looked up at him in surprise. "My...*mate* is below ground, as you know. She will be safe."

Luukas shook his head. "No. If something happens to her, you will cease to exist." A smirk lifted his lips. "And I'm rather fond of your ornery self."

"With all due respect, Luukas, I'm not bringing her. She is safer here," Dante said, crossing his arms over his chest. Having Laney with him would just be a distraction. Even if the things managed to get into the building, they wouldn't find her. Once they realized the vampires were gone, they would come after them. She was better off where she was.

If she hadn't already left, that is. Dante cracked his neck to ease the tension there. He'd given her the choice, and he would deal with whatever consequences that wrought.

"I'll get Prickles," Aiden told Grace.

"All right, then." Nik rose from the sofa and pulled Emma up alongside him. "We'll meet by the vehicles in thirty."

Dante started walking away when he heard one of the females say, "What about the other people in the building? The people that live here? The humans? What about them and the people nearby?"

Everyone stopped, the vampires exchanging looks. It was Christian that answered Ryan's question. "The guys have security measures in place, and Keira has a ward around the building. It's us they're after, or rather the box we have. All we can do is hope that they won't get in, or if they do, that they'll leave once they realize we're not here." He took her hand. "We'll do all we can to make sure no one is hurt."

Rolling his eyes, Dante took off. He wanted to stop by his apartment and check on the pets. Maybe he would grab Laney another blanket and take it down to her before he left, along with some more food. Brow furrowed in thought as he tried to think of anything else she may need, he picked up his step.

23

Jesse sat stroking Cruthú's black feathers just outside the crumbled remains of Leeha's mountain fortress. The raven preened under his attention, ruffling her feathers against the misty rain and rubbing her beak along his hand. She gave a squawk, tilting her head and staring at him with one intelligent black eye.

"I know, Cruthú. I know. But Shea left us. She made her choice. And she won't even take my calls. Although, I guess that as long as she keeps hanging up on me, I know she's safe." As if on cue, his cell phone rang. The raven jumped up to his shoulder as he dug it out from his pocket. He stared at the number on the screen. Accepting the call, he held it to his ear.

"Jesse?"

Her whiskey voice came across the line clearly, as if she were sitting right next to him. If he closed his eyes, he could imagine that she was.

"Jesse, I know you're there. I don't have a lot of time. I need your help. I need to know something." His heart fluttered for a fraction of second. It stopped cold at her next words. "I need to know what Leeha's demons are after. They're here. And we have something they want." A pause. "We think it's a clue."

No. That couldn't be. If they were coming after the box, that means they had found the others and nearly had all of the clues. If the demons got their hands on the last one, the world as they knew it would no longer exist.

Cruthú flapped her large wings, sensing his disquiet. "What do you mean you think you have one of the clues?"

"It's a wooden box with a carving of a dagoba in the bottom underneath the felt lining." She paused again. "You know what it is."

How the hell had they gotten their hands on one of the clues? It should be across the ocean. "Shea, listen to me carefully. You need to get rid of that thing. Immediately."

"We are," she said. "We're taking it somewhere tonight and hiding it."

"They will find it," he told her. "It doesn't matter where you hide it. They won't stop until they find it."

"What is it, Jesse?"

Jesse struggled with the decision to tell her. If she knew what it was, it would endanger her even more. However, to not do so would also put her immortal life in danger. And somehow, in the short time they'd known each other, her life had become very important to him. "It is a clue," he heard himself saying. "When the demons were tied to the altar, thousands of years ago, the witches that performed the spell drained them of their blood so their souls could not find their bodies again. The clues will lead them to where their original blood is hidden."

"What will happen once they find it?"

"They will be able to reanimate their original physical forms...and hell will reign on earth."

Shea was silent for a long moment. "Is there any way to stop them?" Her tone held little hope.

He thought about it. "If we can stop them from finding the clue, it will slow them down. But if they have the others—"

"I'll tell Luukas that Dante was right and we just need to burn the fucking thing. They'll never find it."

He smiled. If only it were that simple. "That's impossible. It won't burn. The old witches made sure of it. They wanted to make sure their descendants would be able to find the blood, and keep it hidden. In retrospect, probably not the best plan."

"Can the blood be destroyed somehow?"

He shook his head, even though she couldn't see him. "It's demon blood. It must exist in some form or another."

"What about you?" she asked quietly.

"What about me?" Jesse fought to keep his tone impersonal. It was very difficult.

"Are you safe?"

"They won't find me or my things, Shea. And I need to stay here. I need to protect the altar, in case there's ever a chance we can bring them back to it. Though I appreciate your concern."

"They'll kill you if they find you there." Her voice was deadpan.

The corners of his mouth lifted at her concern. It was unnecessary, but she didn't know that. "And would that bother you, Shea? Would you shed a tear over my cold body before you walked away? Again?" He was being an ass. But he needed to hear her admit that it would.

She didn't answer his question. "I have to go. Thank you for telling me."

He stared at the pine trees towering around him, like ghostly sentinels in the misty rain. "You're welcome," he told her.

The line disconnected, and he put the phone back in his pocket. Lifting his face to the cold rain, he let it soothe his heated skin. It was coming down harder now, so he pulled the hood of his cloak up over his head and headed back through the trees to the mountain that loomed in the darkness, and the underground labyrinth he'd been unable to make himself leave.

He'd lied. He didn't need to stay here to protect the altar. The altar had been there for thousands of years, and it would still be there long after he was gone. In all honesty, he hated this mountain. Yet he wouldn't leave. For even though she was only there with him for a short time, it reminded him of Shea. And he still held a thread of hope that, someday, she might come back.

24

Laney huddled on the mattress, the slightly warmer blanket Dante had brought her before he'd left wrapped around her shoulders. She'd waited for him to say something, to show some emotion...happiness that she was still there, surprise, anything. But he hadn't said a word, wouldn't even look at her. Just walked in, dropped off the blanket and food, and left again. He'd even brought her a jacket. A jacket she wouldn't need if she were staying.

Maybe he didn't want her to stay. He'd never really said that he did. Only that it would "behoove him" if he kept her around. Maybe the connection she felt was one-sided.

So as soon as he'd left, she'd put the coat on and slung her backpack over her shoulder. Tromping over to the tunnel that led to his torture room and the way out, Laney had every intention of getting the hell out of there. But as she stood there with hot candle wax dripping onto her hand, she couldn't bring herself to leave him.

He needed her. If she left, she'd be condemning him to die. She'd be responsible for another person's death. But more than that, she was discovering it was possible that she needed him, too.

After the death of her son, Laney had died with him. Not physically, of course. Physically she was still in this world. She still woke up every day, went to work, smiled, talked, even flirted at times. But inside she was as dead as the babe she'd held in her arms. She shunned anyone that tried to get too close. Whenever she got asked out for a date, she would politely but firmly turn them down, the fear that she would hurt someone again always lingering in the back of her mind.

The only thing that brought her any semblance of joy were the hours she'd spent hiking the trails, just trying to forget, trying to lose her memories in the harsh beauty of the desert. It brought her temporary comfort, but it never lasted long.

She smiled. The desert had also brought her Dante. And now he knew all of her darkest secrets, and he hadn't judged her for them in the slightest. He didn't fear her.

It didn't forgive what she had done, but since her confession to him, she felt like she could breathe again. Shouldn't she do the same for him? She understood what made him behave the way he did where humans were concerned. In the short time she'd known him, she'd seen that he didn't feel anything halfway. Whether it was a vampire thing or just a Dante thing, he was quick to react and his emotions ran strong. Those that had wronged him were treated to the full fury of his wrath.

Would his love be just as fierce? Was he even capable of love?

Laney was surprised to find that she wanted to find out. But if she was going to stay with him, there needed to be some changes. He couldn't really expect her to just hang out down here with no one to see and nothing to do but wait for him to honor her with his presence. She would go mad. If it weren't for the thick copy of *The Iliad and the Odyssey* sitting by his bed, she would be stir-crazy already.

Dante had only been gone maybe thirty minutes or so when she heard a sound in the tunnel behind her. Fearing rats, Laney jumped to her feet. She hated rats. Her skin crawled as she looked around frantically for something to smack it with. Spotting her backpack against the wall where she'd dropped it, she picked it up again, hefting the weight. It would do.

The sounds came closer. It sounded big; too big to be a rodent. She worried her lower lip between her teeth. What if it wasn't a rat? What if it was some other animal that had found its way down here? Like a stray dog? Or a bear? She'd heard there were bears in this area, although why a bear would be wandering around the city of Seattle she didn't know.

Whatever it was, it was definitely bigger than your normal rat. The shuffling got louder as it neared the room, and now Laney could hear other small noises accompanying it, along with a stench the likes of which she'd only smelled when driving past road kill that had been rotting in the sun for a few days.

Cold sweat beaded on her upper lip as a hand appeared out of the hole, bony fingers curling around the bricks to hoist out the body it was attached to. It was wearing a jacket with a hood that covered its face. Coming completely out of the tunnel, it stood, and Laney's heart stopped as she found herself face to face with a living corpse.

It appeared something else had found Dante's means of escape.

She opened her mouth to scream, but no sound came out, for the thing had spotted her standing there and it was on her before she had time to draw breath. There was a flash of yellow fangs as it reared back, preparing to strike, and she had a sudden flashback of another monster doing this exact same thing less than a week before. Only Dante hadn't smelled like death. He'd smelled warm and vital, even as emaciated and dusty as he'd been. Squeezing her eyes shut, she braced herself for the pain, when the thing suddenly released her.

"Get away from her, you fool! We can use her!"

Laney opened her eyes to find another creature, not quite as decayed, eyeing her up and down. It was another male. Or at least it used to be. Milky eyes peered at her from underneath the covering of its hoodie. Evil seeped from its pores. She stood perfectly still, her blood racing so fast she saw spots, as it strolled up to her and...smelled her?

"She belongs to one of the vampires," the zombie, or whatever it was, told the others. Laney counted five of them altogether. "I can smell him on her, and *in* her." Turning away, he looked around the room. "An old vampire if his décor is any indication." He smiled, a gruesome slash of what used to be his mouth. "This will save us a lot of time and trouble, boys. The human will come with us somewhere a little more open. The vampires would give their lives for their mates. We'll trade her for the last clue."

One of the others spoke. "What if they won't give it up?"

"They will," the leader assured him. Pointing to one of the others, he said, "You. Bring the female."

"No! Leave me alone!" Laney struggled as one grabbed her from behind and another took her bag. Keeping his back to her, he unzipped it and dug inside as she tried to take it back. Not seeing anything that interested him, he tossed it onto the floor while the one that held her threw her over his shoulder.

Laney kicked and screamed to no avail as they entered the passageway that would take them to the cave-in and out to the elevator.

"Shut her up," the leader said.

Laney braced her hands on its back and lifted her head, trying to see through her unbound hair. A fist that felt more like a boulder slammed into the side of her face, whipping her head around. Her ears rang as spots filled her vision, and the copper taste of blood flooded over her tongue and dripped down her lip. Shaking her head to clear it, she lifted herself up again and opened her mouth to scream when another fist smashed her in the head.

There was no pain this time. Just peaceful blackness.

25

Dante kept his steps measured as he walked through the parking garage to the elevator after the others. They had just returned from hiding the box in the woods outside of an abandoned building that Luukas owned near Fish Town. At least, it appeared to be abandoned to outsiders. It was actually one of their numerous bug-out buildings, in case the shit hit the fan and they needed to get out quick and re-group, far enough away, but close enough to get to it quickly, if need be. Outside, it was impenetrable. Inside, it was decked out with everything a vampire could want or need for weeks. But the area around it was rural, and hiding the box near it posed little threat to the few humans that were around.

Because they'd taken the human females with them, they'd had to drive, which meant that Laney had been here alone for just over three hours when all was said and done.

"Are you coming up, commander?" Aiden asked him as they all piled into the elevator.

He glared at the Brit, but gave the asshole no other indication that the name bothered him. It would only make him use it more, he knew. Aiden was a bastard like that. "No," he told him shortly.

Aiden grinned.

"We'll just see you at sundown," Luukas told him.

Dante gave him a nod of agreement, and as the doors closed, he made his way to the second elevator that would take him to the underground.

He wondered if Laney would still be there.

Sitting up in the front seat of the SUV beside Luukas—the only one that would give him any peace—he'd kicked himself the entire drive for giving her a way out. And the reasons why he was beating himself up surprised even him.

It had hit Dante that, in the short time he'd known her, this particular human was not one that he could easily push out of his mind. Somehow, she had gotten under his skin as easily as the knife blade she had tried to plunge through his heart. And he was...not horrified...at having her there.

The elevator doors opened and he entered his underground. His boots pounded along the walkway, crushing his fears with each step. He refused to entertain the thought that she wouldn't be there. She felt something for him other than fear, he would bet his wretched life on it.

Which was exactly what he had done by telling her how to escape. A deep growl rumbled in his chest at his own stupidity. He should never have said anything. She was perfectly safe down here, and he needed more time with her. More time to cleave her to him, whatever it took. Dante wasn't stupid. He was a killer. And not only that. He enjoyed it. A female like Laney would never willingly agree to stay with him.

So he would force her to submit to him, whatever it took.

Jumping down from the top of the cave-in, Dante stopped. The scent of Laney's blood was in the air, and it was fresh. His eyes fell to the wooden planks he stood upon. Just ahead, about twenty feet away, was blood. Just a few drops, but easily seen with his vampire eyes.

Pain shot through him. Pain as such that he hadn't felt in hundreds of years. He knew exactly what the blood meant. She had tried to claw her way out of the rubble behind him again. Maybe she had tried to get out the other way and couldn't lift the bench top. It would be heavy for a human, now that he thought about it. So she had come back out here and tried to get out this way again.

Dante continued down the passageway, hardening his heart against what he would find when he got to his room, but it mattered not. For when he arrived, he found the room empty, and his cold heart plummeted to shatter upon the wooden floor.

His little mouse had escaped.

He knew this even without checking the other room. Only wisps of her delicious scent hung in the air. She was gone. She had left him. Clenching his fists at his sides, he threw his head back and raged with all of the anger that was stemmed up inside of him, until he felt nothing.

Sinking down onto his makeshift bed, he reached behind him and pulled the small box from where he'd hidden it in the waistband of his pants. The others didn't know he still had it. They thought he'd buried it next to the abandoned building, but he'd gone back for it when everyone was piling into the vehicles again. He'd told them he'd dropped his phone, and no one thought twice about it. It was a stupid fucking idea to leave it there. If the demons were after the box, they needed to keep it close, not leave it somewhere for those assholes to find it.

Throwing it on the mattress next to him in disgust, he picked up the blanket he'd brought her and held it to his nose, breathing deeply. He couldn't give a rat's ass about that fucking box now.

The lingering remnants of his anger slowly withered and died, only to have grief well up in its place. The unexpected emotion hit him so suddenly that a scream of anguish tore from his throat before he realized he meant to voice it. It shook the walls around him, loosening dirt to rain down between the cracks in the wooden ceiling. With a violent jerk, he tore the blanket in two and threw it aside. Then he swept the box off the bed with his arm, sending it crashing into the wall.

It landed next to her backpack lying on the floor near the wall. The zipper was open and some of her things had spilled out. Dante's eyes skipped over the now familiar items, but then his head whipped back around. Lying on top of her other things was the copy of *Goodnight Moon* that she carried with her.

His blood froze in his veins to see it lying there, so innocently. She never would have left without taking that with her. Not unless she'd had to run for her life.

Or she'd been taken.

Relief battled with terror inside of him. Shooting to his feet, he dove headfirst into the tunnel and came out the other side. He didn't need light, he could see just fine in the darkness. The bench top in the back of the room was lifted, the latch broken. Dante tore across the room and peered down the ladder. "Laney!" he bellowed. "Laney!"

There was no answer. Fear struck his soul. What if she was hurt? He stuck his head farther inside, searching the area at the bottom of the ladder for her prone form. As he did so, he caught a whiff of rotten meat, but didn't think much of it, as this was the way he carried out the corpses of the humans he'd fed on once he was finished with them.

With one hand on the edge, he vaulted over the side. His boots landed with a soft thud on the packed earth eighteen feet below. He took off running, not stopping until he hit the end of the tunnel, hidden in a copse of trees near the Sound. He found no other signs of his female. The stench of decay, however, accompanied him the entire length, growing weaker the closer he got to the end. Again, not unusual, as the smell would naturally be stronger closer to his feeding room.

Dante frowned. *Think, you stupid fuck. Think!*

Turning around, he went back the way he had come, slower this time, scenting the air and paying more attention to the scenery around him. By the time he got back to his lair, he was convinced that Laney had not escaped through that tunnel.

Which meant someone, or some*thing*, else had come in that way.

Letting his instincts take over, Dante closed his eyes and "listened" for her blood to call to him, but she must be too far away already. His head pounded and his heart raced as he dried his clammy palms on his thighs. If anything happened to her, he had no one to blame but himself for being so stupid as to leave her down here by herself while he was so far away.

But he knew what had taken her. And he knew what they wanted. Grabbing the box, he shoved it back into his waistband and went up to his apartment.

Shea found him in the bedroom when she came to check on the pets. She eyed the holsters strapped to his bare chest and the pair of Smith & Wesson .500's he was loading. "Trouble in paradise?" she joked.

"Laney is gone. I'm going after her."

"And you need pistols that would stop a herd of zombies to win her back?"

"Or a group of demon-possessed vampires," he growled. He didn't worry about anyone noticing the weapons. Humans tended to keep their distance from him. Even their so-called law enforcement.

Shea stepped in front of him as he made to leave. "Wait," she ordered. "I'll get the guys together and we'll go with you."

"There's no time. I can't hear her anymore. She's already too far away." When Shea opened her mouth to argue with him, he roared, "MOVE."

With a loud sigh, she did. "We'll follow you!"

"There won't be anything left for you to kill," he growled. Then he slammed out the door.

Dante had a sense of déjà vu as he stood in the parking garage, half-expecting a van with blacked out windows to come squealing around the corner. But the garage was quiet this time of night, appropriately enough.

Out on the street, he paused. The never-ending rain had let up, leaving a damp mist hanging in the air, but Dante didn't even feel it. The lights of the city guided him as he headed west, toward the docks. He didn't stop to think about why he went that way, he just did.

He was a little over a mile away when his blood surged and his fangs shot down in his mouth. Chills skated across his skin, the heat behind his eyes telling them that they were glowing with an unnatural light.

Laney.

She was close, and she was alive. He palmed his weapons and kicked it into vamp speed. He would have his female back within the hour, or he would die trying.

26

Laney moaned as pain lanced up the side of her face and into her temple before settling into a dull throb. She kept her eyes closed, not wanting to leave the blissful numbness of sleep, but it wasn't happening. Giving in to the persistent pull of consciousness, she fought her way to the surface. Her eyes blinked rapidly as she forced them open through the haze of agony. Shards of bright light stabbed her vision. Suddenly nauseous, she leaned over and vomited on the cement.

"Well, well, well. Look who finally decided to join the living again. So to speak." Throaty laughter sounded all around her.

Laney rolled her eyeballs up until she could see who was speaking, and realized it wasn't just the pain that was making her sick. It was also the smell. As she stared at the living, reeking zombie in front of her, the events of the last few hours came crashing back into her aching skull: talking to

Dante, the sounds in the tunnel, and getting punched repeatedly in the face until she'd passed out.

"Where am I?" Her voice was raspy to her ears, like she had been screaming again. Maybe she had. Looking around, she saw the rest of her kidnappers sitting quietly here and there on the pavement. A large cargo ship loomed behind the leader, anchored to the dock. She couldn't see much beyond that through the dense mist hovering over the water.

Feeling something hard and cold digging into her spine, she carefully tilted her head back. A steel crane hung high above her. The giant orange neck seemed a mile away as it hung in position over the ship ready to unload the cargo.

"Not far from where we found you, but just far enough to give us some time to be ready," the leader answered.

Laney tried to remember what he was talking about. She'd forgotten her question.

He looked at a watch hanging loosely on his bony wrist. Probably stolen off the last person he'd killed. "Your vampire, whichever one it is, should be arriving any moment now."

"And when he does?" She was shivering now, and not entirely from the cold.

"Then we get what we want."

"Which is?"

He looked heavenward and sighed. She could tell he was getting impatient with her questions, but if all the TV shows she'd watched were right, the longer she kept him talking, the better her chances were of staying alive.

"I think you know what we're looking for, witch." He scrutinized her sitting there on the pavement at his feet. "Or maybe not." He sounded somewhat disappointed, but not necessarily surprised.

She really didn't. But now she knew why Dante had told her about the escape tunnel. Of course, he couldn't have foreseen that they would find it first. He should have told her what was going on. He should have warned her. But it was too late now. "And what will happen to me? To the vampire?"

He shrugged, unconcerned. "For you, it all depends on how thirsty my friends here are."

Laney's stomach plummeted. "And Dante?"

"Is that his name?"

She didn't answer.

Taking a deep breath, he exhaled again loudly. His rotting breath washed over her. "I love the sea air, don't you?"

Laney pulled her legs in and pushed with her feet, scooting a few feet over, away from him and the spot where she'd gotten sick. "Who are you?" she asked when she could breathe again.

The thing cocked its head at a strange angle. Bending at the waist, it leaned over her. Through its decaying skin she saw bone, or maybe teeth, through a hole in its cheek. Dead eyes yellowed from a failing liver sent tingles of fear up her spine. "I'm your worst nightmare, sweetheart," it growled.

Laney shivered harder as invisible fingers crawled over her skin. A cold breeze blew in off the water, the salty air carrying away the stench of death. She breathed it in with relief, then lifted her chin and stared the thing down until it straightened to its full height, a morbid smile lifting its pale lips.

"I like you. Maybe I'll keep you for me. Once we have what we need and I become my true self again, I'll need a few humans for daytime errands." His eyes raked her small form. "And to suck my dick when I feel the urge, which is quite often in spite of my current appearance."

The thought of that decaying appendage being shoved down her throat almost had Laney vomiting again. Swallowing hard, she fought the feeling until it went away. "You'd have to kill me first."

"That can easily be arranged," he replied with a shrug. His head suddenly whipped around to the left. "Ah, here comes your savior now." Pain shot through her skull as he grabbed a handful of her hair and yanked her to her feet. Spinning her around, he pulled her back against him and wrapped one arm around her waist. The other hand grabbed her sore jaw and pointed her face in the direction he was looking. He was big, but not as big as the vampire coming after her.

"Watch!" it cried dramatically. "Your boyfriend will be coming right around that building. Annnny second now—" The others stood and jostled into position around their leader. Two on each side, they balanced on the balls of their feet, ready for anything.

Laney winced, closing her eyes against the throbbing in her jaw and trying not to breathe. The ground rumbled beneath her feet, and her captor threw back his head and laughed with delight. A wet, phlegmy sound that made her stomach heave in spite of her best efforts.

"He's pretty fucking pissed off," he shouted happily. His hand slid up under her shirt, roughly grabbing her breast through her bra. "Maybe I should see what all the fuss is about. Hmm? I don't normally go for such little girls, but I could make do." He squeezed her roughly. "What do you think your vampire will do when he comes around that corner to find me tearing up that tight little ass? Because, you know, this body has a lot of faults. But the one good thing about it is the size of its cock."

Laney struggled in his arms, trying to pull his hand off her. "He's going to kill all of you," she gritted out.

He laughed again. Tightening his grip on her jaw until she whimpered in pain, he whispered in her ear, "And that's where you're wrong, honeybunch. He is only a vampire, and as old as he is, he's nowhere near as ancient and powerful as I am. Mark my words, you little cunt. He will not survive this night."

Only a vampire? What was older and stronger than a vampire? Laney gave up trying to remove its hand from her breast, and concentrated on watching the spot where Dante was about to appear. The pavement suddenly shook so hard it buckled beneath her feet. Her captor stumbled, laughing like a maniac as his hand fell from her breast, unable to keep his grip on her.

Suddenly, two shots rang out. Out of the corner of her eye, Laney saw the two creatures on her right fall forward. They had large holes in the backs of their skulls. As she watched, blood formed a puddle on the pavement where their faces lay. "Dante," she shrieked, scared shitless that he would shoot the thing holding her from behind next, and possibly her in the process.

A familiar gravelly voice, tight with unrestrained anger, echoed around them. "*Release* the female, Steven."

Laney winced as Steven's fingers dug into her jaw. "You know the game, vampire. Give me what we want."

She noticed he left off the "and we will let her go" part.

Long seconds passed in silence. When nothing happened, the creature, Steven, huffed an impatient breath in her ear. Suddenly, her head was wrenched to the side. Something sharp scraped along her neck.

A feral growl came out of the mist coming off the water, and a second later, a wooden box clattered along the pavement toward them at high speed. It slid to her sneakered foot and stopped.

"Pick it up and hand it to me," Steven told one of the others. He released her jaw to take the box, but one arm was still wrapped tight around her waist.

"Now, let her go," Dante growled.

Laney looked around frantically, but she couldn't pinpoint where he was.

"I don't think so, vampire. And as a matter of fact, since you gave us the box without a fight, maybe I won't kill you." Then he laughed like that was the best joke he'd ever heard. "No, no. I'm kidding. Of course I'm going to kill you. But I think I'll let the girl live. We were actually just talking about our new life together once I regain power over this world, isn't that right, sweetheart?"

Laney cringed as wet lips smacked her on the cheek.

A strong breeze blew her hair into her face as something flew past her, too fast for her to track, but her captor stumbled while spinning her around in his arms. He regained his footing again and then she was lifted off the ground and they were moving.

A roar of anguish echoed around them, and Laney kicked with her feet, trying to twist her body around and out of its grasp. Pieces of flesh slid away as she clawed at her captor's face. When they stopped just a few seconds later, she was left hanging by one arm with her feet dangling mid-air. She kicked out hard, trying to loosen his grip.

"Laney! STOP! Don't fucking move!"

The order came from somewhere far below her. Pushing her hair frantically out of the way with her free hand, Laney found Dante standing far below her near the hull of the ship. He was completely out in the open. Looking up the length of her arm to the hand holding her just below the elbow, she found Steven sitting casually on one of the iron beams of the shipping crane. Leaning to the side, he swung her body around in a small circle.

"Yes, Laney. I wouldn't wiggle around too much if I were you. One small slip...." His mouth formed an exaggerated "O" as he opened his hand. Laney's scream was cut off with a jerk as he caught her again around the wrist. Her shoulder twisted painfully in its socket as she spun slowly back and forth like a child's doll.

Dante was directly below now. He smiled up at her, but it wasn't a pleasant expression. "Hang tight, little mouse."

Her shoulder burned, but there wasn't much she could do about it. As she stared down at him with desperate longing, the other two came out from hiding and were creeping up on Dante from behind. "Dante, behind you," she shouted.

Without taking his eyes from her, Dante pointed a large pistol behind him and fired. The thing sounded more like a canon than a gun when it went off, and Laney watched as the creature on the left jerked backwards in surprise and put a hand over the gaping hole in its chest. It wiped the blood off on its pant leg and kept coming.

"Drop her if you want, Steven," Dante said, and Laney's pulse ramped up to double-speed, afraid he would call his bluff and do exactly that. "I'll make sure I catch her."

Somehow that didn't make her feel better. Laney twisted her hand around and wrapped it around her captor's wrist, hanging on for dear life. She felt exposed muscle and bone under her fingers, but didn't loosen her grip.

"I wouldn't press my luck if I were you," Steven taunted. "I meant what I said."

Dante smiled again. "Try it, asshole. I dare you." Spinning around, he lifted both pistols and shot the two things creeping up on him point blank in the face. They flew backward and landed hard on the pavement. Dante turned back around, looking up at them. "Your move," he growled.

Not the response she would've went for, but okay.

Her captor cackled with delight. Then shooting pain burst from her tender shoulder socket as he threw her one-handed into the air and caught her around the middle. Sitting her on his lap, she cried out as he wrenched her head to the side and hissed in her ear. She felt the sharp tips of its fangs push through her skin.

Below her, Dante lost-his-shit. Screaming with rage, he disappeared, and suddenly she was being jostled around as the thing holding her jerked and grunted, fighting to keep his hold on both her and the box. Sharp pains shot down her neck as its fangs ripped through her flesh and tore their way out.

With a satanic growl, one of its hands flattened on her back, and she was suddenly catapulted off his lap and flying through the air toward the water. Wind whipped around her in hurricane-like speeds, her breath knocked from her as she hit the cold water with such force that she tumbled head over heels underwater.

The weight of her clothes immediately pulled her down into the cold, dark depths. The salt stung her eyes and burned the open wound on her neck. Ignoring the pain, Laney kicked her feet and paddled with her arms. Spinning around blindly in the water, she started to panic as she tried to find the way up to the surface. Her lungs burned to breathe, and she sucked in a mouthful of salt water.

I'm going to drown.

The thought echoed in her head as her struggles became less and less frantic. This shouldn't be happening, she was an excellent swimmer. Suppressing the panic, Laney relaxed her body and let it do what it would naturally in the water. A few seconds later, she floated to the top and her back broke the surface of the water. Raising her head, she coughed up seawater, barely catching her breath before she was hit by a swell and sank back under again.

"LANEY!"

She heard his bellow of fear right before she went under. This time she let the water do its thing and help her rise to the surface again. Treading water, she coughed the last bit of seawater out of her lungs, pushed her sopping hair out of her eyes, and searched for the dock, swearing to herself that she was going to shave her head to match Dante's if this was the life she was going to be living from now on.

A body landed in the water next to her. Or rather, a part of a body. A leg, to be exact. After assuring herself that it wasn't Dante's, Laney started swimming toward the dock. She tried not to think of what might be lurking beneath her, attracted to the smell of her blood and the rotting carcass floating nearby. She headed to the hull of the ship, and the ropes skimming the surface of the water. The loose ends looked like they were tied to the dock. Maybe she could pull herself up.

As she got closer, she heard the leader shout, "Sorry, vampire, but play time is over!"

Fear for Dante tightened painfully in her chest. Her vision flickered, and for a moment, she was afraid she was going to pass out, but then everything became clear and sharp. Energy surged through her and her strength returned as she was filled with a renewed purpose—to save her mate.

Grabbing one of the ropes, she braced her feet against the side of the dock and climbed up. Her wet sneakers slid on the slick surface, and the rope burned her hands, but somehow she made it to the top and flung herself over the side. She landed on her stomach and lifted her head.

The scene unfolding in front of her was like something out of a movie. Dante held one of the creatures two feet off the ground with a hand around its throat. Its eyes bulged from its head and its mouth flapped soundlessly as it clawed at his arm with skeletal fingers. Blood ran down Dante's arm as he squeezed. The visible tattoos on his face and arm pulsed with power, adding to the terrifying picture he portrayed. If Laney didn't know better, she would think he was the devil himself, risen from the depths of hell to avenge her.

As she watched, another one came running up from his right. Before she could warn him, Dante whipped his head around without releasing his hold on the first one. Fangs bared, he roared with rage and slashed the air with his free hand.

Without even touching the thing, he sent it rocketing through the air and impaled it on a metal spike sticking off the railing of the ship. With an evil smile, he went back to the first one, squeezing his fist until there was a sickening pop and the creature's head tumbled to the ground.

Dante turned his focus to their leader.

"Enough," Steven shouted. "As amusing as this has been for us all, vampire,"—he glanced at the bodies littering the ground—"well, at least for me, I have things to do."

Dante hissed at him and took a step forward. That was as far as he got, however. His mouth twisted in pain, he slapped his hands to either side of his head. Laney screamed as he fell to his knees, his eyes wild, searching for and finding her. He closed them briefly at the sight of her safe on the dock, then they popped open as his body was flung into the air by an unseen force. Back arched, he roared with pain, hovering mid-air while the leader calmly walked up to stand beside him.

Steven turned the box over in is hands. "Thank you for bringing this," he told Dante as he opened it up and peered inside. "It saves me a lot of time and trouble." Snapping the lid shut again, he looked over at the second two Dante had shot and sighed heavily. "Get up, you fools. And finish him." With a flick of his wrist, Dante crashed to the pavement so hard the concrete busted beneath him, cracks appearing in a spider web design all around his body.

Laney struggled to keep it under control, staring in disbelief as the last two zombies, or corpses, or whatever the hell they were, slowly slid their hands under the front of their shoulders and staggered to their feet. Their faces, what was left of them, were gone, replaced by something that resembled the gore that littered a butcher's floor.

"I can barely fucking see," one of them complained.

"At least you still have your nose," the other said.

Dante got his arms and legs underneath him and rose to his full height. Watching them shuffle toward him, he cracked his neck, pulling a knife from an unseen sheath on his thigh.

The fight that ensued over the next few minutes moved so fast that Laney couldn't really keep track of what was happening, but she'd never been more terrified in her life. Occasionally, she would hear grunts of pain and catch a glimpse of a flying fist or the glint of a blade. Blood flew in all directions to spatter the pavement around them. Dante's roar of rage failed to drown out the sound of popping bone just before one of his attackers went skidding across the ground. It jerked its broken leg back into the correct position, then it rose and went back to the fight.

Laney felt like she had been thrown into a horrifying version of *The Walking Dead*. Dragging her eyes away, she searched for Dante. When she found him, he was face down on the pavement with a booted foot shoved into the back of his head. He was covered in blood, one of his arms lying at an unnatural angle. She covered her mouth with her hand, but he twisted away and sprung back up to his feet with a growl that made the hair rise on her arms. Throwing his head back, he head-butted the thing behind him, then swung his left fist, catching the other one in the jaw. The temperature seemed to drop in direct proportion with his rage, and Laney began to shake violently, her wet clothes doing little to protect her.

Before he could do anything else, the two were on him, taking him to the ground as the leader laughed at his efforts to throw them off. As she watched him go down, Laney no longer felt the cold. When the leader tilted his head and pronounced dramatically, "Off with his head!" her fear turned to rage, and then transitioned to a dead calm. It descended over her like a layer of armor, a purple haze that filled her vision and tuned out the world around her other than the sight of her vampire. A buzzing filled her head until she couldn't hear the grunts of pain coming from the male that was now a part of her. The male that was about to die before her eyes trying to protect her.

The colors around her shifted, converging on each of them in turn, picking out each of the creatures murdering her male. She focused on the one with its hands wrapped around Dante's head. Words came to her lips, words she didn't understand and didn't remember learning. On her knees next to the water, Laney chanted, her voice gaining in strength, yet never rising above a whisper.

Suddenly, the creature dropped Dante as its head whipped toward her. The one eye that was still in its skull widened in fear. "Steven! She's doing something!"

The leader searched the area around them. When it found her kneeling there, it gripped the small, wooden box until its knuckles turned white. Baring its fangs, it snarled, "Do what needs to be done. We'll re-group. I must keep this safe." Then he spun on his heel and was gone.

The one Laney focused on wrapped its arms around itself, like it was trying to hang on to its own body. "Stop her!" it yelled at the other one.

Laney widened her line of vision until they were both included. She'd only felt this way once before, when she was but a child, angry at what her grandfather was doing to her grandmother. Now that it was happening again, she remembered whispering something then as well, though it had escaped her memory until now. Words that she didn't understand, yet were a part of her.

They backed away from Dante in confusion. "What the fuck is she doing?" one of them cried. The words were garbled coming from the destruction of its face. One-Eye started shaking its head in answer. "Ah, fuck. She's a Protector. Fuck!" He fell to his knees and the other one soon followed. Laney focused on the first one as a ball of cold energy rose up inside her. With a softly spoken word, it shot from her to him. Its head fell back and its mouth opened on a scream, then the body it possessed fell to the ground as the demon was forcibly evicted. The second one quickly followed suit.

Laney watched the disembodied souls fly toward her. Their rage hit her first, and if she hadn't been prepared, the force of it would have knocked her back into the water. Their ghostly forms came next, swirling around her, their violent intentions clear by the red of their auras. But they couldn't harm her. With a snarl and a softly spoken word, she sent them scattering into the mist.

When it was over, Laney swayed in place before toppling forward, managing to catch herself on her hands before her forehead smashed into the cement. She was exhausted, but she crawled over to Dante with her heart in her throat. Pushing and pulling, she finally managed to roll his large body over. When she saw what they had done to him, her hand flew over her mouth to stifle her cries.

Besides his broken arm, one side of his face was smashed in, the tattoos sunken into the concave that used to be his cheekbone. A large portion of his throat was torn out, and blood poured from the wound to soak his shirt and the pavement beneath him. Air was rasping through the tear, the blood bubbling up from his windpipe until his breathing slowed down and finally stopped altogether. Everywhere she could see, his skin was cut and bleeding, like it had been lashed with shards of glass.

Laney pulled his head into her lap, her tears falling to mix with the blood on his face. She searched around desperately for something to stop the bleeding, then finally yanked her shirt off. Ignoring the cold, she wadded it up into a ball and pressed the wet material to the wound.

His mouth moved, but nothing came out, and he bared his fangs in frustration as his black eyes focused on her face. She tried to put her wrist to his mouth, but he pressed his lips together and turned his face away.

Her face burned at his rejection. "You have to take it," she told him. "I don't know what else to do."

As his body started to spasm, he grabbed her hand and stuck something in it. It was the knife she had stolen from the room in his underground. With his hand over hers, he brought it to his ravaged throat just above her shirt and pressed.

"No," she cried, sobbing harder. "Dante, no! No. I won't do it!" She fought his hold until the knife clattered to the pavement beside his head. His eyes burned into hers, but she shook her head so hard she could feel her brains rattling around. "No," she told him, softer this time. "You need to live, Dante. I need you to live. To stay with me."

Footsteps pounded on the pavement around them. Acting on instinct, Laney grabbed the knife from where she'd dropped it and jumped to her feet. Adrenaline flooded her system, making her scalp tingle as she crouched over her male to face this new threat. She felt Dante's hand grasping at her leg, and she reached over without looking and pressed down on the makeshift compress again.

"Holy shit, would you look at her," a blond guy said. He looked like he'd just stepped off a movie set.

"Don't let Emma hear you say that, mate," a guy with a British accent teased.

The blond rolled his eyes. "I didn't mean it like that. And don't you dare go starting shit with her, Aid. She wouldn't believe you anyway."

Laney brandished the knife at them, her upper lip lifting in a snarl. "Stay away from us," she shouted.

A woman with black hair pulled back in a high ponytail lifted her hands in front of her. Her green eyes flipped back and forth from Laney to Dante. She took a cautious step forward. "It's all right," she said softly. "We're friends. We're Dante's friends."

Laney looked from her to the four guys. Her attention was naturally drawn to one in particular, a man with dark hair and a stoic face that stood a few feet apart from the others. He had a set to his shoulders and an overall bearing about him that told her he was the one in charge. She directed her question to him. "Who are you?"

He stepped forward, showing her his hands. "I am Luukas. I am the Master Vampire of this territory. These are my Hunters." He waved one hand toward the others. "Dante is my Hunter as well. You are Laney?"

She looked at each of them in turn, and saw nothing but worry and concern as they returned her stare. None of them made a move to disarm her. "You're friends?" Her teeth were beginning to chatter, whether from the cold or from everything that just happened, she couldn't say.

"Yes," Luukas said.

Laney believed him. She lowered the knife. "Tell me what to do. I don't know what to do. He won't take my blood—" Her words were cut off by a sob. She was babbling, but she couldn't stop the flow of words once they'd started. "I was attacked by these...things. Corpses. They used me as bait." She looked down at Dante. "Tell me what to do. I don't know what to do."

The woman approached her. "Laney, I'm Shea. I'm Dante's friend." She smiled, and all Laney could think was how stunningly pretty she was. "I'm going to help you. Okay?"

Laney sniffed. "Okay."

Shea squatted down next to her and Dante. "Get off him now so we can help him."

With a start, Laney realized she was still crouching over him protectively. Leaning her weight to one side, she fell onto her ass, dragging her leg across his hips. She kept the pressure on his throat.

"Can I see your wrist?" Shea asked.

Lifting her free arm, Laney gave it to her without thought.

"Trust me, okay?" Shea asked. Then she brought Laney's wrist to her mouth.

Dante's body bucked next to her, and Laney looked down to see his cold, black eyes burning holes into Shea, but she just smiled. "It's for your own good, you stubborn ass." White fangs flashed in the light of the street lamps just before Laney felt the female's fangs pierce her skin. The ground shook beneath her as Dante bared his fangs and let out a gurgling roar of rage. His good hand tightened on Laney's thigh, but in spite of his obvious fury, he made no move to get the other vampire off her wrist.

Shea released her fangs. "Put it in front of him now," she told Laney, licking the blood from her lips.

Laney did, letting the open wound hover just above his mouth. Dante closed his eyes, clamping his mouth shut again. But she saw his nostrils flare at the scent of her blood. "Please, Dante," she begged. "I can't stand to see you suffering like this."

Something in her tone must have gotten through to him. His eyes opened. They were full of pain, but they were lightened with warmth as they travelled over her face. Yet, he still wouldn't open his mouth, even though she could feel his broken body trembling with the effort it was taking him not to drink from her.

She looked to Shea for help. "Why won't he drink?"

Shea shook her head. "I don't know. He's not one to open up to people, you know?"

Laney looked around at the rest of them, but no one seemed to have an answer. "Would you give us some privacy please?"

"Sure," Shea answered. "We'll be right over there if you need us." She pointed at the building on the corner.

Laney watched them leave, then turned back to her male. "All right, you son of a bitch. You're going to listen to me. Do you fucking understand?"

He narrowed his eyes at her in warning, but she would not be put off.

"You took me from my home against my will. You keep me locked up like an animal underneath a perfectly comfortable and safe apartment. Drink my blood whenever you damn well feel like it, treat me like shit half the time, and barely remember to feed me. But you're the first person, or vampire, I guess, to really know me. You *know* me. And I know you. So somehow, in spite of all that, you've become important to me, blood bond or no blood bond. I need you, and you need me. And I am not going to let you die on me now that I've just found you. So whatever fucking macho shit this is, get the fuck over it." Biting down on her wrist again to keep the wounds open, she shoved it back into his face. "Now drink," she ordered.

At first, she didn't think she'd gotten through to him, but then something touched her face, and she realized he was brushing away her tears as he so often had before. "Please drink," she whispered. "Don't leave when you've only just found me."

With a low sound that was somewhere between rebellion and submission, he opened his mouth and bared his fangs. Laney quickly pressed her arm against his lips, and felt the sharp pain of his bite with an overwhelming sense of relief. She could feel him swallowing beneath the wad of her shirt, now soaked through with his blood. His legs moved restlessly, the muscles twitching, and then the lacerations on his face began to heal before her eyes.

Lifting his distorted arm, Dante slammed it back down beside him, forcing the bone back into place with a grunt of pain. Then he wrapped one hand around her elbow and one around her hand, holding her wrist to his mouth as he drank.

A low growl rumbled through his chest, a possessive sound she was beginning to recognize. Laney responded instantly, her pulse quickening and her body pulsing with desire. His nostrils flared again.

Suddenly, he sat up, taking her wrist with him, until his ruggedly handsome face was only inches from her own. Her shirt fell from his neck, and underneath the streaks of blood, Laney could see the gaping wound was nearly completely healed.

Dante licked the blood from her wrist with languid strokes of his tongue, and Laney could feel her face heating for an entirely different reason now. He kissed the spot where his fangs had just been and lowered her arm to her lap. They stayed like that, connected only by their heated gazes, until a throat cleared next to them.

"How about we get you two home, yes?" the British guy said.

Coming back to reality, Laney blinked, still a bit dazed from what had just happened. "Okay, yeah." Pulling her legs under her, she tried to get up, and would've fallen if Dante wasn't suddenly there, lifting her up into strong arms.

"I've got her," he growled at the others. One large hand attempted to cover her breasts, barely covered by her lacy bra.

Laney laid her head against his chest. "Take me home," she whispered.

27

Dante stood just inside the elevator door with Laney passed out in his arms. Noticing the gooseflesh on her bare torso, he pulled her in closer to his chest, trying to keep her warm. The doors closed in front of him, then opened again, then closed again as he stared at the panel of buttons. His immediate instinct was to take her below ground where she would be safe and he could watch over her.

But she hated it down there.

Dante's fangs shot down, aggression overtaking him as he wrestled with the demons in his head. He couldn't protect her upstairs, and he couldn't stay up there with her. He was ready to jump out of his skin even for the short periods of time he was required to be up there. If he took her up there to recover, she would be alone. Vulnerable.

But the others were all up there. And just because she was his fated mate didn't mean they had to be attached at the fucking hip. She didn't even have to like him, just give up her blood whenever he needed it for him to survive. Hell, he could set her up in her own place. As long as it was somewhere nearby....

He immediately squashed that thought. *Fuck, no.*

Dante heaved a sigh. But maybe he should give her the choice.

Dante stared down at her small form, indecision wracking him. Her earthy sweet scent rose around him, overpowering the mix of sea air and car oil that permeated the garage, and the smell of demon gore and seawater on their bodies. She had saved him today. She had saved them both.

The doors opened again. He growled low in his throat, shifted Laney's weight to one arm, and punched a button with his finger.

Less than a minute later he was kicking open the door to his apartment, startling the dog, who in turn began to bark his fool head off. Dante silently ordered the dog to hush while he carried her back to the bedroom and laid her across the bed. Reaching over her, he tugged the comforter up and tucked it around her.

Then he straightened to his full height and exhaled, slowing his breathing to almost nothing so he could listen. After a moment, he relaxed. Her heartbeat was strong and steady, her lungs expanding and contracting as they should with no abnormalities. Dante took a relieved breath, brushing the stray hairs off her face. Her skin was damp and pale from exertion, but she was sleeping soundly. Yes, his mate was strong. Probably stronger than him.

He would get one of the other witches to come sit with her so she didn't wake up alone. He needed to secure the underground. It wasn't safe there anymore now that the demons knew of his secret exit. Or entrance, depending on how you looked at it.

But first he would bring up her things. He'd made up his mind. He was leaving her here. They could buy her a table and a couch and whatever else her heart desired. The vampire council had plenty of money stashed away. She would be better off staying up here with the others, much as it hurt his pride to admit it. The witches would make sure she was fed, and she could be with her pet. She would be happier.

The last few days had proven that he was worthless as a mate for her. Her own words earlier only confirmed it, as did his inability to protect her. He had no fucking idea how to take care of her, or how to comfort her.

Laney thought they shared a bond, and he supposed that was true—to a point. They'd both lost a child. But whereas her son, he was convinced, had died of completely natural causes, his had not. His had died for no reason other than his father...that *he*...had failed to protect him. There was no comfort to be had there, from her or anyone else.

And other than his own personal convictions, he now *knew* it was impossible for Laney to have killed her own child. She was a Protector: a special breed of witch that came from a long line of magical ancestors who passed down the ability to fight true evil from generation to generation. There was normally one or two in each coven at all times. They protected their kind and the ones connected to them by blood. The sorcery that bred them would not allow them to do otherwise even if they wanted to, similar to vampires with their mates.

It all became clear to him now. This was the reason she was cleaving to him, the only reason. It was the only thing that made sense to him. They had a blood bond now. But she deserved better than a brutish male like him. Dante had spent his entire immortal life hating humans and punishing them for everything they'd done to him. He didn't even know how to fucking talk to her.

Hell, a human male could do better by her. Dante couldn't even save her from a few limp-dicked demons. She was one of the most important witches of her generation—one of the most important people to him—and he had failed her in his efforts to keep her safe.

And thanks to him and his fucked up ego, Steven now had the exact thing Luuk had been desperately trying to keep away from them. The Master Vampire had immediately sent out scouts, including Nik and Aiden—and Aiden's demon—to try to track him. But Dante knew that demon would not be found unless he wanted to be. And who knew where the rest of those bastards were or who they were possessing now. The vampire bodies were no longer viable, and would soon be nothing but ash when the sun came up. To make sure humans didn't find the carnage before that could happen,

Christian was keeping watch over the scene of the fight. He'd hightail it back home just before he was barbecued himself.

Tucking the comforter closer around Laney, he leaned down and pressed a tender kiss to her hairline, breathing the scent of her into his lungs. Then he turned away, left her there, and went to check on the pets. Noting that they had plenty of food and water, he hunkered down onto his haunches to scratch the dog's ears and ruffle the cat's fur.

He locked the door behind him, and went back down to the underground. After confirming the latch on the bench was repairable, he set about reinforcing it until he was comfortable that nothing would be getting in or out unless he wanted them to.

When he was done, he wandered around the room, his eyes touching on each piece in turn. Past memories assaulted him along with the way—voices begging for their lives, a blood curdling scream as he carved a piece of flesh from a face.

He had come upon that particular male while hunting one night, his interest piqued when he heard the sounds of a scuffle. The guy was beating an elderly woman when Dante found him. Apparently, the woman wouldn't give the asshole her purse. His fangs ached at the recollection of that guest. He had lasted longer than Dante would've wagered.

Turning his head, his eyes skimmed over the bench he had just fixed. Screams of a different sort echoed through his head as he saw a woman with blonde hair and extra flesh strapped face down upon it with her ass in the air as he fucked her from behind—right before he'd dug his hands into all of that hair and yanked her head back until he heard the soothing sound of cracking bone. The screams had stopped abruptly as he bent over her and sank his fangs into her shoulder just before he came. He'd been stalking that one for days. She left her young daughter home alone every night while she whored herself out. Strangely enough, the memory did not make him hard, as it normally did.

But he was no hero. Sometimes he killed just for the fun of it. He could count on one hand the number of times he'd fed on a human without taking their life. He preferred to kill them. Less risk that way.

When he got to the table that held his assortment of "tools," Dante scrubbed his hand over his mouth. His skin felt tight, the muscles underneath twitching restlessly as he admired the assortment of blades, whips, and other pain-inducing gadgets. Picking up a small knife in his right hand, he shoved his sleeve up on his opposite arm and laid the cold blade against his skin. The tip bit into the edge of one of his tattoos.

Dante paused. The markings had been done by hand with a sharp stick and the ash from a sacred fire by one of the elders in his camp. It was supposed to protect him from the evil lurking inside his body after the vampire had attacked him. An ancient spell tattooed permanently into his skin, but only on the left side, where the bites festered.

Needless to say, it didn't work, and he turned soon after. But he moved the tip to avoid cutting into it, just in case. Slowly, he drew the blade across the unmarked skin of his forearm. His upper lip lifted, exposing his fangs as the blood welled and spilled over to run down his arm and drip onto the floor.

He repeated the process until both arms were decorated with red diagonal lines, but the bloodletting wasn't enough to release the restless self-loathing and agitation churning inside him.

He needed to hurt someone. Maybe a couple of someones. Alone in this room, all he could smell was the blood, sweat, and fear of his victims. It made him hungry for the hunt just thinking about it. This was who he was.

Less than a minute later, he was roaming the city streets. A light drizzle fell, washing away the blood on his skin and gradually soaking his clothes. Dante paid no attention to it, sticking to the shadows as he made his way to The Jungle, Seattle's infamous homeless encampment. When he got there, he remained under the cover of trees, observing the huddle of tents, searching for something that caught his interest. He was familiar with most that lived there. Some were there because they'd fallen on hard times and had no other recourse. But others chose to check out of society, and he couldn't really say that he blamed them. Others preyed upon both groups.

It didn't take long before Dante spotted exactly what he was looking for. A punk ass and his buddy appeared from the other end of the camp, picking their way along the center path. Their eyes were shifty as they crept through the encampment, peaking inside the tents where they could.

A quick connection of his mind to theirs confirmed his suspicions, and Dante smiled. These two were the perfect reciprocals for his aggression.

His hunting instincts took over as he watched them get closer. A quick look around confirmed that everyone else was asleep. Not that it mattered. He cared not whether he was seen here. Everyone thought these people were nothing but crazy meth addicts. Nothing they said was taken seriously. A moment later, and he was crouched on the branch of a large oak. He hadn't made a single sound. Watching them closely, he waited for the exact right moment.

Dante liked to toy with his prey.

One of them ducked into a tent, only to reappear moments later. He shook his head at his friend, and they kept going. Dante waited with the eternal patience of the damned as they made their way toward him.

Come on, you fuckers. I want to play.

They walked beneath the tree, completely oblivious to the angel of death crouched directly above them. He let them pass, then stood and stepped off the branch, landing behind them with a soft thud.

They spun around at the same time, and Dante smiled at their matching looks of horror as he towered above them. "Wrong place, right time, assholes."

Grabbing them both around the throat, he dragged them further into the underbrush that surrounded the camp. There were still a few cars on the nearby highway, the sounds of the traffic muffling the sounds they made as they tried to kick and claw their way free.

Dante pulled the one with the greasy black hair in closer until his fangs were front and center in the idiot's line of vision. He caught the terrified gaze with his own. "You will remain calm, sit quietly, and wait your turn." Then he dropped him to the ground where the guy obediently sat up and wrapped his arms around his knees to wait.

He then turned his attention to the one he still held. Panic-stricken blue eyes shot from Dante to his friend and back again. Shaking his head back and forth, Dante tsk'd at his bad behavior. "Stealing from the poor. That's pretty fucking lame. Even for a piece of shit like you." The guy's eyes bugged out of his head as he clawed at Dante's hand, still wrapped around his windpipe. It was a good look on him. Dante flashed his fangs with anticipation.

The human's gurgling screams, however, were beginning to grate on his nerves. He squeezed his fingers closer together until the guy's lips flapped like a fish out of water. But at least he was fucking quiet.

Much better.

The smell of urine reached his nose, and Dante cocked his head to the side with mock sympathy. "Don't feel ashamed, asshole. I tend to have that effect on people." Then he narrowed his eyes and brought him in closer. "What shall I do to a thief and a liar, hmm?"

"He never lies," the one on the ground informed him in a monotone voice. "But he does steal. I think he even stole off me once."

Dante gazed down at his greasy head, considering. "I'll keep that in mind. Thank you for telling me." Then he smiled, and tore the jacket from his victim's shoulder with his free hand. Rearing back, he prepared to strike.

"Dante."

He froze with his fangs barely touching the homeless man's throat. Dante didn't have to look to see who it was. He knew. "Leave me be, Shea." His victim whimpered in his arms, and Dante tightened his grip around the guy's throat to shut him the fuck up.

"Dante, what are you doing? They're just kids."

With an impatient sigh, he twisted his head around to look at her. "Old enough to steal from others who have nothing to spare." On that note, he tore into the guy's throat with relish.

A second later, he threw him to the ground with disgust and spat out the vile blood in his mouth. "Godsdammit!" he roared, and spit some more. "This is fucking disgusting." He shoved the human with his booted foot. "What the fuck are you on, asshole?" The human turned eyes wide with shock upon him as he pressed both hands over the gaping hole in his throat. It did nothing to stem the flow of blood, however, and he soon passed out.

Or bled to death. His friend watched it happen with no reaction.

Shea crossed her arms over her chest. "Who exactly are you punishing?" she asked. "That human? Or yourself?"

Dante did not have the time nor the inclination to defend himself. Grabbing the human that was still alive by the hair, he hauled him up off the ground until they were face to face. "Follow me," he ordered. Then he dropped him and walked away, the human on his heels.

Shea jogged to catch up to him. "Look. You can tell me to fuck off if you want—"

"Fuck off."

"But I think I know why you're acting out this way, and why you've done it before." She paused. "Okay, I'm lying, I have no idea why you do this. Maybe you're just old and cranky." She hurried on when he shot her a look. "But Laney's awake. She's asking for you."

Something lurched inside of him. He gritted his teeth and ignored it. "She doesn't need me."

"She seemed pretty out of sorts when you weren't there."

When she didn't expand on that, he stopped, turning to glare down at the human when he walked right into him. Giving his attention back to Shea, he cocked one eyebrow. "And?"

She smiled at him. "She's worried about you."

A fragile thread of hope wound its way around his gut. But then he remembered what a piece of shit he was. With a grunt, he kept walking, the human on his heels. "That means nothing to me."

"Dante—" She quickly caught up to him.

"I'm done here, Shea."

"You can't live without her. Like, literally. Maybe you should give her a chance."

"I'm *done*."

With a sigh of defeat, she stopped talking, and they walked the rest of the way in silence. When they reached the apartments, she said, "Luukas wants you to come and see him."

I bet he does. "Tell him I'll be up as soon as I am finished down here." Dante left her at the elevators and took his dessert down to his feeding room.

He had no idea how the "new" Luukas was going to react to his major fuck up. But he would not run from the consequences of what he had done. It had been a stupid move. More than stupid. Ever since he'd brought that female here, he hadn't been thinking straight. His decision to keep the box, and to then take it with him to barter for Laney, was all because of her. And now the demons still had the clue they were looking for, and he'd gotten his ass kicked in return. He deserved whatever punishment he had coming to him.

Hell, he hadn't even bothered trying to use it as a trade. No fucking way. Instead, he'd gone in there thinking he was all badass as soon as he had her in his sights—guns blazing, starting a fight, and almost getting them both killed.

And they'd gotten it anyway.

In a fit of temper, he raised his fist to lash out at the human standing next to him. The human stood calmly awaiting the blow, still under the mindfuck Dante had bestowed upon him. He didn't even flinch.

With a snarl, Dante lowered his fist and stepped back. Everywhere he looked, he saw Laney's accusing brown eyes. No, not accusing. Disappointed. She would be disappointed if she found out he killed this one in here. Or had killed any more humans at all. And somehow, that was even worse than her anger.

Why do I even fucking care?

But he did care. Godsdamn her.

He laughed out loud. It wasn't a pleasant sound. But it was downright fucking amusing, this turn his long life had recently taken. Laney would never care for a monster like him. Not the way he needed her to. And she shouldn't. She was all that was good and light, a Protector. Even the way she tried to accept her fate with him proved that she was too good for him. He didn't deserve her. But Shea was right: he needed her. And Dante wasn't like Nikulas. Fuck, no. He was entirely too fucking selfish to walk away from her, and not entirely because he needed her blood.

Smashing his fist into the brick directly above the human, Dante roared with frustration. He began to pace the room, tearing at his skull with both hands. Every once in a while, he would stop and destroy something. By the time he got it all out, there wasn't much left for his entertainment.

Numb, he sank down onto the bench with his head in his hands.

28

Laney sat on the side of the bed staring at the nightstand. On it laid her copy of *Goodnight Moon*. The rest of her stuff was in her backpack on the floor. A glass of juice waited for her to drink it. It had all been there when she'd woken up. She also had one of Dante's T-shirts on over her jeans. It nearly swallowed her whole, but she didn't change out of it.

She'd woken up with a sense of panic, shooting straight up in the bed. The first thing she noticed was that the sun was up, and she quickly scanned the room, looking for Dante. But he wasn't there.

However, the female vampire and two others were waiting for her, sitting on the floor against the wall. "It's okay," the strange dark-haired woman had said. "You're safe."

"Where's Dante?" Something was wrong. Laney could sense it. He'd seemed okay before she'd passed out. "Is he okay? Where is he?"

She smiled. "He's fine."

"I'll go find him," the vampire assured her, rubbing the dog's ears on the way out. She didn't appear worried.

Still, Laney couldn't relax. "Why am I here? In the apartment," she clarified when the other two looked at each other and then back at her in confusion. "Why is my stuff here?"

"Dante brought you here and brought your stuff up for you," the same woman answered.

"Why?" That sense of panic increased.

"I don't know," she answered. "But I'm glad he did. We were worried about you."

The other woman nodded and smiled in agreement. She had long mahogany hair and an "I love girls in wellies" T-shirt on. It was too big on her. "Can we get you anything? Are you hungry?"

Laney shook her head. Her stomach was in knots.

The first one got up off the floor and came to sit on the side of the bed. "You're Laney, right?"

Laney nodded, looking around the room nervously. She couldn't shake the feeling that something was off. It wasn't the women, she felt nothing negative coming from them, only warmth.

"Laney, I'm Keira. Keira Moss. I'm a witch. As are you." She smiled when that got Laney's attention. "And this is Grace Moss." The woman on the floor, Grace, gave a little wave.

Wait. "Moss? Your last name is Moss?"

Keira smiled. "Yeah. We're family."

Laney looked at her again, closer this time. She couldn't deny the uncanny resemblance. "How is that possible?"

Making herself comfortable, Keira tucked her legs to the side and leaned over onto one hand. "From what I was told growing up and from the guys here, the Moss witches all belonged to the local coven in this area until it was overthrown by the new High Priest. A few of the families scattered, taking their children—us—with them. Fate and a little help from yours truly here has brought us all back together. Here and now."

Laney rubbed her forehead. It was gritty from the seawater. As a matter of fact, her entire body felt salty. "I don't understand—"

"We were scattered all over the world," Grace spoke up from her spot on the carpet. "Four of us have found our way back to each other. Keira and Emma are sisters. Ryan and I are cousins."

Laney tried hard to stay focused and keep up. "There's more of you?"

"Five. Including you," Keira said.

"Where are the rest? Your parents?"

"They're gone," Keira said sadly. "All taken by 'accidents'."

"Doesn't seem very accidental to me," Grace muttered.

"And there's that," Keira agreed. "But we can get more into the family history later. So, what happened out there? Luukas said when they found you that Dante was beaten to a bloody pulp and you were trying to protect him. He also said there were dead vampire bodies littering the ground, curiously empty of their demons."

"I don't really know—I think I killed them," she said in a small voice. Glancing at them each in turn, she confessed, "I don't really feel very bad about it."

Keira sat up and touched her leg through the comforter. "Can you tell me what happened?"

Laney tried to put what she'd experienced into words. "Um. I heard them threatening Dante, and everything just got really sharp and clear. I wasn't scared, or angry, or anything. And it was like the air turned purple, and I could see their... spirit? Aura? I don't know. Then I just imagined it being squeezed from their bodies." She hung her head and plucked at a loose thread. "It's not the first time this has happened."

"Laney, those things that took you? They were vampires that were created by Luukas, but they'd left this colony to serve another vampire." Her voice dropped. "A real bitch."

"They were also possessed," Grace said.

"Possessed?" Laney asked.

Keira nodded. "That bitch I just mentioned, she found an ancient altar hidden deep underground. There were demons chained to it, well, their spirits were anyway. At least, until she figured out a way to free them. And she did that by finding bodies for them to live in. Vampires created by a powerful Master Vampire work the best and last the longest."

Laney recalled the stench of rot and the decomposing bodies. "They didn't seem to be taking very good care of themselves."

"I think the bodies are dying, because Leeha—the aforementioned bitch—is dead now. And since she was technically their creator because she re-animated them after the possessions with her own blood, they won't survive long in those bodies."

Vampires, demons, witches...if Laney hadn't seen the stuff she'd seen with her own eyes, she'd think these two were crazy. But she had seen it. Still, she was confused. "What happened to the original owners of the bodies?"

The two women looked at each other. "We're not sure, " Keira admitted.

"Um, one thing you should know," Grace said. "My mate, Aiden. British, dimpled chin, sexy grey eyes...he has one of those things inside of him." Her face grew cautiously hopeful. "Maybe you could get it out?"

Laney stared at her.

"Grace, I think we should wait," Keira said quietly. "We don't know enough about Laney's magic. None of the vampires survived her exorcism."

Grace refused to be deterred. "Can you do it, Laney? Can you get that fucking demon out and leave my Aiden in there?"

"I...I don't know."

"You said this has happened before," she coaxed. "What happened? Were they humans or vampires or...?"

"They were humans," she told her.

"And?"

"They died," she whispered.

A heavy silence descended upon the room.

"Well, shit." Grace covered her face with her hands.

"Grace, it'll be okay," Keira got up from the bed and went over to soothe her. "When you're cleaned up and fed, we'll talk more about this," she said to Laney. "See what we can figure out."

Laney didn't respond.

Eventually, they'd gone to let Luukas know she was awake, and with nothing else to do, Laney had taken a quick shower and put Dante's shirt back on over her last clean pair of jeans. Now she sat staring at the book on the nightstand with one hand clenched in the comforter and one hand over her stomach, trying to hold in the butterflies.

She wanted to see Dante.

The front door opened and closed, and Laney jumped up off the bed and ran out to the other room in her socks. It wasn't her male, but the female vampire. "Where is he?"

She smiled and opened her mouth. Then she snapped it shut and the smile fell from her face. "He's not coming."

"What's your name?"

"Oh, sorry." She strode forward on long, graceful legs and held out her hand. It was pale and delicate, but her grip was strong when Laney took it in her own. "I'm Shea."

"Hi, Shea. I'm Laney." She gave her a small smile. "Do you know where he is?"

"Sure do," Shea said. "But I think you should wait for him to come up here."

Laney laughed. It sounded bitter to even her own ears. "Yeah, no. Dante has no plans to come here. Take me to him. Please," she added. "I need to see him."

Shea eyed her up and down. She must have passed the inspection. "He's underground. I'll get you in there."

"Thank you!" Acting on impulse, Laney hugged her.

Shea stiffened for moment, then her arms came around her and she hugged her back. "Go get your shoes," she told her.

29

Her scent came to him first.

Dante lifted his head and his burning eyes shot over to the empty tunnel.

She's here.

Standing up, he triggered the secret latch underneath the bench he'd been sitting on and raised the seat. In a flash, he was in front of the human male, still waiting for his turn near the smashed bricks in the wall. "Time to go, asshole." Lowering his head until he was eye to eye with the shorter man, he said, "Go back to the homeless camp and find your dead friend. You won't remember me, or what happened to him. It must have been an animal."

"An animal," he repeated obediently.

Dante could hear Laney in the other room now. "Yes, a bear. Now get the fuck out of here." He pointed toward the bench.

"Follow the tunnel to the other end. Don't speak to anyone until you get back to your friend."

The guy started shuffling toward the escape hatch, and when he didn't move fast enough, Dante came up behind him with a snarl. Grasping him by the collar and the back of his pants, he hitched him over the side and dropped him through the opening.

"Dante?"

Her voice washed over him, soothing his raw nerves. He didn't respond right away, watching to make sure the human male got up and walked away, and then he slammed the bench closed and secured the latch. Steeling himself, he turned to face her, and felt like he'd been punched in the gut.

Laney stood before him in one of his plain black T-shirts and jeans, holding a candle. The shirt fell nearly to her knees and hung off one bare shoulder. He could see the outline of her bare breasts, the nipples jutting against the soft material. Her hair was partially damp and tumbled around her face and down her back in disarray. She was still too pale, too thin, her tawny eyes worried and too large in her delicate face.

She was fucking exquisite.

It took him a moment before he found his voice. "What are you doing here, little mouse?"

"I came to find you," she simply said. "Who was that?" She glanced around. "And what happened in here?" He could see her coming to conclusions—the correct conclusions. Her voice lowered to a near whisper. "No. Dante, did you hurt him?"

Dante narrowed his eyes at her, unused to being questioned, nor having someone to answer to. But he felt compelled to do exactly that. He tried to swallow past the dryness in his throat. "No. I—" The words wouldn't come. He'd wanted to hurt the human. Craved the release it would have brought him. And he still might have done it if she hadn't shown up.

She studied him, her perceptive eyes roaming from his face to his clenched fists and back again. Somehow, he managed to remain still, even though he wanted to hide, afraid as always that she would see right through to his black soul.

"Why did you leave me upstairs?"

He ground his jaw, though her directness shouldn't surprise him by now. His heart palpitated in his chest. "Because that's where you should be." His voice was gruff. He tried to swallow again.

She took a step toward him. "I should be with you, Dante."

"No, little mouse." He gave a snort of disgust. "You should not be with me." His voice became strained. "You should have finished the job you started last night, the job the demons started out there on the docks. You would be free now." A razor sharp pain lanced his insides at what he was about to say, yet he heard the words come out of his mouth as if in a dream. "I should still free you."

"Dante—"

He interrupted whatever she had been about to say. It was too late now for her. "And yet, I can't let you go. Not without forfeiting my own damned life. And I'm entirely too fucking selfish to do that." He paused. "Letting you live upstairs is the best I can do. I will only bother you to feed when I have to. The others will make sure you have everything you need and will keep you safe." His instincts screamed in denial. No one could keep her safer than he could.

But we both know that's nothing but a fucking lie, don't we?

She was silent after his little speech. He longed to know what she was thinking, but couldn't bring himself to reach out to her thoughts, half-hopeful and half-terrified at what he might find there.

Finally, she spoke. "But that's not what I want. I want to be where you are."

That tiny tendril of hope threatened again. In an act of sheer desperation to save himself before it was too late, he changed the subject. "Why are you wearing my shirt?" The question may have come out a bit harsher than he had intended.

Full of defiance as always, she lifted her chin. Her gaze was steady as she stared daggers across the room at him. Witnessing the way she stood up to him, his chest swelled with pride.

"Because mine are filthy. And because I wanted to. It smells like you."

His blood warmed at her answer. "Laney—" He stopped, not quite sure what it was he had been about to say. A plea, or perhaps a warning. Talking had never been his forte. Especially when he had so many emotions eating away at his insides.

She came closer, so close he could reach out and touch her face. And that's exactly what he did, his fingertips skimming lightly over her cheekbone. Setting the candle down, she took his large hand in both of her small ones and held it to her chest, over her heart. "I want to be with you, wherever that is."

Her simple words struck him harder than any elaborate speech would have, all of the raging thoughts and emotions screaming inside of him settling into a low hum. He ran his free hand over his shaved head. He wanted to believe that she meant what she said, but perhaps she just didn't want to be alone. The other witches lived with their mates. "I can't live upstairs, little mouse. It's—"

"Not safe," she finished for him. "I know."

"I'm not—"

"A good person...or vampire...or whatever. I know."

Pulling his hand from hers, he paced away. He didn't understand. He hadn't been kind to her. As a matter of fact, he'd treated her little better than any other human he'd run across. "Laney, I'm no good for you."

"I know. It doesn't change anything. It doesn't change the way I feel."

In the face of her unwavering perseverance, Dante began to do something that he hadn't done in a long, long time. He let that tiny thread of hope spin into a rope. Tentatively, he reached out and touched her thoughts with his, but immediately pulled back again, still frightened that he'd find out it was all a lie.

Her features softened, a small smile lifting the corners of her mouth. "Go ahead," she told him.

He stared at that mouth, transfixed by the curve of her lips. This tiny female that was more threatening to him than a group of hell's demons. Swallowing hard, Dante reached out again. What he discovered made his heart stall out in his chest, then begin to pound sporadically. There was a touch of fear, yes, but there was also hope, longing, passion, and the beginnings of an honest love. He didn't know if that love was a natural occurrence or brought on by the blood bond, and honestly, he didn't fucking care. "Little mouse...Laney." Unable to stop himself, he hauled her up into his arms and took her mouth with his. It wasn't a tender kiss. It was a kiss of hunger, of disbelief, of euphoria and possession. Her soft body molded perfectly to the hard planes of his chest.

He broke it off, working his way along her cheekbone to her ear. "Don't be frightened of me. I would never hurt you."

"I'm only frightened of what I feel for you," she whispered.

His hand tightened in her hair. "You are MINE, little mouse." With a hiss of longing, he flashed his fangs and kissed her again.

Her arms wrapped tight around his neck and her legs wrapped around his waist, her moans of surrender blending with his. He kissed her until their hearts beat in rapid unison and their every breath depended on each other. He kissed her until his body trembled with wanting her. With a low growl, he made his way over her jaw and down to her throat, barely stopping himself before he plunged his fangs through her tender skin.

She tilted her head away, exposing her throat to him. Dante groaned with the need to consume her in every possible way, but somehow he refrained. She was too pale. He had taken too much blood earlier in order to heal. However, he couldn't resist running one fang along her pulsing artery before dropping a kiss there.

"Dante, please," she begged.

"No, Laney." Kissing his way back up to her mouth, he pressed a soft kiss to the corner of her mouth. "You're too pale." Glancing around, he scowled.

"What's wrong?"

"You don't belong in here. In this room." Still holding her, he strode over to the tunnel and set her down to go first. "Go. I'm right behind you." He nearly regretted his decision as the sight of her deliciously plump ass in front of him nearly drove him to take her there in the dark, and he couldn't resist touching her as they made their way into the other room.

When they arrived moments later, he was surprised to see the candles had all been lit. Her backpack was there, along with her book. She had laid it on top of his, the green and red cover a bright contrast against the black. A few bottles of water and some juice were lined up along the wall, and there was a paper bag. He could smell the food inside. On the bed was the thick comforter from upstairs. And pillows.

"Do you think you can figure out a way to keep rodents away? I swear I've heard them on occasion. And some hot running water would be nice, too. To bathe? But I guess that can be done upstairs." She clasped her hands in front of her. "I hope it's okay that I brought a few things down here."

Dante had no words. The fact that she was willing to stay down here with him at all was hard for him to believe. He stood there like a fucking idiot, at a complete loss, his body raging with desire.

"I can take everything back upstairs," she said when the silence stretched on.

He finally found his voice. "No!" he told her. "No. This is fine."

She watched him carefully. "Are you sure you're okay with this? If you don't want me here—"

That was as far as she got. "Take off your clothes, little mouse."

Laney blinked, and her mouth snapped shut with an audible click.

"Take them off now," he growled. So many thoughts clamored for dominance in his head, so many emotions, but there was one that overruled them all.

He needed to possess her. He needed her submission.

The air between them was simultaneously too heavy and too thin. Dante's blood raced, his muscles tensed, his sex throbbing within the confines of his pants. Inhaling deeply, the scent of her desire filled his nose. His mouth watered. She was already wet for him, her breasts rising and falling with her quickened breaths. He waited.

She glanced around, then back at him. Backing up a few paces, she braced one hand on the brick wall as she kicked off her sneakers. After a slight pause, she undid her jeans and pulled them off, taking her socks with them. Straightening up, she stood before him in nothing but his oversized T-shirt.

"All of it," he ordered.

Blood flooded into her cheeks, making them flush, but she did as he ordered, pulling off the shirt and tossing it on top of the rest. She didn't try to cover herself.

A low growl rumbled in his chest. She wasn't wearing any underthings. There was a buzzing in his head as his eyes traveled from the lock of hair curling around one dusky nipple, to the curve of her hip, to the scars on her belly, to her shapely legs and the "V" of dark curls in between, and even her small feet.

Grinding his jaw against the urge to spin her around and take her against the wall, he ripped off his shirt, still wet from the rain. His skin felt tight, his fangs ached, and his manhood was so engorged it was painful. But he welcomed this pain. "Lie down on the bed," he told her as he knelt down to unfasten his boots. "On your back."

Again, she did as he told her. But he wasn't fooled. His little mouse only obeyed his commands because she chose to do so. Her sweet, earthy scent was only tempered by the musky smell of her sex. There was no stench of fear.

As he rose and unfastened his pants, kicking off his boots much as she had, her hungry eyes were rapt on his manhood. When he was as nude as she, he took the heavy length in his hand. It filled his palm, and he stroked himself as he walked over to her and dropped to his knees.

She immediately sat up, reaching for him, but he pressed her back down. "No, Laney." Kneeling beside her, he released his sex as he ran his free hand over her soft skin, afraid he would come merely from the sight of her. Laney arched her back, pressing her breasts into his palm, and he pinched her nipple. "Spread your legs. I want to see you."

She did, and he moved until he was lying between them. Her sex was soaking wet, the scent of her desire strong. Placing his hands on her thighs, he pushed them even further apart. He could see her opening, and lower, her ass.

He would possess her there one day also.

Sliding one hand up her leg to her pelvis, he ran his thumb through her satiny folds, spreading the moisture to the hard nub hidden within.

Her hips bucked. "Dante, please..."

He kissed the inside of her thigh. "Shhh, little mouse." Dante was fast discovering that he enjoyed this particular type of torture, both for her and for himself. But more than that, he was determined to take his time and enjoy this gift that had fallen into his hands against all the odds.

He circled her clit a few more times, eliciting a groan from her before moving his thumb down through her wet pussy to press inside of her. Her hands fisted in the blanket as she arched her back again, trying to force it in deeper. Pulling out, he replaced his finger with his mouth, inserting his tongue. Her taste made him moan.

She rocked against his face shamelessly as he licked up the length of her, flicked her clit with his tongue, and then took his mouth away.

"Touch your breasts," he ordered.

She immediately covered them with both hands, moaning when her fingers brushed over her nipples.

With the sounds of her pleasure in his ears, he lowered his head back between her trembling thighs. As his tongue went to work on her clitoris, he cupped her ass in one hand and pressed his thumb back inside her. In and out, in and out—until she was panting and moaning his name. He longed to bite her, to taste her sweet blood mix with her desire, but he made himself wait.

When he sensed that she was on the verge of coming, he slid his thumb out and moved down to her ass. He circled the outer ring, spreading her moisture, readying her. She stilled when she realized what he was doing, but he pressed his other arm across her hips and held her there. Baring his fangs, he bit her at the same time that he invaded her tight ass with his thumb. The blood from her swollen clit covered his tongue as he swirled it around the hardened bud.

Laney came instantly, her body jerking uncontrollably as her cries echoed around them. He pumped his thumb in and out of her as he held her in his fangs and continued to flick her with his tongue. When she stilled beneath him again, panting heavily, he didn't give her any time to recover. With one last taste, Dante rose over her and lined himself up with her pussy. A guttural cry escaped him as he pushed his thick length inside of her. She was hot and wet, her body squeezing him as he withdrew and slammed in again. And again. And again. Faster and faster as she bent her knees and raised her legs to give him better access to her body.

Gathering Laney's wrists in his one hand, he raised them above her head. She laced her fingers through his as he held them there, bracing his weight on his elbow as he slid in an out of her slick heat. When he felt his balls tightening, he lifted his free arm to his mouth and bit down. Pressing it to her mouth, he ordered her to drink. "Take it. Take me."

She moaned at the taste of his blood, every pull on his vein sending sparks of lust straight to his sex. Lowering his head to the curve of her shoulder, he reared back slightly and sank his fangs into her warm flesh. Lancy cried out against his arm, and Dante moaned in ecstasy as he began to drink, every swallow sending her lifeblood shooting through his body. He felt *everything*, heard every tiny sound of pleasure that tore from her throat. Dante pounded into her, barely keeping himself under control, trying hard not to hurt her.

She bit down on his wrist, and lust surged through him. Lifting his head, he roared with the strength of his release as Laney tensed beneath him. Waves of passion escalated through his body as his seed pumped from his manhood, continuing for long moments after the pulses of her orgasm had wrung him dry.

Dante released his fangs from her neck, licking the wound clean, and then doing the same with his wrist. Holding her leg around his hip, he rolled to his back, taking her with him until she was sprawled on top of him with their fingers still laced next to his head.

He ran his free hand down her back and over her ass, overcome with the power of what he was feeling, in spite of the release he'd just experienced. "If you ever try to leave me, little mouse, I will hunt you down. There will be nowhere for you to run, nowhere for you to hide. I won't ever stop until I find you."

Bracing her arm across his chest, she lifted her head. Her silky hair tumbled around them, shielding them from the rest of the world. Her face was flushed, her eyes bright as she smiled. "Promise?"

As he gazed spellbound into her beautiful face, Dante's black soul was engulfed by light. He was home.

EPILOGUE

That night, Shea roamed the rain-slick streets of downtown Seattle. She had just left a meeting of the vampires and witches at Luukas's apartment. Luukas was edgy with everything that had happened. There'd been no word from Nikulas or Aiden yet, nor from any of the other scouts he'd sent out. He didn't blame Dante for what he had done. He'd even admitted that if it had been Keira, he would have done exactly the same.

Dante had brought Laney upstairs with him, where she was properly introduced to everyone, and the girls were already planning ways to "brighten" up the underground for her, since she insisted on staying down there until Dante could bring himself to stay upstairs with her. Though Dante had quickly shut down that idea, promising Laney that he would do everything he could to make their room comfortable for her. He even took their pets down there with them when they left. Laney was hoping her cat would turn out to be a good mouser.

While they were there, Dante had sat down with her and explained to her that she was a Protector, filling her in on what exactly that meant with help from the other witches. He also told her that because she was a Protector, there was no "fucking way in hell" that she had killed her own child. The baby shared her blood; it was impossible for her to hurt him. The others backed him up on that point until she believed him. Her grandfather, she'd admitted, was her grandmother's second husband. They'd wed after Laney's mom was born, so there was no actual blood bond. After more questioning, they'd all come to the conclusion that he had been possessed. His body had probably already died before she had exorcised the demon. She'd cried in his arms then as he'd silently held her.

At one point, while the witches had Laney surrounded, Dante had pulled Shea aside with a jerk of his head. When she'd joined him, he'd said under his breath, "About that human at the homeless camp—"

"We'll keep that just between us," she assured him.

He'd given her a grateful nod. "Thank you, Shea."

"Anytime, commander." She'd grinned when he'd narrowed his eyes at the name. Then he shook his head and went back to his female. The pull between them was so tangible, Shea herself could feel it. Dante would never be cheery, but maybe he would find a measure of peace with her. Shea was very happy for him.

Then why did she feel so damn crappy?

She walked until she got to Capital Hill, the notoriously gay neighborhood of Seattle. Shea wasn't gay by nature, but being that she couldn't so much as touch a male without horrendous pain shooting through every nerve of her body, she often found herself in the area looking for a meal. Sometimes, she even had sex with the girls she found; just to be able to have some skin on skin contact.

Up ahead on the corner, she saw the dark brown walls of her favorite dive gay bar. Refurbished from a nineteen thirties vintage gas station, the place was small but quaint. And more importantly, it had a patio that was open year round thanks to a retractable cover and a fire pit, providing room to avoid accidental touching and a quick escape if the need ever arose.

The bouncer eyed up her combat boots, tight black jeans and green silk tank top with appreciation. With a smile and a wink, he let her in. He didn't even bother to card her anymore. Which was good, because she never brought her fake ID with her.

It was disco night, hence the silk shirt, but Shea was early. The place was only about half full, and she made it to the bar without having to dodge any friendly male greetings. She ordered her usual, a Jack and Coke, and while she waited, she admired the porn stapled to the walls. All male, of course. Drink in hand, she thanked the bartender with a fat tip and wandered out to the patio. Once out there, she found her favorite corner table and settled in to wait. It may take a bit to find a female that caught her fancy. The crowd tended to be overwhelmingly male.

The rain seemed to have taken the night off, and Shea did a little star gazing as she sipped her drink and waited for more people to show up. She was restless tonight, and she couldn't quite nail down a reason why. A group of males came out, celebrating a birthday it seemed. She gave them a once over and proceeded to ignore them, not sensing any threats.

Suddenly, Shea froze with her drink halfway to her mouth. A large raven had landed on the half wall next to her. Tilting her head, she stared at Shea with one beady black eye and then squawked in greeting.

It couldn't be.

Shea's eyes skittered around the small patio and her fangs shot down in her mouth as a faint scent drifted on the light breeze. She knew that scent. Setting her drink on the table, she rose from her chair. Her heart pounded, her skin so sensitive she felt every tiny nuance in the change of the air.

The birthday boys broke out into raucous laughter and headed back into the club as a particularly campy song came on. Shea stared past the spot they'd just vacated into the opposite corner of the patio. A pair of topaz eyes glowed by the light of the fire, piercing her to the core.

Slowly, she made her way across the floor. His eyes wandered leisurely down her body and back again as she approached. When she reached the table, they dipped down to her breasts, and her nipples hardened against the sensuous rub of the silk. Those eyes seemed to grow brighter before making their way back up over her bare shoulders and to her face.

"What are you doing here?" she whispered.

"Hello, Shea."

Jesse's deep raspy voice stroked her like a lover's caress.

The Series Continues With
<u>A Vampire's Choice</u>.
Keep reading for a sneak peak!

PROLOGUE

THE MOUNTAINS OF WESTERN CANADA - CURRENT DAY

Shea's thick-soled boots made no sound as she ran through the wet underbrush with the light-footedness of a wraith. She dodged the towering hemlock trees with little thought or effort, ignoring the icy drops of water dripping from the branches after the afternoon's rain. Her steady breathing left a trail of clouds floating behind her, barely discernible in the shadowy moonlight.

The smell of blood lured her from ahead.

The stench of death pushed her from behind.

A huff of warm breath touched the back of her neck, and the tiny hairs all over her body stood at attention as a shiver of revulsion skated across her skin. Her fangs shot down, preparing for a fight. She forced herself to run harder. Pumping her arms and pushing off her toes, she increased her speed, as impossible as it seemed.

Just a little farther. She just had to make it a little bit farther.

He was waiting.

CHAPTER ONE

LONDON, ENGLAND - 1826

"What are you doing, sister?"

The woman froze, one hand stretched too close to the fire. After a slight pause, she pulled her arm in and straightened. Turning only her head, a string of golden ringlets fell over a bare shoulder to cascade down a thin back. Green eyes, much like Shea's own, narrowed in on her face. "What do you want, Shea?"

Remembering her place, Shea dropped into a quick curtsy, her brow furrowed with confusion. "I am only concerned that you were about to hurt yourself." Her older sister had been holding her hand directly over the open flames in the fireplace, with no concern for the pain or what she was doing to her skin. Even now, Shea could smell the nauseating stench of burning flesh and could see the burned edges of

CHAPTER ONE

her sister's sleeve. If she hadn't spoken, her gown would have caught fire.

"Why would I do that, Shea? I am about to marry the man of my dreams and live in this beautiful home." She swung her arm in a wide circle, taking in the entire sitting room and the rich furnishings that filled it. "You should be grateful that I took you out of that hovel of a home father raised us in and brought you with me, not sneaking around spying on me."

Shea let her arms fall to her sides and she straightened her back in indignation. She took a step forward before again remembering their agreement and retreating to a proper distance. "I am very grateful, Elise, you know that. However, that doesn't mean that I'm going to allow you to set yourself on fire." Anxiety and concern swiftly spun into annoyance. "And I wasn't spying for the gods' sake, I was only passing by the doorway on my way to fetch the tea and biscuits, and saw what you were doing."

"Watch what you say!" Elise's haughty demeanor was completely unlike her, even if she *were* about to become a great lady. "Do not speak of your gods here, or we will both be burned alive."

A thread of unease wound its way around Shea's heart. This wasn't the first time in the last few days her sister had spoken as if they didn't have the same upbringing, and the same history, despite their current positions in society. "*My* gods? Are they not *your* gods anymore?"

Elise turned away with a swish of her full skirts, stretching her hands back out to the fire, with no reaction of pain to the red, scalded skin on her left palm. "Of course they are. We just shouldn't speak of them. There's a reason our bloodline has been 'lost' in the family records."

Her tone was dismissive, yet Shea hovered, afraid to leave her sister. The door opened, and she was relieved to see Matthew, Elise's fiancé, enter the room. He gave Shea a polite smile when she curtsied to him, before moving past her to take his place at her sister's side. "There you are." Raising her hand to his lips, he placed a chaste kiss on the back. With a frown, he turned it over and gasped. "Elise! What have you done to your hand?"

Elise smiled politely up at him. "I was only trying to chase away the chill, and I got a little too close to the flame. I can't seem to get warm enough today."

"Mrs. Richards will know what to use to ease the pain for you." He turned to Shea. "Please go fetch the cook."

But Elise shook her head. "Do not interrupt her in her daily duties. She's very busy getting everything ready for the wedding. And besides, I'm fine. Truly."

He smiled down at her, an adoring expression on his face. "Yes. The wedding." Matthew immediately turned back to Shea. "Would you please fetch us some tea?"

Shea dropped into a curtsy. "Right away, sir." Still in the submissive pose, she asked, "Is there anything else *you* require, my lady?"

"No, Shea. That will be all. Thank you."

CHAPTER ONE

Leaving her in the capable hands of her future husband, Shea murmured the correct response and left them to their wedding talk. Her fingers twisted together in her apron as she rushed to the kitchen to get the tea and cakes.

Elise was acting strangely. So strangely, in fact, that Shea was becoming convinced that woman was not her sister at all.

Then who is she, if not my sister?

Shea didn't know, but that was not the person she had grown up with. Not the person whose friendship she valued more than anything else in the entire world. The thing in that room, though it resembled her sister in appearance, made Shea's skin crawl and the blood freeze in her veins.

There. She'd finally admitted it. If only to herself.

The closeness she and her sister shared was the reason Shea was here with Elise, in her new home, with her future family.

Her sister had met Matthew by chance at the market, and sparks had flown at first glance. He'd asked to call on her, and though she'd tried to refuse him, telling Shea he was too much the dandy for her, he hadn't given up until she'd agreed. The fact that she came from a lower social status, and was actually barely above living on the streets, made no difference to him. Matthew was the fourth son in a long line of sons up for the title of earl, and therefore, was given free reign to live his life as he wished for the most part, especially when he really wanted something. And he had really wanted Elise.

CHAPTER ONE

Within a month, he had proposed the union of marriage, and her sister had accepted, on the condition that Shea could come with her. Matthew had agreed, and had even been gracious enough to hire her into his household as her sister's lady's maid. She would make her own money, and would be included in everything they did.

Well, maybe not everything. Shea blushed at the thought. But when they traveled, Shea would go also. And when they had children, Shea would take over as nanny.

And if, by some chance, Shea met someone, Matthew had offered to give her a small dowry to take to her new husband. It was a perfect situation for both of them. Their father could barely support himself and her mother, never mind his two daughters. But he had done his best by them, and besides, material comforts were not important. What was important was that they stay warm and fed—and alive.

For Shea and her sister came from a very special bloodline. A secret bloodline. One that was only known by certain members of the holy community, and one that needed to survive for the good of the world.

Or so she'd been told since she was three.

Shea retrieved the tea tray and took it back to the sitting room. As she approached the closed door, she heard Matthew's voice, raised to a high pitch.

"What do you mean, Elise? Are you changing your mind?"

"Matthew, please don't shout."

CHAPTER ONE

"Don't shout? Don't shout? My bride-to-be is telling me she has changed her mind the day before our wedding, and you're telling me not to shout?"

Shea stopped outside the door and set the tray down quietly on the stand. Leaning in closer, she pressed her ear to the wooden door.

There was a rustle of clothing, and then her sister's voice. "You're being dramatic. I'm not cancelling our nuptials, I only want a little more time—"

"Time for what, Elise? What exactly do you need time for?"

"You wouldn't understand."

"You're correct. I don't understand. I don't understand any of this. Not at all." A pause. "I thought you loved me."

"Matthew, please." There was a grunt. More rustling of clothing. And then her sister's voice again. Only it wasn't her sister's voice. Not at all.

"Get off me." Followed by the sharp sound of skin striking skin, and then absolute silence.

Shea straightened up, her heart pounding as she heard footsteps coming toward the door. Leaving the tea tray on the stand where she had set it, she picked up her skirts and hurried away.

She rounded the corner to the dining area just as the door to the sitting room was flung open. Peeking around the doorjamb, she watched as her sister—or something that

CHAPTER ONE

looked like her sister—marched in the opposite direction and headed upstairs to her rooms.

A few seconds later, Matthew stumbled out into the hallway. Their eyes met, the bewilderment in his matching her own feelings, and for a moment, Shea thought he was going to come talk to her. But he walked past, striding down the hall and out the front door.

Shea ran outside after him. "Matthew! Please wait!" She realized belatedly that she had called him by his first name, but it wasn't important. Not right now.

He stopped and turned to her, waiting for her to catch up.

She dropped into a curtsy. "If I may speak to you a moment?"

"Of course you may, Shea. Please stand up, and tell me; what the bloody *hell* is going on with your sister?"

Clasping her hands in front of her, Shea glanced up at her future brother-in-law. "I apologize for listening. I brought the tea and heard raised voices—"

He waved a hand in dismissal. "It's fine, Shea."

She closed her eyes, praying he wouldn't think she was crazy. She supposed there was no way to say it other than to just come right out with it. "I have reason to believe that woman is not my sister."

"I'm sorry?"

Opening her eyes, she lifted her chin. "That isn't my sister, Matthew. That isn't the woman you proposed to."

CHAPTER ONE

Thick dark eyebrows rose nearly to his hairline. "Then who, pray tell, is it?"

She could tell he was frustrated, but also that he wasn't taking her seriously. "I don't know. I don't know who it is. I only know it's not Elise. But please don't kick us out just yet. I promise I will get to the bottom of this."

His handsome features softened. "I'm not going to kick you out, Shea. I just want to know what's wrong with my bride-to-be."

He didn't understand what she was trying to say. He thought her sister was having her woman's flow or something. The fight drained out of her as she realized it was very likely that he would call the men with the white coats to take her away in their carriage if she kept on. With a polite smile, she promised him she would talk to her.

Matthew gave her a grateful nod, and continued to the stables. A few minutes later, she saw him astride his new black stallion. He gave her a wave as he kicked the horse into a trot, and then a gallop, as they headed off toward the meadow on the other side of the fence.

Once he was gone, Shea hurried to the stables and requested a carriage. She needed to talk to her father. He would know what to do. If she didn't tarry and got straight to the point, she would be back in time to help Elise get ready for dinner.

Funny how fate can wreck even the most meticulous of planning.

CHAPTER TWO

TWO WEEKS EARLIER - CURRENT DAY

"What are you doing here?" Shea whispered.

A light breeze lifted the loose tendrils of her hair, and raised chill bumps across her sensitized skin. Or maybe it was the way the dark warlock's topaz eyes stared all the way through to the deepest secrets of her soul.

His scent drifted to her on the light breeze. It filled her nostrils, making her upper lip twitch, exposing her fangs before she could stop herself. The taste of his scent made her mouth water and the back of her throat burn with thirst. She ached to pierce the firm skin stretched tight over the strong pulse in his throat until she could taste the dark essence of him. Her blood pounded, keeping beat along with the music coming from inside the renovated building that was now a popular gay club in Seattle's infamous Capital Hill neighborhood. It was 70's night, and the place was filling up

CHAPTER TWO

fast. Soon people would start spilling out to the outdoor patio, but for right now, it was just the two of them.

And Cruthú, of course. His raven.

"Hello, Shea." Jesse's low timbre stroked her like a lover's caress. He looked different somehow, and after a moment, she realized it was his clothing. Instead of the usual black, a burgundy cashmere clung to his muscled torso. Her hand twitched toward it, to feel the soft material stretched across the hard muscle of the arm beneath. But she pulled it back, even though he was nowhere near touching range. His long, lean legs were covered in tailored charcoal slacks, and expensive shoes had replaced the black, heavy-treaded boots she was used to seeing on him. His dark hair was different, too—a bit longer—the wavy ends falling just past his collar.

He sprawled casually in his chair as she took in his changed appearance, one large hand resting on the small table in front of him, fingers wrapped around a sweating bottle of local beer. It was still full.

A trickle of fear slid down her spine as she watched him trace designs in the condensation with the tip of one finger without taking his eyes from her face. It had only been a few weeks since he'd released her from his mountain prison, but it was obvious he'd been following her. No one could have told him she came to this club, even if he'd had the nerve to ask them. No one else knew. Shea glanced around, ensuring herself they were completely alone, at least for the moment. "What are you doing here?" she repeated, louder this time.

CHAPTER TWO

His fingers stilled on the bottle, but despite his calm demeanor, she knew he was aware of her proximity. Very aware. Yet, while her pulse paused and stuttered as if it tried to relay everything she felt in Morse code, she could hear his beating strong and steady beneath the orchestral sounds of disco.

"Won't you sit down?" He nodded at the chair across from him.

Shea hesitated. A quick glance around ensured her they were still the only ones on the patio. She swallowed nervously. He'd never hurt her in any way while she'd been with him, but she still didn't trust him.

One side of Jesse's mouth quirked up in a sardonic mask of a smile. "I mean you no harm, Shea. I just want to talk."

Pulling the chair out from the table, she angled it so her back was to the half wall surrounding the patio and she was facing the door that led inside to the dance floor. As soon as she sat down, the raven hopped along the wall to stand near her and squawked in greeting, picking up a strand of Shea's long hair and running it through her beak. She reached back and stroked the silky feathers of the bird's cheek. "Hey, Cruthú."

"She missed you." He paused, allowing Shea to absorb the heavier meaning implied with those words before he continued, "I wanted to come and check on you after our phone call. I was concerned. I'm glad to see you are safe and well."

Shea didn't know how to respond. "There was no need for you to do that."

351

CHAPTER TWO

"Of course there was. I had no idea you were in possession of one of the boxes the demons are after, or I would have checked on you sooner."

Shea didn't know how he hadn't known. He seemed to know everything.

Jesse lowered his eyes to the untouched bottle of beer. He spun the bottle with his fingertips, until it balanced on a tilt. Removing his fingers, it continued to spin for a few seconds by itself.

Shea watched the bottle spin, fascinated, until he grabbed it and stopped the momentum.

When he lifted his gaze again, the intensity within made them glow bright as the sun. "I missed you, as well." Clearing his throat, he glanced away and went on before she could respond to that surprising statement. "What happened to the box?"

It took her a moment to answer him, unsure if he was friend or foe at this point. "It's gone."

His eyes flashed back to her face. One eyebrow lifted. "Gone?"

She nodded, not seeing the harm in telling him what happened in either scenario. "The demons got their hands on Dante's mate and threatened her life. He gave up the box to save her." Jesse knew vampires, and therefore, she knew he was well-aware of the weakness they had for their mates. She wasn't giving any secrets away.

CHAPTER TWO

The warlock cocked his head and stared at her. "They didn't kill her."

"No. They tried, but Dante and Laney both survived."

"Good." His face was grim. "But the demons got the box anyway."

"Yes." Her tone was bleak. During their phone call a few days earlier, Jesse had warned her of the consequences if this were to occur.

"If they've found the others, the last clue will lead them to their original blood. It will allow them to reanimate to their true forms." He gazed past her shoulder, his forehead creasing. "They will destroy this world, you know."

Shea stopped petting the raven and dropped her hand back into her lap. She waited until his attention once again focused on her. It took a few seconds, and she knew he was seeing a future they could not allow to occur. A future of hell on earth. "Luukas plans to find it before they do."

"The blood?"

"Yes."

He didn't appear reassured. "And how will he do that? When I last spoke with you, you didn't even know what it was you had until I told you. Does he have any idea where the blood is hidden?"

With a sigh, Shea shook her head. She didn't bother arguing the point that he could have saved this all from happening if

CHAPTER TWO

he had just told her about it from the beginning. "No. But finding it first is our only hope."

"He won't be able to stop them now, Shea. I can't stop them. No one can."

"But you released them—" She slammed her mouth shut with an audible click before she could say anymore. She wanted to ask him why. Why he had done such a thing. What did he hope to gain from it?

However, she didn't really need to ask. She knew. He'd helped free them because he was evil, like Leeha. Like the demons.

"Releasing them was easier than sending them back will be. They wanted to be free. They don't want to go back. It would take more blood and magic than I alone possess to do so."

The implications of his words began to truly sink in. Fear loosened her bowels and clenched at her heart. "There has to be a way to send them back to hell...to chain them to the altar again. It was done once before, it can be done again." For if what he said was true, they were all well and truly fucked—humans, animals, and supernatural creatures alike.

"The first time it was done by a full coven of witches using a lost form of dark magic. Keira is powerful in her own right, but even if I wanted to help, it wouldn't be enough with only the two of us."

"What if there were six of you?"

He cocked his head at her. "Six?"

CHAPTER TWO

"There are five Moss witches residing with us now. Keira and her sister, Emma, Grace, Ryan, and Laney. Some of them knew of their heritage, some didn't. Keira is working with them, strengthening their magic and their control. Laney is a Protector." She stuttered to a halt before she said too much. "With your help—"

"No, Shea. I'm sorry."

She would think he was upset about being unable to help her, but for the stubborn set of his jaw.

Shea sat back in her chair and averted her eyes from the enticing male. There was more going on here than he was telling her.

The silence stretched between them. It would have been deafening if not for the music and the small sounds the raven made as she tried to get Shea to stroke her again. A human couple wandered out into the area, the males heading to the opposite side of the patio to make out in the corner.

Shea ran her hand down Cruthú's soft feathers one last time, then stood. "I should go."

Jesse stood also, reaching for her hand across the small tabletop.

She tensed, pulling it out of his reach with a quiet hiss, flashing her fangs at the male. "Don't touch me."

Pain darkened his golden eyes, but he pulled his hand back and held his clenched fist at his side. That tiny glimpse into his soul was gone so fast, Shea wondered if she had imagined it. "I'm sorry. I only wanted to try to convince you to stay a bit longer."

"I can't, Jesse. I have to go." *Away from you.* His masculine scent permeated her nose, causing the thirst to burn with an intensity that tilted the world around her. She needed to feed, and as much as she wanted to, she couldn't drink from him. Instinct told her such intimacy would be devastating for her, and not just because of the physical pain it would cause. "I need to go," she repeated.

"Let me come with you—"

"No!" She wanted to tell him that she preferred to be alone, wanted to tell him that out of all the males she knew, his company was the one she wanted least, but she couldn't force herself to form the words. It would be a lie, and she couldn't bring herself to lie to him. Not with the way he was looking at her, seeing right through to her soul. She lowered her voice. "No. You can't. If the others saw you here, they would kill you."

His expression hardened. "They could try."

He wasn't being cocky. It was the truth. She'd heard about the battle between Jesse and Luukas. Even with Keira's magic thrown in to help, Luukas was convinced Jesse had only been toying with them. They'd survived for one reason: because Jesse had left the scene and allowed them to leave.

"I need to go. Goodbye, Cruthú." She paused, the next words catching in her throat for reasons she didn't want to define. "Goodbye, Jesse."

CHAPTER TWO

Turning away before he could say anything else, she made her way through the burgeoning crowd inside the dark club. A few males bumped into her accidentally as she edged around the dance floor, but Shea's hisses of pain were drowned out by the thumping beat of the music.

Once safely outside again, she waved to the bouncer and strolled down the street with a casual swagger until she reached the corner, so as not to raise suspicion. But as Cruthú circled the sky above her, she felt anything but calm.

An icy chill slithered down her spine.

The raven's eyes weren't the only ones watching her.

Read **A Vampire's Choice** now.

ABOUT THE AUTHOR

L.E. Wilson writes romance starring intense alpha males and the women who are fearless enough to love them just as they are. In her novels you'll find smoking hot scenes, a touch of suspense, some humor, a bit of gore, and multifaceted characters, all working together to combine her lifelong obsession with the paranormal and her love of romance.

Her writing career came about the usual way: on a dare from her loving husband. Little did she know just one casual suggestion would open a box of worms (or words as the case may be) that would forever change her life.

On a Personal Note:

"I love to hear from my readers! Contact me anytime at le@lewilsonauthor.com."

.